Where the MONEY Is

A Novel

By Bruce MacDonald

Midpine Books
P.O. Box 526
Cummaquid, MA 02637
www.bhmacdonald.com

Book and Cover Design by Kristen vonHentschel

ISBN 979-8-9924709-1-8

Dedication

To my wife, Sharon, who has helped me stay
focused and on task every day.
She is my biggest fan.

And to all my friends who encouraged
me while I was writing this book.
Thank you!

Preface

I was driving to Cape Cod when I saw a guy driving a Porsche Panamera who looked like a banking professor I had in graduate school. He was a retired executive at Bay Bank. That is how I started this book. I just tried to imagine what he was doing after he retired, and I came up with this story.

This story is about friendship and greed, and the consequences that one can inflict on the other. Where The Money Is takes you through the ups and downs of the banking world from a leadership perspective and then through the various and ever-increasing cycles of greed.

Remember what one of the most famous bank robbers, Willie Sutton, was reported to have said when asked in prison by a reporter named Mitch Ohnstad why he robbed banks. He said, "Because that's where the money is." He commented that he loved the feeling he got when he robbed a bank.

But remember that greed ultimately ruins it for everyone.

Chapter One

Charlie had just left the Hyannisport Club, where he enjoyed a beer after golf. He was on his way home when his wife, Barb, called him. Charlie had been a member of the Hyannisport Club for almost five years. While he could have joined any other private club on Cape Cod, he chose the Hyannisport Club because of its beauty and history. The Club was built in the late 1890s by Donald Ross, one of the most famous golf course designers. It reminded Charlie of the Pebble Beach Golf Club in Monterey, California, with similar ocean views and lots of hills sloping down towards the water. Hyannisport even looked a little like St. Andrews over in Scotland. The Hyannisport Club was also the course that President Kennedy loved to play, and it was just up the street from the Kennedy Compound – another feature that pleased Charlie. In some ways, Charlie felt he was as successful as any of the Kennedys. He was wealthy, nationally recognized, and well-liked by his family and friends. It felt good to know that he and President Kennedy had played some of their best rounds of golf at the Hyannisport Club.

Charlie answered the phone and heard his wife's stress-filled voice. "Get home, Charlie; something's happened to Doug. Oh my God, he has had a stroke or something. Jenn just called me, and we must get over there right away! She's already called 911. Where are you,

Charlie? Please hurry!"

Charlie cut her off. "Barb, I'm almost home. Take a deep breath. I'll meet you out in front of the house."

"Please hurry!" she said.

Charlie hung up the phone. Even though he and Barb lived just a few miles from the Hyannisport Club, Charlie put his foot to the floor and sped home. The Porsche's engine gulped in lots of air and gave back more horsepower.

As Charlie rushed past the big homes on Wianno Avenue, his smile turned to a frown as he wondered what might have happened to his friend Doug. "Heart attack, stroke? Oh god!" he thought. He had just spoken with Doug the night before. Everything was fine with him physically, even though they had quarreled. Charlie was uncomfortable with the way they left things, but surely, he didn't want anything to happen to his friend and partner.

Charlie rounded the corner onto Seaview Avenue and hoped an ambulance was already at his friend's house. 911 calls in the area were routed through the Barnstable County Sheriff's office, where a room full of dispatchers was available. They took 911 calls from all seven villages that comprise the Town of Barnstable and from all the towns that comprise Barnstable County, which covers most of Cape Cod. In this case, the nearest fire department with an ambulance was not too far from Doug's house, so Charlie prayed that help would arrive quickly.

As Charlie pulled into his driveway, his wife, Barb, was waiting for him on the front steps. He was undoubtedly a lucky guy to have married Barb. She was tall and slender, with beautiful blond hair lightly blowing in the afternoon breeze. She was someone who loved him unconditionally, and she was his best friend. She was a good listener and always tried to understand his complex needs and desires. Yes, Barb helped Charlie grow emotionally while he climbed the corporate ladder, always in an upward direction.

Barb jumped into the Porsche, and Charlie turned left out of his driveway onto Seaview Ave. He slipped the Porsche into second gear, then pounded the accelerator. They sped down Seaview Ave. to Eel River Road and were turning left into Doug's driveway in no time at all. Both the front gate at the driveway and the front door were already open. He and Barb ran into the house and found Jenn kneeling over Doug's body in the library. Charlie had always liked this room - it was circular, and all the outside windows looked directly out onto the river. It had a beautiful view, particularly around sunset, when you could see across the river to West Bay and the gated community of Oyster Harbors. Yes, Charlie had lots of fond memories in this room with Doug, Jenn, and Barb. All that changed now that he saw Jenn sobbing as she knelt next to Doug's body.

Jenn looked up, her face streaked with tears and her dark hair hanging in her face.

"Jesus, Charlie, I think he's dead – I don't know what happened; I found him this way when I got back from Hingham a few minutes ago, and I think he's dead!" Jenn stood up and started to cry again. Barb reached out to her, put her arms around her, and pulled her close.

"Can you do something, Charlie? Can you please help him?" Barb asked frantically.

Charlie knelt next to Doug and got a good view of the blood all over the floor under Doug's head, neck, and shoulders. Doug was lying on his back with his eyes wide open, motionless. Charlie's knee was now stained with the sticky blood that covered the floor, but he didn't seem to notice.

"Oh my God, what's happened here?" asked Charlie, more to himself than to Jenn or Barb.

"He must have fallen and hit his head," Jenn sobbed. She had no real idea what had happened to Doug, but she certainly believed this was a terrible accident.

"You called an ambulance. So, where the hell are they?" Charlie touched Doug's hand and neck, then looked up at Jenn, who was shaking her head, sobbing, and still mouthing the words, "I think he's dead!"

"No, he's not dead; he's got a pulse," Charlie then roared, "What the hell happened?"

But Jenn had no answers. She'd been up to Hingham to visit her youngest daughter Emily and her new baby, so Doug had been home alone all day.

"I don't know, Charlie. I just don't know!" she said with tears streaming down her face. Barb cradled Jenn in her arms as if to protect her from Charlie, who was shouting out questions like the CEO he used to be. Barb held Jenn even closer and squeezed her shoulders to comfort her.

Two EMTs, a paramedic, and a police officer arrived and brought a stretcher into the library. They immediately conducted a triage, an initial assessment of the patient's condition and the determination of the urgency of treatment, and then went to work on Doug to stabilize him. They wrapped the wound on the back of his head and lifted him onto the stretcher. One of the EMTs announced there was a faint pulse. While the paramedic and the EMTs continued to work on Doug, the police officer asked Jenn if she knew what had happened. However, Jenn was now hysterical and couldn't even focus on the officer's questions.

"We'll get him right over to the hospital," said the paramedic. Then, he turned to Jenn and added, "You can ride along with us in the ambulance." Barb asked if she could ride in the ambulance too, and both Jenn and the Paramedic said "Yes."

"I'll be right behind you, Jenn," said Charlie.

They were taking Doug over to Cape Cod Hospital's emergency room in Hyannis, about 7 miles away. The hospital was the epicenter of all healthcare in this part of the Cape. Furthermore, it was summer on Cape Cod, making this the busiest time for the hospital. This was one of Massachusetts's most active ERs primarily because the Cape's population nearly doubled in the summer. Doug would get excellent attention and care, which is what he needed.

As the ambulance pulled out of Doug's driveway, Charlie followed. Charlie was getting very anxious and kept shouting for the ambulance to speed up. The ride to Hyannis was pretty quick, but the hospital was on the far side of town, so it took a little longer, even with the sirens blaring. The ER entrance for the ambulance was an underground ramp located out back on Park Street, providing undisturbed access away from the parking lot traffic in front.

The ambulance backed through the ER gate as Charlie pulled into a nearby parking space across the street. He followed Jenn, Barb, and Doug's stretcher into the ER, but they were stopped at the admitting lobby, where a doctor pulled Doug, the EMTs, and Jenn into one of the many patient treatment rooms across the hallway from the ER entrance. He began checking Doug's vital signs while speaking with Jenn. Charlie tried to get closer to the conversation, but the doctor and Jenn spoke in hushed tones. Barb pulled Charlie back out through the main corridor and into the ER waiting room.

"What the hell do you suppose happened with Doug?" Charlie asked, not thinking that Barb didn't know any more than he did. "What happened to him? It doesn't look good at all, does it? He looks like shit… and all that blood," Charlie said, staring at Barb, who was standing right next to the Emergency Room receptionist.

Barb shook her head, and Charlie saw that she was crying. He walked over to Barb, grabbed her hands, and closed his eyes. The image of Doug lying in a pool of blood with his eyes wide open and not moving still haunted him.

Charlie put his head in his hands. He had a million questions running through his mind. Out loud and to no one in particular, he asked, "Damnit, Doug, what the hell happened to you?"

"I don't know, Charlie," Barb responded, thinking he had asked her. She was in shock seeing her best friend's husband in a pool of blood and was worried for both Doug and Jenn. "I don't know how he fell and hurt his head. Maybe he had a stroke or something. We'll see what the doctors say. They'll know what happened; they'll know what to do."

"I can't make any sense of this, Barb. Doug is as healthy as a horse. Today's the 28th. He had his annual physical earlier this month, just a few weeks ago, maybe on the 5th? I thought they gave him a clean bill of health." But Charlie knew more than he let on. "He must have had some type of stroke, maybe a heart attack, right? And that must have caused him to fall and hit his head," Charlie postulated while shaking his head back and forth.

"Charlie, let's just wait and see what the doctors find out. We should check in later and see if Jenn needs anything," Barb responded.

"Okay… I just can't help thinking about why Doug fell and hit his head. Something big happened here," Charlie said as he slumped back in his chair. Charlie was used to finding answers when he asked questions.

They sat in the ER waiting room, surrounded by a multitude of very busy nurses, police, and EMTs coming and going with patients who had various injuries. Charlie saw a woman who looked like she was going to give birth, then noticed a young man who had been shot in the neck and was bleeding all over the sheets on his stretcher. Barb was quiet, just waiting to hear how Doug was doing.

About half an hour later, Jenn came out to the waiting room to tell her friends that Doug had been stabilized and was now safe. Barb gave her a big smile and a hug and asked if there was anything she needed at this point. Jenn thanked her, turned to Charlie, and hugged him. Both Barb and Charlie thought of Jenn as a best friend and knew she was a wonderful wife to Doug. She had helped Doug polish his image, making him feel much better about himself, both personally and professionally. She was the best thing that could ever have happened to Doug; he loved her for that and for giving him two beautiful daughters. As Doug would say from the time he met Jenn, "She's the best; she's the very best."

"I know he'll be okay now that he's here at the hospital. I just don't know what could have happened to him, Charlie." Jenn searched her friend's face, hoping to find an answer there. Charlie always knew what to do in any circumstance.

"Jenn, I know he'll be all right; Doug is a fighter," Charlie said in a positive tone. She gave him a quick kiss on the cheek and whispered she'd call them as soon as she knew more. She then turned toward the ER and walked back into Doug's room.

Chapter Two

Charlie was a big deal in the banking industry. In most banking circles, he was known as the Chairman of the Board and Chief Executive Officer of one of the country's largest banks. His friend Doug was also a big deal. In accounting circles, he was known as the Chief Accounting Officer of one of the country's largest banks, the same bank where Charlie worked. Both were at the top of their game as far as their career were concerned.

Charlie was tall and "imperially slim" like the character Richard Cory in Edwin A. Robinson's poem, Richard Cory. Charlie had a full head of hair highlighted with brown streaks and a touch of grey around the ears. His voice was deep, and he always took command of conversations, even in a room full of people he didn't know. And most people were envious of him, just like they were envious of Richard Cory. Charlie had always loved that poem and, in some ways, thought that he was a lot like Richard Cory minus the suicide thing.

Doug was significantly shorter than Charlie, with a slight paunch, sporting a mostly bald appearance with graying wisps of hair around the sides and back of his head. He was a bit of a loner, maybe even shy, with a whisper of a voice, and rarely spent time with people he didn't know very well. Instead, he focused on counting numbers and was extremely good at running them in all directions.

Charlie and Doug were best of friends and had worked together at the same bank for over 20 years. Even their wives were best friends and had been roommates at Wellesley College, which is how Doug and Charlie first met. At the time, Charlie was a graduate student at the Wharton School of Business at the University of Pennsylvania in Philadelphia. Doug was at Boston College, getting his undergraduate degree in accounting. Doug spent most weekends at Wellesley College with his girlfriend, Jenn, and became quite well acquainted with Barb. By a stroke of luck, Charlie came home to stay with his parents in Wellesley the same weekend that Wellesley College hosted a mixer. It was there that Charlie first saw his future bride. Barbara was a tall, shapely young woman with long blond hair and a beautiful smile. He was instantly drawn to her and enjoyed spending time with her friends, Jenn and Doug. Even though Doug was quiet at first, he warmed up to Charlie rather quickly. They all liked each other's company and soon became the Four Musketeers. Whenever Charlie would come home for a weekend, he'd meet up with all three of them.

Wellesley was a "dry town" – no liquor served or sold unless the seating exceeded one hundred persons – so there were only two places to buy a drink. One was the Wellesley Inn in downtown Wellesley, and the other was the Wellesley Country Club, a private golf club on the way to Needham. Both were old-fashioned, stuffy establishments, not the type of places where younger people would be comfortable socializing. Charlie sometimes drove over to Newton to one of the package stores for beers they drank in one of the remote parking lots at Wellesley College. "Road tins," they were called. But most of the time, they would find themselves heading to the bars and restaurants in Cambridge or Boston, and sometimes they would journey out to the suburbs of Arlington, Medford, and even Somerville.

Charlie had attended Harvard College as an undergraduate student, so he knew his way around the city. On the other hand, Doug only went out occasionally, so he was only familiar with a few places around Boston College. He typically stayed in the well-charted territory of Cleveland Circle at MaryAnn's bar or at the Circle

Cinema, where he would go to a movie alone. Both girls were happy to have Charlie guide them through Harvard Square in Cambridge, where there were great pubs and many eateries with good food. Jenn liked Harvest on Brattle Street, and Barb enjoyed Grendel's Den over on Winston Street.

Doug and Charlie loved special nights with the girls at the Hyatt Cambridge, a pyramid-shaped hotel on the Cambridge side of the Charles River, right on Memorial Drive. The hotel had a restaurant and lounge on the top floor called the Spinnaker Lounge. It turned slowly and offered great views over the Charles River, showcasing the entire Boston skyline and most of Cambridge. Doug liked the food, the gorgeous views, and their imported beer. The bartender, Al, would occasionally give Doug free beers in exchange for some simple tax advice. Charlie liked everything about the Hyatt, from the dining to the rooms. He and Barbara would always stay there if the chance presented itself. Doug had a dorm room over at Boston College, and since he was a senior, it was a single room with plenty of privacy. Jenn preferred the Hyatt but couldn't always get Doug to spend the money. He was cheap – even in college.

Sometime over the summer during Charlie's second year at Wharton, he asked Barbara to marry him. That same week, Doug gave Jennifer a ring he bought for her at Kay's Jewelers at the Chestnut Hill Mall. Both Charlie and Doug thought it might be fun to have a double wedding, but the girls emphatically said, "No!" So, the couple decided that Doug and Jenn would get married first, and Charlie and Barb would follow a few weeks later. Of course, Charlie was Doug's Best Man, and Barb was Jenn's Maid of Honor. And yes, when Charlie and Barb were married, Doug and Jenn held those same titles. Doug and Jenn held off their honeymoon until after Charlie and Barb's wedding so they could honeymoon together. They went to Bermuda for almost two weeks and stayed at the Southampton Princess, one of the better hotels on the island's south shore. They had a blast, exploring the island on scooters, and it was there that they all fell in love with island life.

For years, Charlie and Barbara lived in Wellesley in a lovely house on Cliff Road that Charlie's folks helped them buy. Doug and Jenn lived in Doug's grandmother's house on Pearl Street in Newton for a while, which she had left to Doug's family after her passing. A few years later, Doug and Jennifer had a daughter, Hannah, so they moved to a bigger house out in Dover, southwest of Boston. Shortly afterward, they had a second daughter, Emily, so moving to Dover proved to be a good decision, as the house had more space for their expanding family.

After college, Charlie worked in corporate finance at the First National Bank of Boston. The bank was headquartered in downtown Boston. At the same time, Doug interviewed and accepted a position in Fidelity's corporate accounting department. Fidelity, a prominent Boston-based mutual fund and financial services company, was run by the Johnson family as a private company. One of the largest investment companies in the world, it was perhaps best known for its highly successful Magellan Fund, managed by Peter Lynch.

In the summer, they all rented a house together on Cape Cod in the beach town of Dennis. The cottage was right on the beach on the bay side of the Cape. The water was warm, and the beaches were less crowded than on the Atlantic side. The house was a duplex with two sides, each a mirror image of the other. The first summer, Doug and Jenn rented the right-hand side of the house, and Charlie and Barb rented the left side of the house. The following year, they switched sides so that each couple felt like it was a new adventure. It was a great location – walk down a few steps, and you were on Mayflower Beach.

The couples enjoyed a lot of summer fun, including watching shows at the Dennis Playhouse and devouring fried clams and soft-serve ice cream at Captain Frosty's. Two full weeks off for the boys and then down every weekend. After a couple of years of renting, Charlie surprised everyone by purchasing the house, which he said they all could share.

A couple of years later, Doug finished graduate school with an MBA from Boston College. Doug now had degrees in accounting and business and was a Certified Public Accountant as well as an Enrolled Agent (a federally certified tax specialist). Doug was definitely on the fast track at Fidelity. Charlie became the head of the Mergers and Acquisitions Department when the bank absorbed several small and mid-sized New England-based banks. The bank made seven separate acquisitions in just one year, including BayBank, a prominent bank throughout New England. The old-line name of First National Bank of Boston was changed to Bank of Boston, which was then rebranded as BankBoston in 1999 following the merger with BayBank. That summer, Charlie was promoted to Division President due to his outstanding performance in managing all the acquisitions. After his promotion, he asked Doug to leave Fidelity and join him at BankBoston, which Doug was delighted to do. In just a few more years, Charlie was promoted to Chief Operating Officer – the number two position at the bank. Then, he immediately pushed the Board of Directors to promote Doug to Chief Accounting Officer. Best of friends and best buddies at work, life was grand!

After all the promotions (which naturally included significant pay raises), Doug decided that he and Jenn could afford to buy their own summer home rather than share Charlie's place in Dennis. He and Jenn chose to buy on Martha's Vineyard, where Doug had always dreamed of summering. The house was on the shore road in Vineyard Haven, not too far from where Walter Cronkite, the CBS News host, lived in the summer.

About a month later, Charlie sold the duplex in Dennis, and he and Barb bought a beautiful home in the fancy village of Osterville on the Nantucket Sound side of the Cape. The house was on Sea View Avenue – one of the nicest streets in town. It ran along the Nantucket Sound, with most homes on the left-hand side of the road sitting up on a high bluff that offered spectacular views down to the water. The house was just down the street from the Wianno Club, where he and Barb, Doug, and Jenn became members. Charlie purchased the home in 2004. Barb thought he was crazy to sell their house over on Mayflower Beach in Dennis. Still, Charlie wanted to live on Nantucket Sound, and everyone knew that one of the best places to live was Osterville, and one of the best addresses in Osterville was Sea View Ave. – a perfect place to live.

The house was set back from the street with two garages – one on the right side of the lot and the other on the left side of the lot. The left garage had space for two cars and a large studio apartment on the second floor, which they used when hosting big parties for their overnight guests. The garage to the right had space for two cars and had a storage loft with a full stairway from the first floor. They almost looked like two additional houses set on each side of the main house. There was a swimming pool on the left side of the main house, offering a beautiful view down over the back lawn and beyond to Nantucket Sound. Formal gardens surrounded the entire property. Barb planted hundreds of flowers and shrubs and loved to tend to them, even though Charlie was spending a small fortune with a local landscaper. Charlie didn't mind; he thought he had one of the prettiest homes in town.

Doug and Jenn followed them to Osterville soon thereafter. They sold their summer place on the Vineyard and bought a beautiful home in Osterville, only a few minutes away from Charlie and Barb on the Eel River, where Doug had direct deep-water access to Nantucket Sound. There was also access to the Crosby Boat Yard and the Wianno Yacht Club upriver. Doug loved to go fishing almost as much as he enjoyed evading his taxes, and he was now on his third boat. It was a Post convertible with twin engines, a 56' blue-hulled beauty named Bonanza, which, as you might have guessed, was not named after the TV show of the same name that ran from 1959 to 1973!

Life was pretty good for Charlie, and yes, life was pretty good for Doug, too. The years flew by, and the four of them found themselves traveling to Europe, skiing in Colorado, taking trips to South America, and seeing almost every city in the United States. Doug and Charlie continued to receive substantial cash bonuses that sometimes exceeded $1 million a year. By the time they heard about the Fleet Bank acquisition, Charlie was one of a handful of executives running BankBoston, and Doug was his right-hand numbers guy. Even though their appearance would lead you to believe they were opposites, Charlie and Doug had a lot in common, including their wants and desire for more and more money. In addition, they had a solid friendship, including the friendship their wives shared. All of this spilled over into work, so it was no surprise that Charlie continued to look after Doug, and Doug continued to look after Charlie.

Chapter Three

Fleet Bank was an old-line Rhode Island-based bank that had also grown rapidly through acquisitions, including the buyout of the venerable Shawmut Bank of Boston, which made Fleet Bank the largest bank in New England. But that's never enough – so the Fleet executives hatched a plan to become one of the largest banks in the country. Fleet had attempted to merge with the First National Bank of Boston on a couple of occasions in the past. It didn't work out then, but in 1999, with greater size, assets, and a new leader, Bill O'Brien, Fleet put together a buyout plan referred to as a "merger of equals" to ensure everyone would support it. The Fed gave its blessing, and so did the shareholders at Fleet and BankBoston. Charlie and Doug watched as the boys from Rhode Island put their strategy into place in Boston.

Ultimately, after just six months, the merger was completed. Charlie was no longer the CEO of BankBoston, and the new bank had a new name, FleetBoston. Fleet's top-tier management moved into the existing BankBoston home office building at 100 Federal Street, known to locals as the "pregnant building" because it bulged out in the middle. It bulged out even more after the merger due to all the Fleet personnel who moved in. In less than a year, the storied old-line Boston bank was essentially gone, and the new bank would push to continue to grow through acquisition. With this tremendous growth would come significant and irreversible change. Charlie and Doug were in an excellent position to be part of the change; even better, they could help influence it. Charlie became FleetBoston's Chief Operating Officer, and Doug was promoted to Chief Accounting Officer. Both would have higher pay levels than they had before the Fleet acquisition, but they felt they missed out on some hefty bonuses being passed around during the acquisition. They knew that if they could orchestrate a subsequent merger, then they would both reap even greater rewards.

Right after the Fleet acquisition, Charlie made it clear to Doug that he wanted both of them to gain significantly from any subsequent mergers (which he hoped would happen sooner rather than later). Charlie figured that, at a minimum, he and Doug should receive no less than $5 million each over the next few years if they played their cards right, just like those guys at Fleet did when they initiated the merger with BankBoston.

"What do you think you need for retirement – $5 million, Doug? Do you think you could live better if you had an extra $5 to $10 million?" Charlie asked with a smile.

Doug said he'd be happy with half of that amount, but Charlie quickly chided Doug and said, "Listen, don't sell yourself short – don't ever sell yourself short!"

"Good point! In that case, $5 to $10 million is perfect," Doug nodded his agreement. Charlie always had big plans and a certain air of confidence that was hard to deny. So, Doug invariably followed Charlie's lead with a resolute spirit.

"It's our vote, our influence, and our connections that will push the Fleet guys to take some risk and go for the stars," Charlie said. "We can certainly get them to buy up another big bank or even some smaller banks, maybe one a year. If we receive our rightful bonuses for one major acquisition, it may amount to $10 million each. Or maybe if we get a bonus for each small acquisition, like one every year for five years, we'll still have that $10 million to take when we retire." Charlie paused and lowered his voice. "And Doug, $10 million is just a starting point – we've got some other things, you know that we can do, and they'll be worth a lot more than $10 million, my friend." Charlie just smiled at Doug and repeated himself, "A lot more than $10 million!"

The first day working at the new FleetBoston had been exhausting, and it was almost impossible to stay sharp. But Doug and Charlie had managed to sit through each of the Fleet senior managers' presentations without droopy eyes or snoring. Even Bill O'Brien's presentation was boring.

To make matters worse, Charlie kept thinking the acquisition should have been the other way around. BankBoston should have acquired Fleet Bank. The recent addition of BayBank had made the First National Bank of Boston slightly larger than Fleet Bank, and Doug and Charlie had been at the helm. But once the Fleet and BankBoston merger was announced, Charlie predicted what would happen. Sure enough, he and Doug lost the edge that had kept them on top for so many years. Now, the Fleet boys were in charge, and Charlie and Doug were nothing more than two highly paid servants to the Fleet royalty. It was all about control and timing, but for Doug and Charlie, neither worked in their favor this time. And forget about getting big bonuses; those were all going to the Fleet boys, while Doug and Charlie just got small rewards and a big thank you.

Chapter Four

Jenn came back into the waiting room with the ER doctor in tow when she saw that Charlie and Barb had returned.

"Charlie and Barb, this is Dr. Nick Kosta. He is the head of the Emergency Department. Dr. Kosta, these are our dearest friends." She introduced them and asked Dr. Kosta to explain to Charlie and Barb what was happening with Doug. He told them that Doug had been put into a medical coma to ensure that his brain would not shut his body down due to the extreme trauma caused to his head when he fell.

"It's the safest way to protect him until we find out what happened to him," the doctor explained. "It is still too early to tell if he had a stroke or tripped and fell. Either way, he had a severe concussion as a result of the fall, and that needs to be observed as well." Then Dr. Kosta excused himself and went down the hall.

"Everything will be all right; I know it will." Charlie got up and put his arm around Jenn's shoulders. Then he sat down, closed his eyes, rubbed his cheeks, and fell back asleep, thinking of Doug.

Doug had grown up in a blue-collar section of the City of Newton, which happened to be a fairly well-to-do town, while Charlie had grown up in Wellesley, a very high-income town. Even though Charlie's mother drove a Mercedes and Doug's mother drove a

Chevy, Doug and Charlie got along quite well, especially at work. If Charlie had any questions about the source of a particular external banking influence (the Fed, Euro, or Asian banking), he would summon Doug. Then, after listening to the problem, Doug would dash back to his office, run a series of numbers, and stumble back into Charlie's office with two or three different scenarios that could explain almost any influence on their banking cycles. Doug was an exceptional "numbers guy," and Charlie loved it.

Charlie was a "people person" – everybody loved Charlie and wanted him to be their friend. He was always the first choice on a pick-up team for baseball or basketball when he was growing up. Charles Henderson was always the captain of the school's sports teams, and his classmates voted him Prom King in his senior year of high school and Class President in his senior year of college. He was also elected to the College Hall of Fame for being the most "well-rounded" student in his class at Harvard. Yes, Charlie was a leader, and yes, Charlie loved people – a great combination and one of the reasons that Fleet Bank kept Charlie on the management team after the merger.

On the other hand, Doug was almost anti-social and didn't like participating in sports or anything else that required people skills. Doug Wood was a loner and enjoyed going fishing by himself. As a child, he'd been teased – the other kids would always call him Doug "Would," making fun of his name. "Who will drink their piss? Doug Would!" When Doug arrived at college, it was more of an escape – a new start and new people. By the time he met Jenn, Barb, and later Charlie, attending college had proven to be a perfect way for Doug to forget the teasing and pretend it had never happened. He was safe in the solitude of sitting in classrooms dealing with numbers. Doug's professors loved him, which went a long way towards helping Doug feel better about himself. Once he entered the workforce, he felt safe in his office, in the solitude of his work, and with his friend Charlie.

From the moment Doug and Charlie met, the relationship solidified. Doug looked up to Charlie, and in a sense, he felt like Charlie was an older brother. If Doug needed to talk with someone about problems, he asked Charlie, who could always help Doug see a solution. Doug went to Charlie if he required guidance regarding his relationship with Jenn or his parents. Charlie just knew the right words to say, and the problem was solved in no time at all. If Charlie had a problem understanding numbers, Doug could explain them with ease. Doug was available to assist if Charlie needed to discuss anything related to taxes, financial statements, or corporate values with someone, which proved invaluable with banking acquisitions. Doug helped Charlie, and Charlie helped Doug. It was a great relationship and a great friendship. It also helped that their girlfriends had been roommates in college and were best friends. They spent considerable time together both at work and during their off-hours.

Charlie woke up in the waiting room to Barb saying good night to Jenn and asking her if there was anything she and Charlie could do. Jenn said no and thanked them both for their support. Hannah and Emily, Doug and Jenn's daughters, were coming down together from Hingham and Cohasset and would be there shortly.

"Thank you both. I don't know what I'd do without you. You're such good friends." Jenn tried to smile through her tears. The strain was showing on her face. It was clear that Doug was still in danger.

"He'll be okay, I promise!" Charlie turned and said to Jenn.

"It's much worse than I thought. Dr. Kosta wants to consult with the neurosurgeon about Doug's head wound and with Doug's primary care doctor, Dr. Moran. And there are some other complications." Jenn shook her head as she leaned toward Charlie and Barb.

"Doug will be okay, Jenn. He has good doctors, and they will do their best." Barb said as she embraced her friend. Charlie started to tear up as he embraced Jenn and turned away, trying not to show his worry.

When Charlie and Barb finally left the hospital, Charlie let Barb drive home, and he promptly fell asleep from the stress of the day without any help from a glass of wine.

Barb pulled the car into the garage on the right and waited a minute before turning the engine off. She looked at Charlie's new Porsche next to her and shook her head ever so slightly. "Why had Charlie spent all that money on a second Porsche when the first one was still practically brand new?" she wondered. Of course, Charlie had justified the need, explaining that since the new Porsche was a Panamera, a four-door sedan, it would be a more practical vehicle to take four passengers because it had four doors. Barb had just laughed at the thought that her family's first house cost less than what Charlie had just paid for this new Porsche.

Chapter Five

Charlie realized early on in his banking career that a substantial amount of money passed through the hands of bankers every minute of every day. As far as he could see, nothing could stop you from reaching out and taking your fair share. So, maybe it was time for Doug and Charlie to reach out and take their fair share. Only time would tell if they could line up Fleet Boston to be acquired by an even bigger institution. Acquisitions were becoming a way of life in the banking industry, so it would make sense that Charlie and Doug would have more opportunities to bring in some additional banks and get bigger bonuses for any acquisitions they participated in.

Charlie called Doug into his office the following day to have a heart-to-heart talk about what they should do next. It turned into an all-day meeting, with Charlie telling his administrative assistant to get them some lunch and not to let anyone disturb them.

"Doug, we need to get the most out of this while we can. The Fleet boys will be getting massive checks once this merger is complete, and we're not going to see any of that money. It's all going to be for them – just for them. So, we need to find another bank, a big national bank, and position ourselves to be acquired again this year."

Charlie always had a slight glint in his eye whenever he was scheming. This time, his blue eyes were shining. He stood up behind his desk and said, "Now is the operative word – we need to sell FleetBoston as soon as possible to someone – to Bank of America, Wells Fargo, or Citicorp. It doesn't matter which, but we need to do it right now!"

Doug loved it when Charlie started scheming because it always meant some fun accounting magic and a big payday for him. He smiled at Charlie and got up out of his chair. As he walked out of Charlie's office, he started thinking about a new boat. Doug spent the next week examining several large national banks to determine which would be the better financial suitor and whether any of them would present unique challenges as a partner.

It was clear to Doug that the Bank of America had a strong balance sheet and was as well-positioned as the others to merge with FleetBoston. The strength of the management team was a little more challenging to quantify. Still, because Doug was Doug, he was able to build a spreadsheet that ranked each bank's management team on a scale from 1 to 100 across various skills.

In the end, Doug was able to provide Charlie with best-case and worst-case scenarios that all but eliminated Citi, Wells Fargo, and the rest of the big national banks in terms of the "best fit" opportunities for Charlie and Doug.

When Doug presented his findings, there was only one question from Charlie: "Can we take 'em?"

"I think so, Charlie! Bank of America has everything we'll need. Even better, they have a broad and rather sloppy upper management. Besides Bill O'Brien, none of the upper management has any real banking experience, as they came to Bank of America from other industries. It appears they are not qualified to run a large multi-state bank, leaving a huge opening for us to sweep in and set some new rules. I'm confident that Bank of America is the one we should go after, and it's the one that will fit best with our goals as we move away from FleetBoston."

Charlie listened to Doug with a thoughtful look on his face. He could imagine taking an offer from the Board of Directors and getting a couple of extensive checks in return when the deal went through. But that wasn't the only thing that Charlie was thinking about.

"Listen, Doug, we've got a huge opportunity to make good if you want to," he began. "It's all about that transition from one entity to the new entity and how vulnerable the new operation will be in the first year. Hell, look at FleetBoston; they're still struggling after the acquisition and will be for another two years. Even if we had been in the early crowd there, it still wouldn't have worked in our favor. But Bank of America looks promising," he smiled at Doug across his desk. "I'm excited that your data confirms what I was thinking.

"It's right here for us, Dougie," he continued. "Let's get into the driver's seat as quickly as possible to set our plan in place. The sooner we get control of the process, the sooner we'll be at the front of the line when Bank of America is handing out those big bonus payments," Charlie explained.

"Right!" Doug smiled and nodded in agreement. Both men remained quiet for a few minutes, each contemplating the next steps.

The plan was simple. They would connect with Bank of America, now based in Charlotte, North Carolina, and inform them why FleetBoston would be a fantastic acquisition and how well it would align with their plans for national growth. Charlie knew the Chairman and Chief Executive Officer of Bank of America, Bill O'Brien, quite reasonably, not only from O'Brien's time as President of Fleet Bank, but also from their two summers of study at the New England School of Banking at Williams College.

At first, Charlie thought spending two summers in Williamstown, Massachusetts, would be a big bore, but it turned out to be a significant opportunity. He met several mid-level bankers, including Bill O'Brien, and the sessions turned out to be both educational and enjoyable. Plus, the Williams College golf course was pretty nice. He and Bill O'Brien became good friends at Williamstown, and Charlie knew he could convince Bill to take a hard look at FleetBoston. Knowing each other well enough, Charlie suspected Bill was already looking into the bank due to his previous ties with Fleet.

Sitting in a well-appointed office overlooking Boston from the top floor of the bank building gave Charlie and Doug a broad perspective on what could be. The two friends smiled at each other. Doug's round face alight with anticipation of the potential challenge and the money he could earn. Charlie had a calmness, with almost a smirk on his face as he thought of the possibility of getting what he felt was due – more money than either one of them could imagine. And he thought that was just the beginning; more could happen as they learned their lesson from a new acquisition.

"Doug, once we get the nod from Bill that he'll make a real run at FleetBoston, we'll be able to jump on top while everyone else is still in the dark. We'll be the ones getting the big checks and BOA stock, while those folks from Rhode Island will still be asking us what's going on. We'll be in control, Dougie – just like the old days," Charlie exclaimed.

"Listen, Charlie, I'm all over this with you, and I want us to be successful this time – it's our time, right? I am entrusting you with my career, and I am confident in your ability to handle it. So, let's give them hell… and more."

Charlie just smiled, then nodded and said, "Right-O, Dougie, right-O! We're gonna have more money than we ever dreamed of, my friend. And who knows, maybe later, even more than that."

They both hugged, and Doug nodded in agreement, "Thanks, Charlie, you're the best friend I could ever have."

Chapter Six

In June of 2009, Alison Abrams was on special assignment at the Federal Reserve Bank in Boston. She was on loan to the Federal Reserve System from the U.S. Department of the Treasury, where she had made quite a name for herself as the youngest forensic accountant on staff and the one who almost single-handedly confirmed the Bernie Madoff financial fiasco. She had listened to Harry Markopoulos when he complained to the Securities and Exchange Commission in 2000 and again in 2001 that Bernie Madoff's investment company was stealing money from its clients, despite nobody else listening. In the end, Bernie Madoff and his company would steal almost $65 billion from his nearly 4,800 clients using a very effective and old-style Ponzi scheme.

It went like this: The early investors in his funds were paid huge annual returns, which were sourced by the newest incoming investors. The process was called the Ponzi Scheme, made famous by Charles Ponzi in the 1920s. Ponzi was a swindler and con artist who offered investors a 50% return on their money within the first 45 days and a 100% return on their money within the next 90 days. Ponzi gave early investors their returns from payments made by new investors. He was eventually arrested and charged with 86 counts of mail fraud and spent almost fifteen years in prison. Following in the footsteps of Charles Ponzi, Bernie Madoff was arrested in December 2008 and subsequently sentenced to 150 years in prison. In a previous life, Bernard Madoff was the non-executive Chairman of the NASDAQ stock exchange. Greed has no boundaries.

Alison, in many respects, felt that the underlying structure of the Social Security System mimicked parts of the Ponzi Scheme. Social Security is based on the simple fact that retired people receive their Social Security payments from the money they paid into the system. However, their Social Security payments are also funded partly by contributions from new workers of the following two generations. It's pretty neat until everyone who is a Baby Boomer (approximately 75 million people) asks for their money a bit early, like at age 62, or they all decide to retire and start collecting at age 65. Then, like a Ponzi scheme, the shit hits the fan. But Alison kept her thoughts about the Social Security System to herself.

She called her mother when she arrived in Boston, as she always did when traveling, and told her that "the Boston Fed was a funny looking building – sheathed in an aluminum skin like tin foil and so it looks as shiny as a new dime." In contrast, her room at the Intercontinental Hotel was unbelievably beautiful.

"Mom, it's right on the waterfront next to a building called the Russia Wharf Building, which was constructed in the 1800s, and behind that building is the boat where they had the Boston Tea Party. I'm only a few blocks away from Anthony's Pier 4, the biggest restaurant in the country, with the old Peter Stuyvesant boat from New York City acting like a floating bar sitting in the water right next to the restaurant! And I can walk from my hotel to the Fed, where I have unrestricted access to all their facilities. Can you believe it?" Alison was thrilled to be in Boston, enjoying the sights of a new city. She was eagerly looking forward to this new assignment. And she knew she could find out what the problem was at the Boston Fed.

Alison was brilliant; she graduated from Georgetown University with honors and dual degrees in accounting and finance. At graduate school, she also studied forensic accounting at Georgetown. She earned a certificate as a forensic accountant, partly because she could visualize the pathways that led to financial ruin long before others could and long before they occurred. She was also able to see the thousands of external factors that might have even the slightest effect on a living or dead balance sheet. Alison could see what were called financial ghosts. It was no surprise that she was asked to visit the Federal Reserve Bank of Boston for some ghost hunting.

Before she hung up with her mother, her mother asked if she would meet any potential husbands at the Federal Reserve Bank of Boston.

"How would I know, Mom? I just got here." Alison hung up the phone and stretched her legs out on her hotel bed. She thought about how many times her mother had asked her if there were any new prospects in her life and how many times Alison had to tell her no. There was never any time for nights out on the town or even a quick coffee date. Alison was a 32-year-old attractive woman who loved her job. She was intrigued by the chase, watching to see who was doing what and then deciphering the puzzles she needed to solve for the U.S. Department of the Treasury. In this particular case, in Boston, the mystery involved lost transactions between the Federal Reserve Bank of Boston and its client banks in the New England Region.

For the most part, Alison found that her best sleuthing was accomplished after everybody else went home, and she could work alone. She was much better off alone. Luckily, the hotel was very close to the Fed building so that she could return to work anytime, day or night. Plus, she had weekend access to the Fed's data storage facilities and servers.

Alison thought about what she had learned already at the Federal Reserve Bank of Boston, and it was not very comforting.

First, she knew that a handshake was a computer-based transaction between two or more computers. If you sent an email or any banking transaction between two or more computers in any location, there would be the actual data sent and an acknowledgment of receipt by the receiving computer back to the sending computer. If the data were not received or only partial data was sent or received, then the acknowledgment would indicate that. She also knew some handshakes between the Federal Reserve Bank of Boston and other district banks were sometimes incomplete transactions. More importantly, she knew that some of the handshakes between the Federal Reserve Bank of Boston and its member banks (also known as regional banks) were occasionally incomplete. Lastly, she knew that she'd have to look at a lot of handshakes before she could discover what caused these infrequent failed transactions. But the good news was that Allison had time and was very patient. She had been extremely patient while watching the handshakes between all the Federal Reserve Banks and the banks used by Bernie Madoff and his clients.

All she had to do now was watch and wait. If she could scrub enough data from the millions of daily handshakes, she could likely isolate why some of them were not completed correctly. At this point, they were losing data and could not provide the high level of performance necessary to manage the transfer of money between the Fed regions and other banks. These banks rely on the Federal Reserve System to provide financial and monetary clarity. Incomplete transactions, even just a few each day, were unacceptable and possibly symptomatic of a substantial problem.

If Alison were to be of any help to anyone, she would need to focus her extensive skills on this issue to determine the cause of the errors. Nothing short of complete success would be acceptable to Alison or the Department of the Treasury. Luckily, Alison was ready and able to figure this all out.

Chapter Seven

When Charlie and Barb got home from the hospital, Charlie called Billy Flynn, his former Head of Security at the Bank of Boston, to discuss Doug's accident and his current condition with him. Billy was a friendly kid who grew up in Chelsea, a rough-and-tumble part of Boston, and he'd never lost his neighborhood toughness and that neighborhood language. Billy was precisely the type of character you'd expect. He was of average height, had a dark Irish complexion, and had a scar on his left cheek from a bar fight he'd won years earlier. He was meticulous and invariably well-dressed, a surprising contrast for someone with his background.

"What the fuck, Charlie? What the fuck happened? This isn't very good. So, what are we gonna do?" Billy's response was always right to the point.

Charlie explained what they knew so far: Jenn had been up in Hingham, so nobody had been home when Doug had fallen. Unfortunately, he was probably bleeding for a long time before his wife got home and called an ambulance.

"There was a lot of blood on the floor all around Doug's head and shoulders; it was awful!" Charlie said.

"What the hell, Charlie? Do you want me to let anyone else know about this?" Billy asked. "Do you want me to come down there?"

"No, and don't, talk to anyone about this! I'll be in touch later. I'm not kidding, Billy, not a word!"

"What was that all about, Charlie? What's the matter with Billy Flynn?" Barbara asked.

"He's okay – just worried about Doug, that's all," said Charlie. Then Charlie moved from the desk where he had been sitting to the couch where Barbara was, sat down, and took her hand in his.

"Hey, dear, let's get out of here. Let's go get a glass of wine over at the Wianno – we need to relax."

Charlie loved the Wianno Club; he called it the best beach club on the Cape and more. The Wianno Club was a very nice "old line" private beach and golf club established in the 1800s. It provided a beautiful oceanside clubhouse, restaurant, and hotel facility on the ocean side of Sea View Avenue, right down the street from Charlie and Barb's house. The main clubhouse sat overlooking the Nantucket Sound and the Atlantic Ocean. There was also a beautiful inland golf course about a mile away. While Charlie enjoyed his membership at the Hyannisport Club, he also played the Wianno course, which offered a different set of challenges that helped improve his golf skills.

When Charlie joined the Wianno, Doug said he wasn't interested and kept a slip at the Crosby Boat Yard upriver from his house. Crosby had all the amenities Doug needed: maintenance, repairs, storage, and a bunch of fishing folks, just like Doug. The dockside restaurant on the property was also a nice place to grab a drink and some oysters after a day on the water. Jenn was okay with the Crosby Boat Yard for Doug, but she loved to go to the Wianno with Barb – the beach was beautiful, the restrooms were spotless, and it was a perfect beachside spot for lunch or the traditional Sunday buffet. Jenn even raised her daughters at the Wianno every summer, with a lot of help from Barb. Eventually, Doug gave in to Jenn's wishes and joined the Wianno.

Barb and Charlie walked together hand in hand down the street toward the middle of Sea View Avenue and entered the club from the side door into the Seaview Room. The long, sweeping porches were empty, so they grabbed a glass of wine from the steward and sat in two rockers looking out at the Atlantic. It was dark, but you could still make out the beach cabanas and the lawn chairs closer to the water. The only sounds came from a few people walking together on the beach in the distance.

"Charlie, I'm so worried," Barb said as she moved her chair closer and whispered, "I don't know what will happen with Doug, and I feel so bad for Jenn. What do you think happened, Charlie? What did Jenn mean by other complications?" Barb took a sip of her wine, and the tears started falling again. She looked up at Charlie, hoping he had an answer. He always had answers, didn't he?

"I don't know, Barb. It looks like he fell backward and didn't brace himself before he hit his head. Maybe a stroke or his heart or something. I don't know why the doctors won't tell us. Tell Jenn – that is." Charlie stared out over the manicured lawns, past the heavily laden blue hydrangeas, toward the ocean. "He just had his annual physical and didn't say there were any problems. He would have told me," Charlie considered aloud.

Barb wiped her eyes and had another sip of her wine. They sat there, each lost in their worries, watching the gulls and the osprey glide over the water. Eventually, Charlie dozed off again when he sat down.

When Charlie woke up, Barb was down by the water, kicking at the surf like she used to do when she was a kid. She'd pick out a wave that wasn't too short or too tall, run at it, plant her left foot in the sand, and kick the breaker with her right foot like a placekicker trying for a field goal. Charlie smiled at the vision of his beautiful wife relaxing for a few moments, and promptly fell back to sleep.

Chapter Eight

Six months after the Fleet-BankBoston merger, a new suitor knocked on FleetBoston's door. It was the Bank of America – one of the largest banks in the world and, by all counts, the second-largest bank in the United States. Bank of America sought to merge with a large eastern bank to expand its market share and asset base by acquiring additional customers. After the Fleet merger, they decided that FleetBoston was just the right size and could provide them with the type of non-organic growth they were looking for.

Of course, when Charlie and Doug heard about the potential merger, they had already considered it and planned something big. It turned out that when Fleet merged with Bank Boston, the only people who made any significant money from the takeover were the Fleet people. Charlie received a stock package worth just under $2 million, while Doug received a package worth $1 million – a fraction of the stock bonuses that the top managers from Fleet received. Doug and Charlie agreed they deserved much more. Following the Bank of America merger, they expected to receive at least $5 million in their stock package, as a bare minimum. Doug had researched similar mergers and found that the average package value for most of the acquired companies' senior managers averaged between $5.5 million to $10 million, so he thought they should ask for a reasonable and appropriate $10 million.

Charlie figured this was a perfect time to jump to the front of the line. And so, a plan was hatched to ensure they'd be paid a "rightful" amount this time. Doug was more than happy to receive a buyout package totaling $10 million just for being in the right place at the right time. Charlie thought similarly.

It became clear to Doug and Charlie that the Bank of America was able, prepared, and ready to acquire FleetBoston. So, they decided to explore all the near-term and long-term advantages this could offer them, particularly in terms of position and power–oh, and don't forget the money. They hadn't forgotten how much money the Fleet boys received as bonuses when the Fleet buyout had occurred or how little they were offered in comparison. They certainly weren't going to let that happen again! So, Doug spent several afternoons in Charlie's office putting the steps of the strategy together. It wasn't based on greed; Charlie was not a greedy man. Instead, his plan was based on fairness. Charlie wanted Bank of America to treat him, Doug, and all the FleetBoston employees fairly, which meant equal money for equal effort, as noted in their job descriptions. If they did more for the bank than another employee, then they deserved more in their buyout bonus.

"Doug, for Christ's sake, the guy who founded Bank of America was an immigrant from Italy. You'd think he'd have taught everyone how to be equitable in their banking practices. Wouldn't you think he established a banking foundation based on fairness? How else could he have made the first step in banking?" Charlie asked.

Doug smiled and agreed, but he knew things had changed in the last hundred years, and fairness was not part of the equation today.

"Charlie," Doug began, "it's not a matter of fairness. It's more about the haves and the have-nots. Remember, I grew up in that part of Newton where the have-nots lived, and we didn't mix so well with those who had."

Doug thought back to a line, maybe in a Kurt Vonnegut book, when one of the characters was discussing his large amount of personal wealth and said in passing to a friend, "It all comes down to this, my friend, and there's only one way to say it, and here it is… 'The hell with you, I've got mine...' No need to explain. Doug and Charlie were in a position and had the power to effect change during the acquisition and would make sure they "got" theirs.

Remembering Doug's suggestion that they dig their heels in and hold tight for a large package once the merger was announced, Charlie called his old friend, William "Bill" O'Brien who had left Fleet Boston after the merger and became Chairman and Chief Executive Officer of Bank of America, Bill O'Brien was down at its headquarters in Charlotte, North Carolina now. Bank of America used to have its headquarters in San Francisco, California, until it underwent a merger in 1998. The bank was founded by Amadeo Giannini, who had also founded the Bank of Italy upon his first immigration to the United States.

"Hello, Charlie – any chance you're calling to let me know that you're interested in moving down here and taking over the day-to-day operations of the whole thing? I'd love to have you sitting next door to me down here at BOA Central! Hell, you can have my office if you like," Bill offered with a laugh.

"Let's talk about the money first," Charlie began. "You know, Bill, it's all about the money, and I want to make sure we're in complete agreement about how much and when! So, let's get that out of the way before we start talking about where."

"Okay, Charlie, you win," Bill laughed. "The deal is just what you asked for – $10 million for you, half in stock and half in cash. Of course, your hard-working accountant friend gets the same deal. Is that good for you and Doug, or are you thinking of becoming bank robbers?"

"Ha-ha!" Charlie said the money was right, but added that he wanted one more thing. "Bill, you know I love the New England Patriots. What a great team we've had with Tom Brady! I know they have a few more Super Bowls in them, right? So, when I do retire, I'd like to retain lifetime access to four of those seats the bank owns right along the fifty-yard line at Gillette Stadium. Can you do that, Bill? I don't want access to the private jets or anything like that; I want four of those Patriots' tickets.

"It's easy to add to the deal, so yes, you can have the four tickets for life," Bill said. Then he asked, "But are you sure you wouldn't rather have access to the jet or the house in London? What's the big deal with Patriot tickets, Charlie?"

"Bill, you know those tickets you have behind the Patriots' bench are invaluable. Even today, I can't get anything as perfect as those were. They are priceless! I want the money and the four seats forever."

"Okay, done!" Bill laughed, and with that, their contract was sealed. Then Bill said, "You and Doug should expect your financial packages by noon tomorrow. Thanks for everything, Charlie. And don't forget – we have a home for you and Doug down here in Charlotte. Please join us if you can."

Charlie again said he'd think it over, and they hung up with a friendly goodbye. Then he thought, "This is a $47 billion buy-out, one of the largest bank mergers ever. It's the least we should get, you cheap bastard."

Charlie had other plans that did not include moving to Charlotte, North Carolina, or anyplace else, for that matter. Instead, he and Doug would be putting together a multi-step plan that included a retirement for both of them as soon as their new employment contract was up and they were free to leave. For now, they had two years to persevere, and worst case, they could jump at a moment's notice. The $10 million each was pretty good, better than what those Fleet guys got, but not nearly the amount Charlie was dreaming about. It wasn't greed, but it was envy. Charlie saw these venture capitalists making vast amounts of money for hardly doing anything. He knew some of these hedge fund managers who were paid millions of dollars just for investing other people's money and felt envious. He indeed ran a tighter ship than they did, so he knew he deserved the big payday and planned to get it very soon.

Charlie called Doug and told him all about his most recent call with Bill O'Brien at Bank of America. Doug was almost as happy about the Patriots seats as he was about the buy-out offer and the payments for him and Charlie.

"Great, the sooner we're on our own, the better off we'll be," Doug responded. He thanked Charlie and told him he loved him like a brother. Charlie smiled and said the same. They decided to meet at the bank the next day to pick up their stock, checks, and Patriots tickets and discuss Charlie's next steps.

"All right then, see you tomorrow," Charlie said. "This might call for a celebratory dinner with the girls!"

"See you then." Then Doug picked up the phone to check in with his youngest daughter, who was up at Bates College in Lewiston, Maine. She was in an internship program that required her to stay at school for six additional weeks, which meant spending most of the summer there. With this type of program, Emily could either graduate in three years instead of four or apply her additional credit hours toward a Master's Degree. Doug hoped she'd continue her focus on pre-med and apply to medical school after graduation.

Charlie had another sip of scotch before he went to the kitchen to see what Barb was planning for dinner. With a big grin on his face, he had difficulty not spilling the beans.

Barbara immediately noticed the look on his face and said, "Charlie, you look like the cat that swallowed the canary; what's going on?"

Charlie's smile grew, and he began to laugh. Then he raised his arms widely over his head.

"Big cat and bigger canary, dear. We've just secured a deal with Bank of America, and Doug and I will make a small fortune with this new buyout. Like eight figures each. Plus, I got Bill O'Brien to give me four of their Patriots seats on the fifty-yard line. How's them apples?"

At first, Barb was speechless. Then her look of shock turned to delight.

"Oh, Charlie, you're the best! I'm so impressed. I love you, and so do Doug and Jenn. What fun, our own Patriots seats!"

She leaned over and gave Charlie a big kiss on the cheek. Charlie took another sip of his scotch, then put it down, extended his arm, and invited Barb to dance with him. They danced all around the kitchen to music only they could hear. Finally, Charlie gave her a big hug and kissed her on the hand.

"Barb, you're the best thing that ever happened to me. I'm so happy we met over at Wellesley College, and I'm even happier you said you'd marry me. You know, you're my soul mate, and that makes me the luckiest guy in the world."

"Charlie, I love you to pieces and forever." Jenn smiled lovingly at her husband.

"Thank you for that, Barb," he said as he took her hand.

They moved from the kitchen into the living room and then headed toward the master bedroom. Dinner was late that night; for now, there was passion and lovemaking.

Chapter Nine

On her first day at the Federal Reserve Bank of Boston, Alison walked five minutes from her hotel to the bank and entered the small lobby from the large plaza out on Atlantic Avenue. The Federal Reserve Bank of Boston had two forty-story towers with elevators on each side and floors positioned between them. It looked a lot like a shiny washboard standing on end.

Alison spent most of her time that first morning getting the requisite clearances, including the bright yellow and blue Federal Reserve Bank badge that would allow her access to paper files, storage, and cloud storage facilities that she'd need to access locally. Her contact and full-time assistant at the bank in Boston was a woman named Agnes, a kind and welcoming person who had worked for the Fed for the last thirty years. She had worked at the old Fed building over on Franklin Street and moved to the new building on Atlantic Avenue when it was completed in 2004. She knew her way around every part of the new complex and had worked in storage and archival in the old building. So, she was very well versed in the retrieval portion of the bank's paper systems, including the on-site warehouse and archival facility, which was located in the basement of the new complex. She would be extremely helpful to Alison, who was not as well-versed in the particulars of the Fed's storage and retrieval systems. So, on her first day, Alison asked Agnes for a tour of the physical storage facility in the basement.

"We'd better bring a sandwich; it's a huge warehouse. We'll be down there for the rest of today and a good part of tomorrow, too," Agnes said with a motherly smile.

Alison smiled back at her and nodded, but was not sure this basement area would rival the sheer size of the Treasury's on-site physical storage bunkers in Washington, D.C., at the Treasury's main building on Pennsylvania Avenue. "In that case, let's start tomorrow morning," she told Agnes. Alison wanted to get a good night's sleep so she could start the day early in the morning.

"I'll meet you right here at 8:30 sharp tomorrow, Agnes. Thanks."

Before she left, Alison took out a small bowl from her briefcase, along with several small bags of candy. She filled the bowl and left it on her desk. She had always believed that offering candy to co-workers was a nice gesture and one that separated her from other employees.

"Well, that should help," she said.

Agnes was already waiting at Alison's temporary office the following day, holding a cup of coffee and a sweet roll for Alison, just in case she hadn't had time for breakfast. Alison smiled and thanked her as Agnes led her toward the eastern tower. There, a bank of elevators would take them down to the sub-basement floors that contained most of Fed Boston's paper storage. In addition, each Federal Reserve Bank held copies of all important documents from each of the other twelve Federal Reserve Banks to create redundancy and ensure that nothing would ever be lost. Unfortunately, it turned out that this was not always the case, as Alison had learned during the Bernie Madoff trial. But she was able to work around all of the shortcomings that confronted her then, and she was prepared to do the same thing here in Boston if necessary!

Alison spent the entire day reading various reports that highlighted the Fed's handshake procedures with its partners, the regional bank members that made up the Fed System in the Northeast. She was looking for the slightest anomalies that might indicate why the

Fed system was out of sync with its member banks. The problem, as it was explained to Alison, was that the Federal Reserve Bank of Boston was not always able to hear and see all the activities of its member banks.

When member banks closed their books each night, they reported all actions back to their Fed partner, and in some random cases, and with no particular pattern, the Fed handshake with their reporting partners was faulty. The member bank reported almost all of their daily transactions – but sometimes, not all of them were captured or they were captured but with empty data slots. This was not a traceable occurrence, and surprisingly, it occurred without any repeating pattern. It looked almost like a completed handshake but without the warm and fuzzy confirmation back to the partner. The reporting and closing of the daily numbers were accurate, just not always noted at the end of the day.

Alison's first task was to look and listen to these rare but continuing anomalies where a member bank was not telling the Fed about all of its transactions. Alison decided to name these anomalies "ghost transactions" because they might have taken place, and there might have been a handshake between the Fed and the member bank or not. So, like a "ghost," the transaction was not visible and, more importantly, might not have occurred. If it did happen, it might not have been seen or if it was seen some of the data slots were empty. In general, the visibility of any transactions was vital to the record-keeping of the Federal Reserve System. If one transaction was passed but not seen, the viability of the entire system was at risk. So, Alison was there to find these ghost transactions and determine their cause before the frequency increased.

On her first full day at the Fed in Boston, Alison was not able to see any of these random anomalies. On her second day at the Fed in Boston, she was not able to see any of the random anomalies. And on her third day at the Fed in Boston, she was still not able to see any of these anomalies, be they random or sequential.

When Alison got back to her hotel room, she called her mother to check in and tell her that the banking system in the Northeast was a bit odd. But she was very careful not to divulge any pertinent information about lost data, even to her mom.

"Something very funny is happening here, Mom and I can't figure out how or why," Alison sighed. Alison liked to use her mother as a sounding board for some of her work things. She also wanted to check in with her regularly because her mother was alone in Alexandria, Virginia.

"You'll figure things out dear, just like you always do." Alison's Mother said. Alison smiled and told her mother she'd be in touch tomorrow. Then she put her head down on her pillow and promptly fell asleep.

Alison's next visit to the storage facilities was more directed. She hoped to look through some of the transaction files dating from the early 1970s. At that point, there was no indication of ghosting, and the Fed believed that all transactions were properly recorded and confirmed in both directions. The amount of data stored in hard copy was almost unfathomable, genuinely unbelievable. Alison had a hard time resolving the vastness of the files available for review. In her first week in Boston, she had reviewed nearly 20,000 separate file folders, some dated as early as June of 1970 but most from the last two years. In total, these files contained almost seventy million transactions. But as everyone already knew, Alison could see through the clouds and into the sunlight; it was her way of separating the invisible transactions from the visible ones. In this particular batch of transactions, Alison spotted approximately twenty-five ghost transactions that should not have existed.

She had a slow first week, and Alison wasn't used to having slow weeks. For the most part, Alison was accustomed to getting to the bottom of things immediately. Since the start of this investigation, everything has been a big fat annoyance! No ghost accounts were spotted, very few ghost transactions, and no help from anyone else besides Agnes. She vowed to get things moving in the second week.

Over the weekend, she took a little time to walk around the streets near her hotel. She strolled along the edge of Boston Harbor along the new Rose Kennedy Greenway, which ran along Atlantic Avenue from South Station to the North End. It was filled with beautiful gardens, promenades, and plazas with fountains and street art. It was constructed after the demolition of the old expressway during the Big Dig project. From the North End, Alison could take the train back down to South Station, which was just across the street from the Federal Reserve Bank of Boston building. While it was nice to explore a bit, her mind kept wandering back to the ghost accounts.

Alison was back down in the basement over the weekend, but it was almost the same as the first week. No clues indicated why the handshakes between the Fed in Boston and its district and regional member banks were sometimes not detected. It was starting to infuriate her, and she was happy to let her mother know just how she felt when she called Saturday night.

"It's a standstill at this point, Mom. I don't have a single idea of what's causing this problem, and I'm not sure where the problem exists, it might be here in Boston or it might be out at one of the Regional banks. Either way, I may have to be up here in Boston for a couple more weeks if I'm not careful, if I don't start to see a pattern!"

Her mother didn't have any idea about what Alison did for the Treasury Department or what she was doing up in Boston at the Federal Reserve Bank. However, she was always quick to tell her daughter everything would be all right, given enough time and patience. She also reminded Alison to get out and maybe meet some young people if she had a chance, including some single young men.

Alison just smiled at her mom's suggestion. She explained, "Mom, I'm too busy right now. I don't have much spare time. I'm only 31, there'll be lots of time for dating later. Just not right now. Okay?"

"Well, Alison, I'm just thinking about what's best for you. Before you know it, you'll be 40 and still single, and then what will we do?"

Her mother was right; one of these days, she'd wake up alone in some hotel room on the weekend and regret that she spent all her time working and none of her time playing.

"Hey, Mom, you're right. I know I need to get a move on this dating thing. I'd like to find a boyfriend so I can spend time with him and maybe not work constantly. Making time for it can be tough, though."

Alison said good night to her mother, sat up in bed, and thought to herself, "She's right; I'm throwing away some of the best years of my life working instead of playing. That's gotta change… and it's gotta change sooner rather than later." So, Alison smiled, threw on some clothes, and took the elevator down to the lobby. She entered the hotel bar, got a drink then sat down, on a couch next to the bar. She looked around the bar to see who else was there just after 9:00 PM. To her chagrin, it was a mix of old-timers staying at the hotel and a few other guys in their mid-forties looking for some fun.

Alison shook her head and thought, "I'm not going to find my boyfriend here at this bar, certainly not tonight." So, she finished her drink, hopped off the couch, and headed up to her room. "Maybe tomorrow," she thought, "or maybe not."

Chapter Ten

Jenn stayed at the hospital with Doug the entire first night, then took a cab home around 10:00 a.m. the following morning. When she got home, her daughter, Emily, called to say that she and the baby would be coming down to the Cape to visit Dad later that day. Worn out from a stressful night, Jenn had drifted back to sleep after a shower and some breakfast. She woke up to Charlie calling. He wanted to know how Doug was doing and what the doctors had to say. Jenn was happy to talk to Charlie.

"He's not at risk while he's in a medical coma, but the doctors still don't know how he lost so much blood without dying. Emily is headed over this morning, and I'll be going back in a few minutes. Are you and Barb going back to the hospital?" Somehow, she always felt better when speaking with Charlie. He always seemed to know just what to do or say in any situation.

Charlie was dumbfounded that the doctors couldn't figure out what happened to Doug other than that he hit his head and bled a lot. Charlie assumed that was pretty obvious when he saw Doug lying on the library floor in a big pool of blood. He told Barb what Jenn had said. Charlie thought he might just call over to the hospital and see what they had to say this morning.

"Don't do that!" Barb said to Charlie. "Just let it be. They'll just tell you he hit his head when he fell, and the bleeding was a result of the scalp being cut open from the fall! We should go back over to the hospital and keep Jenn company. Let's give Jenn some support, Charlie; let's get back to the hospital right now, please!"

Charlie decided he should reach out to Billy Flynn at the bank to get his impression of the next steps and which steps they should take. He nodded at Barb and made a mental note to make the call after he and Barb returned from the hospital.

The medically induced coma was designed to stabilize the patient instead of transitioning toward death and dying. It allowed the doctors to take a closer look at the specific issues the patient was dealing with while not allowing those issues to overtake the patient's ability to continue living. In short, medically induced comas were a "stop-gap" measure to halt or slow down most critical conditions.

In Doug's case, it was the last measure, a "fleeting moment" to help save his life. Unfortunately, it was not able to bring him back to that moment in time before his head crashed into the side of the fireplace hearth, it was not able to bring him back to that moment in time just before his scalp was ripped open, and it was not able to bring him back to that moment in time before his occipital artery was slashed open from the punishing fall.

The occipital artery runs behind the internal carotid artery and, like the carotid artery, provides blood flow to the brain. Once the occipital artery was breached, Doug began to bleed out slowly. It was several hours before his wife came home to find him on the library floor, and in that time, he'd lost a lot of blood. Doug was in the fast lane to death, and few measures were available to slow him down.

Even though the ER surgeon was able to close up the gash in Doug's artery and address the other scalp issues, Doug's autonomic system, which runs his organ blood flow, had begun to shut down as a protective measure. His body shifted major organs into neutral to save energy and reduce the demand for oxygen from the limited blood supply. But even these internal safeguards did not wholly protect Doug's organs, since he had been running on half his blood supply until he reached the hospital. Seeing his condition, the surgeon and

ER staff almost immediately decided to put him in a medical coma. This would slow the internal systems from demanding more oxygen from the blood.

In terms of the cause of the accident, the doctors were confused. In particular, the neurological specialist and the ER doctor both wondered how Doug could have fallen backward. Generally speaking, most people tend to fall forward or straight down if they trip or have an episode that could cause them to fall. Additionally, neither doctor seemed to think that Doug had had a stroke, heart attack, or any other medical condition that would have caused him to collapse. So the inducement of a medical coma was a good stop-gap measure for now.

When Charlie and Barb met Jenn at the hospital later in the day, there was hope in Jenn's eyes. She had spoken with a neurological specialist, Dr. Rick Spencer, who had started a second blood transfusion into Doug's body. The hope was that Doug's body would accept a certain amount of blood, and the rejection rate would be minimal due to the medical coma. If the doctors were correct, then it would only take one additional full body transfusion of blood to get Doug back up to his normal blood levels.

Doug experienced a Class III hemorrhage with a loss of between 30 to 40 percent of his circulating blood, causing a dramatic drop in his blood pressure and dramatic shock to his heart. Fluid resuscitation with crystalloid and multiple blood transfusions was deemed necessary. But Jenn was worried that all these measures might be a big if – no promises yet.

After listening to all of the opinions, Charlie thought it made sense.

"Not to worry, we had a guy at the bank who had a skiing accident. He hit his head and bled a lot, and the doctor up at Hitchcock did the same thing. It saved his life!" Charlie and Barb held Doug's hand and stayed beside him for quite a while. They each talked about where they could travel when Doug was better. Charlie told Doug that he'd even go out on his boat and go fishing with him if he liked.

Jenn smiled and thanked Charlie and Barb. They all discussed their hopes that these doctors would take care of Doug and get him out of his coma. Shortly afterward, Jenn's daughters arrived, so it was good timing for Barb and Charlie to leave for a while.

Charlie called to update Billy Flynn on Doug's condition and to find out what people might be saying about Doug. The Boston Globe had just released an article about Doug's accident without contacting anyone, including Jenn. Some nerve! This just confirmed what Charlie already believed – journalists would stop at nothing to sell more newspapers. Even though he was retired, Charlie made a note to call the Bank's PR Department and give them Hell for telling the newspaper anything about Doug's health.

Charlie was concerned that if people started asking questions about Doug, even though he was in retirement, it might cause a problem. He was afraid that the media attention might upset Jenn and the family, not to mention poor Doug. Not all press is good press, and he didn't want his bank shares to be affected by any news. Charlie would rather this whole accident thing just stay amongst family and friends. However, for now, his only focus was to ensure Doug was getting the very best medical attention available. He needed Doug to show signs of recovery so everyone could stop worrying.

After chatting with Billy, Charlie put a call into his brother-in-law, a neurosurgeon at the Mayo Clinic in Minneapolis. Charlie wondered if they should get Doug up to Boston or even out to Minnesota. But his brother-in-law assured him that Doug was in good hands right in Cape Cod.

"Charlie, you've got one of the best neuro guys in the country working at Cape Cod Hospital, Dr. Rick Spencer. There's no need to move your friend at this point. Moving him would be dangerous; believe me, there's no need for any change of doctors or hospitals. He's in a good place right where he is!"

This made Charlie feel much more comfortable, and he told Barb what her brother had said.

"Thank God he's in good hands!" Barb whispered. "Thank God!"

"I'm just happy he's alive and stable, even though they have him in this medical coma thing. I still can't understand how he fell and why there was so much blood. It's so confusing, I just don't get it."

Charlie continued to worry about what had happened to cause Doug's accident.

Barb didn't have an answer, so she just shook her head in agreement.

"Barb, I think we should order some food for Jenn and the girls and bring it back to the hospital."

Barb agreed, so Charlie and Barb headed out of the hospital and drove to Baxter's, a seafood restaurant out at Hyannis Harbor. They ordered sandwiches, drinks, and some brownies for dessert. Charlie had a beer at the bar while they waited. When they returned to the hospital with lunch, Barb suggested that she and Charlie visit with Doug while Jenn and the girls ate in the ER lobby.

Once they were alone, Barb said, "I think once they're finished eating, we should let them visit with Doug and not be in their way. Too many people at Doug's bedside can't be good for his recovery."

So, when Jenn and the girls came back, Charlie and Barb stepped out for a few hours. They headed out for Route 28, and after a few minutes, they turned west toward Dowse's Beach in Osterville. Charlie turned the car away from the sun when they got to the beach, left the top down, and escorted Barb on a path through the dunes. They both sat down and stared at the beautiful waves flowing onto the shore in front of them.

"Charlie, is Doug going to die? Is he?" Barb asked.

Charlie was slightly surprised by the question, but shook his head no and reached for Barb's hand.

"Barbara, Doug will pull through this – he's a strong guy with a solid support system helping him. Let's think positive thoughts and send Doug our prayers and best wishes. I think he'll pull out of this in no time, and we'll be visiting him at home soon. We should stay positive."

Barbara smiled at Charlie and played with his fingers. She thanked him for the support and then closed her eyes.

When they returned a few hours later, Charlie and Barb left the car in one of the emergency room parking spaces and entered the hospital through a side door to the intensive care unit. They bumped into Jenn, who said Doug was still in a medical coma but stable. Jenn said they could go into the room and visit with Doug for a while.

They walked into Doug's room and saw Doug propped up in his bed, appearing like he was simply asleep. His eyes were closed, the bed covers were pulled up over his waist and abdomen, and he looked like he had just drifted off, but, of course, he was still unconscious. And the doctors wanted him upright to help with the circulation of the blood.

Charlie went to his bedside, sat down.

"Hey, Dougie, you're looking pretty good. How are you feeling today?" As he spoke, he looked over toward Jenn and Barb, who were both smiling

. "Dougie, it's Charlie and Barb. We stopped by to see you and say hello. I hope you're feeling better today, and I hope you'll be up and out of this hospital soon. I know you will, buddy. I'm counting on it."

Barb walked over to the chair on the other side of the bed, sat down, and held Doug's hand in hers.

"Hi Doug, it's Barbara. I just wanted to tell you that we all miss you and want you to feel better every day. Jenn is being a real trooper, but she misses you so much, so get better and let us get you home." She started to cry, so Jenn came over behind her chair, put an arm on Barb's shoulder, then leaned over and kissed her head.

Then, Jenn leaned over toward Doug, kissed him on his cheek, and said, "Doug, I love you, and I know you'll be feeling better soon."

Chapter Eleven

Alison had read something about Doug Wood in the Boston Globe that morning while waiting for Agnes to arrive. But she had no idea who Doug Wood was or what had happened to him. She didn't know it then, but she was lucky that this information would be stored in her memory to be recalled later.

When Agnes walked in, the first thing she noticed was the candy dish on Alison's desk. She was pleased that Allison was making herself at home. They said hello, then headed directly down to Level A – the first floor below the bank lobby.

This floor housed all the data indexes (over one million) that pointed to regional bank activities of any type. For example, if a bank in Westwood, let's say Santander Bank, had a teller named Margie who had mistakenly dropped a zero on her clearing at the end of the day, that pointer would bring you to the transactional error and then point to any additional transactional errors Margie or that Westwood Santander Bank had made that year. It was an obvious way to see if balances balanced and identify any useful patterns. Of course, the Fed in Boston would audit these transactions daily to ensure that all of Santander's branches complied with the Fed's "zero error" policy to ensure banking integrity. If another error occurred at Santander in Westwood, specifically a similar error or an error by the same person in the same week, then the Fed would come down on the teller and the bank pretty hard. Zero error meant just that.

But Alison wasn't interested in looking at simple transactional errors that a teller made; she was interested in looking at transactions that disappeared once they left the Federal Reserve Bank of Boston's District (which included all of New England). A transaction can only leave a region if it is sent to a different region by a Fed transaction. In that case, the accepting region must be able to see and confirm that the transaction arrived and was counted; otherwise, there was only a phantom transaction. It turns out, though, that sometimes, and for no discernable reason, a transaction would leave a Federal Reserve banking region and never be seen by any of the other Federal Reserve districts. It was almost like a ghost coming through your bedroom door. But if you can't see it, it probably didn't happen, right? Wrong – at least at the New England Federal Reserve. In these rare cases, the Fed in Washington was starting to see a pattern of ghost transactions leaving a specific region but never showing up anywhere else. Something was not right, and Alison needed to find out why. She was that good and she always found out what was happening and why. So off she went with Agnes to look more closely at these various transactions between the Federal Reserve System and the regional banking partners.

Alison was in a sour mood when she called her mother later that afternoon, since she had discovered nothing else about these occasional ghost transactions.

"Mom, this is starting to make me mad. I can't even see where these problems begin, and I have not been able to see where they end!" She let out a heavy sigh and brushed her dark hair away from her forehead. "I can't see anything! This is getting on my nerves! I'm supposed to be the best in the business but I can't find anything at all!"

Alison had decided to call her mother from work because she didn't know when she would get back to the hotel to call her. Instead, she sat in her temporary office, staring at two big blue computer screens.

"I know, Alison, I know. But remember – be patient, and it will eventually show itself as it did before." Her mother's reference was to the mysteries that presented themselves during the early days of trying to understand and track the accounting chicanery of Ponzi schemer Bernie Madoff.

Alison thanked her mother for the reminder and decided to go out to dinner at that seafood restaurant down the street from her hotel. She stopped at Agnes' desk and asked, "Agnes, would you like to join me for dinner at Legal Seafood tonight if you're not busy? My treat!"

Agnes grabbed her purse, and they headed toward the elevator, chatting and laughing. Both women would enjoy each other's company, and chatting at dinner would allow them to learn a bit more about each other.

When they were seated at their table, Agnes immediately asked the waiter for a glass of white wine. He turned to Alison, and she ordered her favorite, Absolut Vodka and tonic with a twist of lime. Then, Alison asked Agnes if she wanted to split some crabcakes to go with the drinks. Agnes thought it was a lovely idea. As soon as they received the drinks and appetizers, Alison tipped her glass and asked Agnes about her family.

"I'm divorced. I have two kids; one is in her last year at Radcliffe College over there, in Cambridge, the sister college to Harvard. She pointed across the Charles River towards Cambridge. My other kid is in his first year at Babson College over in Wellesley, about five miles away, over there." She pointed in each direction as she spoke so Alison could see first-hand where the schools were. "They're both pretty smart kids and even though my ex-husband skipped out on us, they're well-adjusted and pretty normal. It was tough initially, but now I'm used to being a single mom, and I prefer it to being married – particularly when I was married to him."

Alison asked if Agnes had dated anyone while trying to be somewhat respectful of Agnes being almost twice Alison's age. Agnes said, "A few guys over the years but nothing steady and certainly nothing permanent. I've got more to do with my life than waste time with guys who don't want to commit, so it was always difficult to get a call for that second date with two kids." Then she laughed, and Alison started to nod her head and laugh along with her.

"I'm sure it was tough for the kids not to have their father around," Alison suggested.

Agnes nodded and said, "Yes and no. I have a younger brother who's single, and he's been terrific about spending time with the kids. They both love him just like a real dad, and he loves them just as much, if not more. So, it's a perfect situation for all of us. We do a lot together, like going on vacations, celebrating birthdays and holidays, and even going to church. He's like a dad to them, with all the affection and love they could ever need, and he gets to go home at the end of the day to some peace!

"How about you, Alison? Have you found the right guy yet? Or are you just playing the field as we say?"

"You're starting to sound like my mother" Alison smiled at Agnes. "I'm too busy to date right now, and I'm not sure I'll ever have enough time to do an outstanding job at dating."

Agnes smiled and nodded her head in agreement. Finally, dinner arrived, and yes, it was seafood: fried clam strips for Agnes and a hot lobster salad roll with melted butter for Alison. They were quiet as they tackled their food, and then the conversation drifted back to work. Agnes assured Alison that whatever she needed, Agnes would find it for her.

"Listen, Alison, if there's anything else you need, you know, outside of the storage facilities, please don't hesitate to ask. I know a lot of people here at the Fed, and I'm happy to get you in touch with them to answer any questions you might have."

Alison sincerely thanked Agnes for the offer.

After they finished dinner, Agnes ordered a cup of decaf tea and a piece of ice cream cake, and Alison ordered a coffee latte and a slice of carrot cake. Alison couldn't believe how tasty the carrot cake was.

"Legal Seafood not only has great fish dishes but is also known for their terrific homemade desserts", Agnes responded with a mouthful of ice cream cake.

As they got up from dinner, Alison looked more closely at the restaurant and decided she liked the light wood of the interior and the modern look of the structure. She said she had a fun time and that the food was excellent. Agnes agreed and said she was delighted to know Alison a little better. It turned out that this was the beginning of a very good friendship between Alison and Agnes that would continue beyond Alison's assignment at the Federal Reserve Bank of Boston, just as long as Agnes wasn't involved in any money laundering activities.

"Just kidding" Alison thought.

Chapter Twelve

Doug was holding his own, stable but not improving. The doctors were concerned that the transfusions, coupled with dynamic blood loss to the brain, may have caused Doug to reject part or all of the blood plasma he was receiving. If the rejection were to continue, Doug would be at significant risk. And, of course, the doctors were still not sure why Doug had fallen backward and hit his head on the side of the fireplace bricks.

As part of their investigation, Doug's medical team decided to consult with the Massachusetts Medical Examiner's Office - MME, where the focus is on investigating the cause and manner of death for cases that are deemed violent, suspicious, or cannot be explained otherwise. With their input, the doctors could at least form an opinion as to why Doug had fallen in such a manner.

The hospital's medical examiner called in Dr. Jack Fernald to investigate. When he arrived, Dr. Fernald went to the visitor suite where Jenn and the girls ate their lunches and introduced himself.

Jenn offered Dr. Fernald a seat next to her and asked, "What's this all about? Is everything all right with my husband?"

"Your husband's doctors have asked me to take a look at him because of the unusual circumstances surrounding his accident. I need your permission to look at your husband, so I was hoping to talk with you and get your approval. Also, I was wondering if he'd started any treatments for leukemia."

Jenn looked up with a startled expression on her face.

"How did you know about the leukemia? Did anyone mention it to you?"

Doctor Fernald explained that he had seen the blood screenings and asked Dr. Moran, who confirmed the patient's diagnosis. Jenn explained they had just found out about it two weeks ago after Doug's last physical and were planning a visit to Dana Farber Cancer Institute in Boston.

Dr. Fernald nodded and continued. "First, we want to determine how your husband hurt himself. I don't want you to worry. I'm called in a lot when there is an accident and no witnesses to help. So, Dr. Spencer wanted me to take a look at your husband and provide a second opinion. You see, both Dr. Spencer and Dr. Moran think the way your husband seemed to fall backward is rather unusual and wanted me to check it out for them," said Dr. Fernald.

"Unusual – what does that mean?" asked Jenn. "Was there something unusual about my husband's accident? Tell me, please. What do you know about this accident that may give you pause to think it was unusual?" Jenn was starting to get nervous, and both daughters leaned forward in their chairs.

"Oh no, Mrs. Wood, that's not what I'm saying at all. I'm just saying that your husband fell backward and hurt his head; that's unusual. Normally, if someone falls from a standing position, they would only fall back if they walked into something located in front of them."

"But doctor, there was nothing in that room in front of my husband, so why did he fall backward?"

"That's what I want to look at, Mrs. Wood. I'd like to examine your husband's injuries and maybe see that room in your house where he fell. This may help us to understand how Mr. Wood fell backward."

"Of course, doctor. You're more than welcome to look at Doug and the room where Doug fell. Anything to help him. Thanks." Jenn calmed down at that point and accepted Dr. Fernald's handshake.

Her daughters stood up, put their arms around their mother, and told her everything would be all right.

"I don't understand why there are so many differences of opinion about Dad's accident. He fell, he hit his head, and that's that. No surprises, no mystery, right? I don't get it. Just make him all better – that's all we want, right. This is heartbreaking." Jenn was frustrated by the complexity of Doug's injuries and her lack of knowledge regarding the doctor's approach. She just wanted him to recover, to be all better.

Emily hugged her mother again.

"Dad is in good hands, and the hospital will take care of him regardless of how the fall occurred. And I'm happy to hear that you're planning to take Dad up to Dana-Farber for his cancer treatment."

Jenn smiled and kissed them both.

"Thank you, I love you both from the top and bottom of my heart." Jenn and Doug had used that phrase with the girls their whole lives. They both smiled and hugged Jenn again.

Meanwhile, Charlie called Billy Flynn and told Billy to meet him at the Wianno Club the next day. Billy got there first, and the receptionist brought Billy into a small private room just off the main living room. She looked him over with disdain. Even though Billy was dressed impeccably, he didn't look like he fit into a private club. His polo shirt wasn't the right brand, and the tattoo on his lower left arm looked out of place. Charlie was dressed in khakis and a blue blazer arrived a few minutes later.

"Hey, Billy. Let's get some coffee and talk about Doug's current situation." He was a bit business-like, but only to protect his feelings about Doug's condition. Otherwise, Charlie would be in tears, and he didn't want anyone, especially Billy Flynn, to see him in tears.

"So, Doug's in bad shape," he began. "The doctors put him into a medical coma, and now they're trying to get the blood loss under control. And we know he's got some complications. Anyway, none of this is good, so we need to be careful until Doug gets better. Understand?"

Billy nodded, then took another sip of coffee., "Listen

"Charlie, I've got Felix all over this, and you know he's one of the best computer guys around." Billy had hired Felix when Charlie and

Doug came to him about getting a really good, really smart, computer guy to help them with their business ventures. It turns out that Felix had worked in software development for UNIVAC and then went on to start his own software development company in California. His specialty is building and decoding high speed transaction systems. Billy found him when Felix was contracted to help develop the transaction processing for DARPA (Defense Advance Research Project – a government version of the Internet.)

With that in mind, Charlie took a sip of his coffee and nodded his head.

"Fine, Billy, but I don't want any trouble, and I certainly don't want anyone finding out what's going on. Doug is my top priority, but this stuff should be your top priority. If Felix can't take care of this, then get someone else who can! But do it right now! I want to hear that everything is all set by tomorrow afternoon. Do you understand?"

Billy just nodded his head in agreement. "Don't worry, Charlie. I'll take care of this."

Charlie stood up and said he'd expect a call from Billy tomorrow afternoon or sooner. They walked through the lobby, and all the while the receptionist watched them with a suspicious look. Billy just nodded his head at her and held the door for Charlie.

Walking back to the parking lot, Billy showered Charlie with platitudes about Doug and his health. As Charlie opened the Panamera's door, Billy shouted, "Nice car Charlie, nice ride."

Charlie waved back at him, jumped into the Porsche, and headed back home to pick up Barb so they could drive to the hospital together.

Billy immediately dialed Felix to let him know the meeting was over and to discuss their next steps. "Felix, this is getting a little more complicated. Charlie is in a terrible mood; he's worried about Doug. I'm concerned that this whole thing might fall apart if we're not careful."

"Listen, Billy," Felix assured him, "I'm keeping very close tabs on the accounts. Nobody will be able to see what's happening except you, me, and Charlie. Tell Charlie not to worry." Billy just grunted and told Felix that this should be his top priority – don't let anything else get in the way!

Chapter Thirteen

Dr. Jack Fernald was a coroner and a medical examiner, an MD with a forensic pathology specialty, charged with investigating causes of death. In Massachusetts, the coroners have specific geography to look after, mostly along county lines. However, in Dr. Fernald's case, he was available to any region to ensure that the medical examiner's office was always involved and offered assistance to local doctors where the patient was still alive.

Doug's medical team waited for Dr. Fernald while he received permission from Mrs. Wood. They were hopeful he could shed some light on the accident. If there was anything unusual about Doug's accident, the medical examiner's office could request that the local police department get involved as well.

When Dr. Fernald returned to Doug's room, he met with the Head of the Emergency Department, Dr. Nicholas Kosta, and Doug's physician, Dr. Steve Moran.

"Thanks for coming down, and thanks for your assistance in this particular case," Dr. Kosta said, shaking Dr. Fernald's hand.

"We don't understand how the patient could have fallen backward without attempting to stop himself. It's a bit suspicious, but it's why he bled so much before his wife got home, found him unconscious and then called 911," said Dr. Moran.

He started with a litany of questions.

"Does he have any lacerations on either his front or back? Was anything broken? Was he completely unconscious when the EMTs got there?" Dr. Fernald asked.

"He was on his back, unconscious, and bleeding from a deep wound at the base lobe of his skull. There was no indication of anything broken and no scrapes or wounds anywhere else on the body." Dr. Kosta held up Doug's X-rays on the screen. "He looks like he bumped into a wall, but he was in the middle of the room with nothing in his path to contact. It's an odd one!"

"If you want to go out to the scene, I'd be happy to take you there," Dr. Moran offered.

"Thanks. I already got Mrs. Wood's okay, so maybe we can go over there this afternoon," Dr. Fernald said.

Dr. Kosta had to see another patient, so he excused himself while Dr. Fernald walked over to Doug's bedside. Dr. Fernald asked if he could approach the patient. The ICU nurse on duty stepped aside to allow the doctor room enough to examine Doug.

"Anything you need," said Dr. Moran as he joined Dr. Fernald at Doug's bedside. Dr. Fernald looked at both of Doug's wrists, fingers, and elbows, as well as his knees.

"There are no abrasions or contusions, which leads me to believe that he did not attempt to mitigate his fall," he said. With some assistance from Dr. Moran, they unwrapped Doug's head, and Dr. Fernald looked at the scalp wound. He measured the distance from the temporal zone to the back center of the crown and then felt Doug's upper spine. He focused on the occipital-cervical joint C1, which holds the skull to the spinal column. Sometimes the occipital-cervical joint can be damaged if a patient walks into an immovable object like a tree or a wall. Then the C1 joint can be "whip-sawed" at a damaging speed, which may damage the joint. Sure enough, there was damage to the joint. In addition, Dr. Fernald felt that the joint might have suffered a second "whip-saw" when the skull hit the floor in a backward fall. However, the cause of such a fall is very limited to actions that include walking into something immovable or being pushed backward with extreme force.

"I don't see how this could happen other than by walking into an immovable object," said Dr. Fernald. "Please, let's go to the patient's house now."

Dr. Moran had some questions, but they could wait until they went to the house to look at the scene of the accident. So, he called Jenn to tell her he and Dr. Fernald were going to her house. "Is this a good time, Mrs. Wood?" he asked.

"Yes," Jenn said. "I'll see you in a few minutes. Thank you"

The two doctors drove down Seaview Avenue on their way to Doug's house on Eel River Road. The road contained some of the most expensive homes on the Cape.

"Wow, these are beautiful houses. I'm happy to be in Falmouth, but these are very impressive. The view is priceless," Dr. Fernald commented.

"Yes, all of the homes on the left side down the street look right out onto Nantucket Sound and the Atlantic Ocean," said Dr. Moran.

They drove by Charlie's house and down Seaview Ave to Eel River Road, then pulled into the Woods' driveway and parked the car. Jenn answered the door with her daughter, Emily, just behind her. She had been crying again but wiped her eyes dry. Dr. Moran thanked Jenn for her time then Jenn and Emily led them into the library, where police tape was still hanging from the door jambs. The spot where Doug had fallen against the fireplace was still stained with blood, as were several bricks in that corner of the hearth. There was a larger bloodstain about a foot away on the light oriental rug.

Dr. Fernald looked out to the back windows facing the river and again thought, "What a beautiful view." From where he stood, he could see the expansive back lawn, the boats at the dock on the river, and even across to West Bay and Oyster Harbors Golf Club. It was a picturesque view. The rest of the room was covered with light pine paneling and built-in bookcases. It was a big room, maybe thirty feet in diameter, with three French doors opening onto a back slate patio. It had two large leather couches with several fancy-looking easy chairs, each with a matching ottoman. Dr. Fernald examined the fireplace and desk as possible places for Doug to hit his head.

He turned to see Jenn and her daughter watching him closely. He continued to look around the room for other items that may have caused Doug to trip or fall.

"I'm sorry, I haven't had time to have this all cleaned up. I've been with Doug every day. Please excuse the mess," Jenn said.

"It's okay, Jenn," Dr. Moran said. "You should be with Doug. Plus, this will help us see what happened for ourselves."

Dr. Fernald turned the edge of the rug to look under it and saw that the bottom of the rug was bloodstained, as was the oak floor underneath.

"He lost a lot of blood, didn't he?" Dr. Fernald asked.

"Yes, just about two liters, but we don't have an exact time frame." Dr. Moran looked over at Jenn and Emily for more information.

"I was up in Hingham at Emily's house and I didn't get home until 4:00. I have no idea how long he was lying here," Jenn offered. "If only I had been here." She started to cry again.

Emily put her arm around her mother's shoulder and said, "Mom, it's okay; he's gonna be okay."

"Well, as you may know, the bleed time has an intrinsic start and stop. However, with the patient in a prone position, it is complicated to determine an absolute bleed time which we generally use for the time of death calculations." Then, realizing what he had just said, Dr. Fernald turned to Jenn and Emily and said, "Sorry, that didn't come out the way I intended…I just have a couple of questions, if you don't mind?"

"I'll try to help," Jenn said warily.

"When you found your husband here, did you see any movement from him, or did he seem to be asleep? Were his eyes open or completely shut? Was he breathing deeply, or was he taking shallow breaths?"

Jenn wrinkled her face up and responded that she hadn't noticed Doug breathing, which is why she told the emergency dispatcher that she thought he might be dead. When she bent over his body, she noticed tears around his eyelids and saw the blood under his neck, shoulders, and head.

"I was convinced he was dead," she said, crying again. Dr. Moran looked toward Jenn and gave her a sympathetic smile and then said they had finished. Jenn looked back at him and said she had one other piece of information to share with Dr. Fernald.

"He was quite warm to the touch, not like you'd expect of someone who may be dead, and that's why I had hope. He was warm to the touch like he had a fever or something."

Dr. Fernald smiled and said, "That's great news, he was fighting the blood loss and providing his version of a medical coma, which may be just what saved his life."

"Thank you, that makes me feel a little better," said Jenn.

Emily walked them to the door, leaving Jenn standing in the library, staring at the blood-stained rug. Her shoulders slumped, and all the color drained from her face. Dr. Fernald thanked Emily and so did Dr. Moran and asked her to thank her mother again for them. She smiled and nodded then said "Yes" then opened the door for them and waved goodbye as they walked down the driveway to their car.

When the two doctors got into their car, Dr. Moran turned to Dr. Fernald and said, "After seeing the room, I'm just as confused about how he could have fallen backward without any indication of bumping into anything. Could he have fallen backward without any of those telltale signs? Maybe something startled him."

Dr. Fernald shook his head and said, "Or maybe, just maybe, somebody shoved him and he fell backward. It's not out of the realm of possibility that someone was in the room with him and gave him a shove backward in the heat of an argument. I quickly checked the fireplace mantle and the desk but didn't see any blood there."

"Let's take another look at the patient's upper torso and lower back," Dr. Fernald said as he cleaned his glasses with a handkerchief. "There may be something we missed."

When they returned to Doug's room at the hospital, Dr. Spencer, the neurological specialist, was there with a couple of residents listening to Doug's heart and checking specific blood flow to the extremities. Dr. Spencer shook hands with Dr. Fernald when they saw each other.

"Hi Rick, good to see you again," said Dr. Fernald.

"Good to see you as well," said Dr. Spencer. "It's been a couple of years since we were at that conference in Cincinnati, and I still remember that yours was the best echocardiogram presentation I've ever heard. You kept the attendees spellbound with the data you collected and your analysis."

"Thanks, nice to hear you say that." Dr. Fernald then turned to questions he had regarding Doug Wood's condition. "Tell me, Dr. Spencer, does the patient have any breathing abnormalities – like a lower lobe airway deficiency in either lung? Does he exhibit any cranial blood pressure loss? I want to confirm whether the front of the skull suffered during impact."

"No, Dr. Fernald, no signs of abnormalities surrounding the skull plate or cranial blood pressure that might indicate a cerebral contusion. All functions were normal even with blood loss to the extremities."

"Very, very odd. Thanks. Mind if I take a look at the blood scans? Maybe they will provide us with some additional information that could explain the fall."

"Sure, here they are." Doctor Spencer handed an iPad to Dr. Fernald, who studied the screens representing all of Doug's blood scans.

The blood scans would undoubtedly provide the doctors with a better sense of how Doug fell backward. Still, they were not conclusive in terms of why the body's inertia overtook the normal falling position to the sides or forward. Something made Doug fall backward, and it was probably not something he did on his own. However, Dr. Fernald would need a bit more data before he could provide conclusive evidence that an external force had impeded Doug's natural tendency to fall in a forward motion.

The possibility that Doug might have tripped on something in his path and reacted with a natural startle remained possible but was very unlikely based on the surroundings in the room near the site of the fall. But then, where was Doug when he fell? Certainly, he was not near the fireplace, where he was ultimately found unconscious. If he fell backward, it certainly did not appear to be because he tripped on something near him. There was something very odd about this accident, and Dr. Spencer and Dr. Fernald were not yet comfortable saying what had happened to this patient.

"I think we need to look closer at the body's posture and the damage to the skull before we rule this an accident," Dr. Fernald said to Dr. Spencer.

"I agree," said Dr. Spencer. "Something doesn't fit – just doesn't hold for this type of accident. There's more to do here."

Chapter Fourteen

Alison was almost at her wit's end. She had been all over Fed Boston's online and hard storage facility over the last two weeks with very little to show for it. She could certainly see a few incomplete transactions between Fed Boston and some of their regional bank partners. Nothing unusual and certainly not a lot of incomplete transactions; that was all she could see. There appeared to be no reason for the faulty handshakes, and she had no idea where the funds ended up.

Allison's mother called to see how she was doing. It was a beautiful day, and her mother hoped Alison was taking time for herself. However, she was a bit dismayed to hear that her daughter was working through the weekend.

"But Alison, it's Saturday. Don't you want to do something else while you're in Boston – take a tour around the city, walk the Freedom Trail, go see a Red Sox game or something? How about going over to a museum? You shouldn't stay at work all the time; you'll get tired and cranky."

"Mom, I'm already tired and cranky, but not because I'm at work all the time. It's because I don't have a clue what's going on here, and nobody in this big, stinking building can help me. I have to stay here until I get a look at the real issues and figure out how to fix them.

That's what I have to do now."

"Okay, Alison, but promise me you'll look after yourself and not get run down."

"I'll be fine, Mom. Talk with you later. Bye."

Alison was alone in the server room when she suddenly had an idea. "Hell, why not put a trace on each server?" she mumbled aloud. "All the outbound traffic will be collected and identified; maybe then I'll be able to see the specific traffic going out and coming back. That might show me the traffic that doesn't complete the handshake process. Maybe there's a pattern with the traffic that isn't completing the handshake. This will identify the source of the problem, and I'll have a chance to track why some of the handshakes are incomplete. There's a possibility it will show me something I can't see now – those ghosts."

As good of an idea as it was, there were around a thousand servers at the Fed Boston in-house transaction storage area.

Although it may take some time to set up, Alison was excited now! She may have stumbled onto a way to watch the handshakes in real-time and see which ones failed and why, rather than simply viewing an end-of-day report. This was turning out to be a productive Saturday, after all. Alison sat down at the console that controlled each server as part of a server-nest. MIT in Cambridge originally designed it as a way for large storage sites to qualify as being safe from external events of any type – server externalities. Sort of a protective coating that touched each server individually as well as all servers combined in the nest. Alison wondered if anyone over at MIT had run into the same issues as the Fed had experienced. Too bad she couldn't ask them since her work at the Fed was classified. Oh well, she thought, maybe there's a way to find out without thoroughly discussing her classified work here at the Fed…maybe.

Alison set a trace for each server. She reviewed all the set points and then launched the trace to go into the nest and follow each transaction on each server for the next 24 hours. Then she set a second trace to follow all the combined transactions that came into the nest itself. This would ensure that any incomplete handshakes would be tracked back to the appropriate regional bank and saved to a separate file as proof of an incomplete transaction. Alison could then review each file to see similar incomplete handshakes on an individual server when acting outside the nest. Simple but effective in trying to capture each incomplete transaction.

And then, just for her edification, she looked at the MIT AI Labs website to see who was responsible for developing and supporting the nesting software. Maybe a quick visit to MIT would be something she could do without sharing information about her classified work at the Fed.

Alison felt much better now that she had something concrete to begin to look at and something that could help lead her to the possible cause of these interrupted handshakes. She thought all these issues with the handshakes and the lost money were related, and maybe she could find out ultimately what or who caused the losses.

Chapter Fifteen

Matt Davis was a senior detective at the Barnstable Police Department. He was just one of only a handful of detectives attached to the Town of Barnstable Police Department, which said a lot about the level of crime in the Town of Barnstable and its villages. A lot of Detective Davis's cases were just run-of-the-mill larceny, domestic violence, or drug-related. He had only a few murder cases in twelve years, and most of them turned out to be very straightforward family arguments, followed by someone killing someone or maybe killing themselves.

Overall, the Town of Barnstable, like many towns on Cape Cod, was pretty quiet except for car theft or drug-related problems. So, it was a bit of a surprise when the Barnstable Coroner's Office called to alert Detective Davis that he would be getting a call from the Chief Medical Officer, Dr. Jack Fernald, sometime that morning. A minute later his phone rang, and it was Dr. Fernald calling.

"What's this all about?" Detective Davis asked.

Dr. Fernald said that a person in Osterville had fallen at home last Tuesday and hit his head on the fireplace hearth.

"There was significant blood loss, and he had to be taken to Cape Cod Hospital. The patient is in a medical coma until they can completely stabilize his blood volume. He was alone when it happened; his wife was up in Hingham visiting family and came home just in time," Dr. Fernald explained. "He's a lucky guy. It might have been a job for the local coroner if they didn't get him into the hospital when they did. Everyone on the medical team thinks it was an unusual fall – not necessarily an accident – so I may need your assistance later."

Matt Davis thanked Dr. Fernald and told him to call if he had any questions for the police or needed support.

Matt decided to check the police and fire logs for the past week in Osterville. He found the event on Tuesday the 28th and clicked on the internal notes that the EMTs and the police officer made at the time. The report mentioned that the body was found on its backside, and a lot of blood came from a deep wound on the back of the head; an injury sustained probably from falling backward and hitting the hearth in front of the fireplace. Nothing else near the body and nothing the patient could have walked into or bounced back from. Seems unusual, but the docs at the hospital had not reached any conclusions… yet. Matt picked up his phone and called the responding officer's cell phone. He knew the officer quite well so the call to his cell phone was from memory.

Officer Reid Thomas answered on the first ring and said,

"Hello, Detective. How are you and how can I assist?"

"I'm great Reid how about you?"

"I'm good, but I know you're not calling to see how my golf game is."

Matt said he wanted to talk about the incident in Osterville last Tuesday; Mr. Doug Wood was the patient's name. Officer Thomas asked if now would be a good time since he was at headquarters and could come down to his office. Five minutes later, Officer Thomas stood at Detective Davis's door with an extended hand and a smile.

"How you doin' Matt?"

"Good Reid, thanks for asking, and thanks for coming by so quickly. I have a couple of questions for you, and I'd like to go over to their house to see where the accident occurred. Do you have his wife's name and phone number, or is the alert file good?"

"Alert file is good, but I'd be happy to call Mrs. Wood to see when we can stop by. I still have her number on my cell phone."

"Thanks. Let's give her a call now, and if she's okay with it, we can scoot over this morning."

Officer Thomas picked up his cell phone and dialed Jennifer Wood's home number. "Good morning, Mrs. Wood. Officer Thomas here. Thanks, I'm fine. How is Mr. Wood doing? Good, glad to hear that. If you don't mind, I'd like to stop by with Detective Davis. He has a few questions. All right, that's good for us – see you then." Officer Thomas gave Matt the thumbs up, and they started walking out of the building.

"Let's take my car, Reid. We can talk on the way over to Osterville.

"Sure, Matt, that's fine with me."

Chapter Sixteen

Alison drove over the bridge on the Charles River to the MIT campus in Cambridge. She had two reasons for the trip. First, she had heard so much about the school and was interested in checking out the esteemed campus. She also wanted to reach out to Dr. Aylward, the distinguished Professor of Neuroscience at the McGovern Institute at MIT. Dr. Aylward and his team developed the nest software search system in concert with the MIT/IBM Watson Artificial Intelligence Lab. The prototype nest allowed servers to act more intelligently as a group than individually. It has evolved into a system that can gather requested data as well as data it deems related to the search, kind of like word cashing from the old computer days.

Alison thought that Dr. Aylward might be able to assist and guide her depending on the trace results that she was expecting in the next day or two. Of course, she would not be able to share details of her classified activities, but she could talk with him in generalities in the hope that he'd understand and still be able to assist.

However, after getting lost on Vassar Street and then getting into the wrong lane on Massachusetts Avenue, she mistakenly traveled back over the Mass Ave bridge. Leaving Cambridge and the MIT campus behind her, she found herself driving back to Boston.

"Damn, this is without a doubt the worst-designed road system in the country! Why can't they do what they do in New York City or D.C. and have all the roads, streets, and avenues go the right way? These one-way streets that end at another one-way street are impossible to navigate! If I have to come back to MIT this week, I'll call a cab – I'm never driving in Cambridge again," she decided. She headed back to her hotel to have a little downtime.

Alison couldn't get back to the Federal Reserve Bank of Boston fast enough Monday morning. She was in the outer lobby as the guards unlocked the front doors.

"Good morning, Ms. Abrams. A bit early today?"

Alison smiled and said good morning, then hurried to the bank of elevators on the south side of the building. She inserted her key card and pressed level 5, the basement level that contained the server farm and where she would review the traces requested over the weekend. She was almost running down the corridor into the server room when she heard Agnes directly behind her.

"What's up, Alison? Why are you in such a hurry? Need some help with anything?"

Alison explained the transaction traces she launched on Saturday and said that she expected to see some sort of pattern with the transactions, particularly since she sent traces to each of the servers as well as to the nest.

"You sent transaction trace calls to all the servers and directly to the nest? Oh, my God, I hope you didn't crash the servers or worse, crash the nest!" Agnes gasped. "Let's go take a look."

Alison smiled at Agnes' motherly concern and said, "Okay."

The servers were fine, and so was the nest. The only issues that Alison and Agnes found were almost a million transaction trace call replies and a lot of data accompanying them. Alison was thrilled at the number of responses and was pretty certain that she could extract a pattern. With a pattern, she could see where the money was going if it did not complete a transaction with the Fed or with the Fed's member banks.

"Agnes, this is fucking beautiful!" said Alison. "Oh, Agnes, I'm so sorry! That just slipped out."

Agnes laughed and gave Alison a big hug. "I have two kids under the age of thirty; I've heard all those words."

Alison began to place the replies and matching traces into a separate file, then labeled it private and put a crypto lock around it so nobody could read the contents. Then she wrote a routine that would grab all the replies and link them to any lost handshakes so she could start the tracing process and see where the transactions failed. Hopefully, this would tell her how much money had left the Fed system.

"Agnes, we're going to find out how much money is leaving the Fed system, where it's going, and maybe who is stealing it. This is a great start, let's grab something to drink, coffee, tea?"

"I'd love some," said Agnes. She and Alison went back upstairs to Alison's office to brew a cup of tea for each of them. Agnes smiled at Alison and said, "You know, Alison, this is the most fun I've had in a long time. Thanks!"

Alison nodded her head and said, "Me too, Agnes, me too."

Chapter Seventeen

Before Detective Davis and Officer Thomas could ring the doorbell, Jennifer Wood had already opened the door and reached her hand out to them. She introduced herself to both officers since she didn't remember meeting Officer Thomas on the stressful day of the accident.

"Please come in. Can I get you some coffee or tea?"

"No, we're fine, thank you," said Matt. "But we want to take a look at where the accident occurred, and we'd like you to tell us what you saw when you got home."

"I'm still having trouble with this, but you're welcome to look around." Jenn started to cry but was able to lead them down the entryway into the library. She beckoned them to follow her and said, "Come this way, please." Then she turned to them and said, "The doctors were here yesterday – they wanted to see the accident scene as well." She pointed at the spot where she had found Doug.

"He was right there with his eyes wide open, bleeding from the back of his head. The blood was all over the bricks and the area rug near the hearth. I had everything cleaned up yesterday after the doctors were here. The crime scene folks were over here yesterday. When they finished, they told me that it was okay to clean everything up. I hope you don't mind." Jenn said. Then, while she was pointing to the floor, she started to cry again.

"He wasn't moving," Jenn shook her head, "but I watched him and saw that he was breathing – thank God he was." Jenn couldn't stop crying, so she turned away from both of them, hoping they hadn't noticed. Both policemen apologized. She looked up and said, "Thank you. Anyway, I grabbed my phone and called 911."

"If you don't mind," asked Matt, "was the house completely locked up when you arrived?"

"Yes," Jenn said, "We have an alarm system that we have to log in to. I checked, and there were no other entries displayed on the console. Doug never left, so the alarm system just had me logging in when I got back from Hingham."

Matt took a few notes and asked, "What time did you say you left for Hingham? Did you go straight there or did you stop somewhere?"

"About 9:00, and no, I didn't stop anywhere. I went straight to my daughter's house," Jenn answered a bit defensively. "It takes a little less than an hour to get there," she said.

"Did you come right home? Did you call Mr. Wood along the way? Were either of you expecting any company?"

Jenn looked at him curiously. "I came right home, and no, I didn't call him. Why are you asking me all of these questions? He already asked me," she said, nodding at Officer Thomas. Matt nodded and continued to write notes.

"Mrs. Wood, I must double-check and cover all of the possible scenarios. This is an unusual accident." Matt then consulted his notebook and asked, "How about anything misplaced or missing? Like if someone had gained entry and was looking through the house for drugs or money."

"No, nothing was out of place, and nothing was missing either. We keep about a thousand dollars in cash in Doug's desk drawer in the office. It was still there. I didn't check my medicines, but nothing was out of place upstairs."

"On a personal level," he said apologetically, "was Mr. Wood well? Were there any health issues that might have caused him to lose consciousness and fall?"

"No," said Jenn, "I don't think so. We recently found out that Doug has leukemia, but that wouldn't cause the fall. Would it? The doctors at the hospital said he had no signs of a stroke, or a heart attack, or an aneurysm, or anything like that."

"Mrs. Wood, do you know what your husband was doing at home last Tuesday?"

"Paying bills, maybe reading or working on a project," said Jenn.

"Why didn't he go up to visit your daughter and granddaughter? Did he say anything about other plans?"

"I don't know. Doug said he had some things to do here in the morning and that he'd run up to Hingham later in the week. Normally, he comes with me when I go to Hingham. He loves his new granddaughter and always wants to see her." Jennifer paused for a moment, then said, "Now that you mention it, I'm a little surprised he scheduled something in the morning. He knows I always go up there in the morning because the traffic is so bad coming back here in the afternoon. He could have come with me in the morning and done his things later in the day. I made these plans a week ago, and he knew it."

"Mrs. Wood, do you have any idea what your husband was doing that morning?" asked Matt.

"No, I am clueless, honestly," said Jenn. She started to say something but stopped herself and looked away from Detective Davis.

Matt noticed and said, "Is there something you wanted to say?"

"No, no." Jenn looked away again. Matt couldn't help but wonder what was going on with Jenn. She seemed upset, of course, but was there something else going on behind those tears?

Matt asked if the security system included video surveillance. Jenn replied that they had video cameras around the property. Matt then asked if the crime scene team had access to the surveillance system.

"Yes, I gave them the surveillance system laptop, which held all of the separate files from the video cameras. However, they said the cameras' data files for the 28th were all missing, maybe erased. I don't know who could have erased those files."

Matt then asked if anyone else had access to the video surveillance system, but Jenn said only she and Doug could use the laptop. Matt wrote himself a note to contact the crime scene team to see if they could figure out how the files could have been erased. Then he thought, "Well, maybe Doug didn't erase the files; maybe someone else did that." He looked back over at Mrs. Wood and smiled ever so slightly, and again thought that maybe there was more to this than she was letting on.

After wrapping up, Matt shook Jenn's hand, thanked her for her time, and said that he hoped Mr. Wood was on the mend and feeling better every day.

While Matt and Reid walked back to their car, they began to discuss the circumstances of Doug's accident.

"You know, I just have this funny feeling that someone was here with Mr. Wood. That must be the reason he didn't go to Hingham with his wife. It must have been a really important meeting. I wonder who it was?" Matt turned to Reid and continued, "Maybe this isn't what it appears to be. An accident? Oh, I don't think so."

"Plus, the evidence doesn't point to anyone breaking in. If Mr. Wood turned off the cameras or deleted the video data files after he let someone in, he must have known that person, trusted them, and wanted it off the record. Kinda makes you a bit more suspicious, doesn't it?" said Officer Thomas.

Matt nodded in agreement and said, "Maybe we need to look at some of Doug Wood's closest associates. Have them explain their whereabouts on that Tuesday. What do you think?"

"I think we should do that and see what we can find. And maybe we should check Mrs. Wood's whereabouts. Just as a precaution."

When they arrived at the station, Matt thanked Reid again for his assistance, and then they headed their separate ways.

Chapter Eighteen

A quick look at the data showed Alison that some of the trace results contained several handshake failures, which were all a direct result of interference by ghost transactions originating from a few ghost accounts that were external to the Fed systems. Alison leaned closer to the display with a surprised expression.

"Holy shit Agnes, there are some ghost accounts that I can see as clearly as I can see the back of my hand. They're all unlabeled, just like if someone had hacked into the system, built these ghost accounts, and then hid them by the side of the road. Do you have any idea how strange that looks? Handshakes from the Federal Reserve Bank of Boston to member banks in their district or the Fed in D.C., and some of these transactions are unseen! Wow!"

Agnes peered over Alison's shoulder and said, "That is a bit odd, isn't it?"

Alison moved closer to the display and scrolled down to the next page. There they were again, probably five to ten transactions where the handshake from the Fed had failed to complete. In those cases, the transactional buckets (where the funds are stored) were not passed along to the intended receiver. Instead, the funds in the buckets were hijacked, sent to the ghost account, and then forwarded to another transaction bucket in someone else's network.

"How strange," said Agnes, "How very odd indeed! So, you mean somebody stole the money sitting in the bucket by diverting the bucket to a location outside the Federal Reserve System."

Alison agreed and said, "What the hell? Yes, it seems that someone is making that money flow away from the Fed or away from a regional bank to someplace else. Maybe to a ghost account!"

"Alison, what exactly is a ghost account, and how can you see them if they're not visible?" Agnes asked.

"So, Agnes, ghost accounts, also known as ghosts, are users typically on social media platforms, but in our case, they are showing up on the Fed network with illegal access to your server nest here in Boston. They are users who remain asleep and do not engage in any activities. They can register on a platform, such as Twitter, or in our case, any Fed system. These social media ghost users follow active members but do not participate in commenting, messaging, or posting. The ghosts here do not do anything with an account until they are ready to interrupt a handshake. Their purpose in interrupting a handshake is to divert the data in the packet, also known as a bucket, and divert the associated monies somewhere else." Alison looked intently at Agnes, whose mouth was wide open.

"They're stealing from the Federal Reserve System and our client banks?" Agnes asked incredulously. "Is that what's going on here, Alison?"

"Yes, Agnes. That's why I'm here. The U.S. Treasury owns the Federal Reserve System, so if there's a problem here, that means there's a problem at Treasury. I am the person they send out to find the ghosts and get rid of them," Alison smiled.

"Wow," said Agnes. "I had no idea. We'd better get going!"

Alison smiled again and turned her attention back to the computer screens as the last traces opened and confirmed that there was a ghost account near the failed transactions. She shook her head and said to herself, "Nice job, kid," and finished her tea. A quick look back at Agnes was all that was necessary. Then she thought, "I wonder how much Agnes knows about ghosting, and I wonder why that guy in IT didn't bother to look for ghosts in and around the servers and the nest. Interesting!"

Chapter Nineteen

Dr. Spencer and several of his third-year residents in neurosurgery came back to visit Doug and assess his progress from the time he was admitted to today. Doug's blood rejection rate was still high, but he had taken a turn for the better since the last time they tested it. Doug's body accepted nearly 62% of the blood transfused, and the most recent transfusion was at an even higher acceptance rate. Dr. Spencer was pleased but still somewhat concerned by Doug's circulation issues. Dr. Spencer asked one of his residents to reach out to the staff cardiologist, Dr. Alexander Karimi, to see if he could determine the reason for the lighter-than-normal circulation, particularly to the extremities. Dr. Karimi was unable to determine why the circulation had slowed down but suggested that they do a full body scan to get a better look at blood flow throughout his whole body and through his heart.

Later that day, Dr. Karimi brought some bad news to Dr. Spencer. Doug's second and more detailed blood screen indicated that the patient's late-stage cancer, called acute myeloid leukemia, was already affecting the non-cancerous transfused blood cells, making them cancerous. The prognosis was not good. As a result, they would have to take Doug out of the medically induced coma to provide targeted chemotherapy and help his body actively fight off cancer that was infecting his new blood. This of course would leave him somewhat defenseless against the brain trauma he received when he fell back and hit his head. In addition, Doug had a significant brain bleed that was not yet operable, and once out of the medical coma, continued blood loss could cause heart failure. This was going to put Doug at very high risk for heart failure as well as subdural damage. Dr. Spencer reached out to Doug's primary care physician, Dr. Moran, and gave him the bad news. Dr. Moran, in turn, found Jenn at Doug's bedside. He took her into the waiting room to give her the update and the bad news.

"Jenn, I just spoke with the cardiologist, Dr. Karami, and he told me that Doug's cancer has invaded all the blood cells from the transfused blood. This necessitates that we take Doug out of the coma to start treating the leukemia and get his body to help us."

Jenn was dumbfounded by this news. Her shoulders slumped, and her already worried expression became more solemn and scared.

"Why didn't somebody tell me about the blood issue? Taking Doug out of the medical coma – won't that put Doug at greater risk if you do that? How about keeping him in a medical coma until he's healthier, and then we can battle cancer? What does Dr. Spencer have to say?" Jenn was distraught by the news about the blood and unsure of what to say or do. "Is there an oncologist looking at this?"

Dr. Moran put his hand on her shoulder.

"Listen, Jenn, the best way to combat both issues is to address them immediately, not one at a time. I'll check back with Dr. Spencer to confirm that we can take Doug out of the medical coma. But in the meantime, we are going to consult with the Oncology Department here. I wanted you to know as soon as possible. Go have a cup of coffee and call the girls." Dr. Moran headed out of the room and left Jenn standing there looking totally confused.

Jenn was still crying when she walked over to a quiet corner of the waiting area, talked with her daughters, and then called Barb. Her hands shook as she dialed the number. "This can't be happening," she thought to herself. "How did all of this come to be?"

"Hi, Barb." Jenn paused to listen. "No, everything is not all right. They told me that Doug's cancer is infecting the blood transfusions he's getting. They will have to take him out of the coma to start fighting cancer.

Barb couldn't believe the news. "I didn't know that Doug had cancer, she said." This is awful, Jenn. Did you know anything was wrong?" she asked.

"Yes, Doug learned about this after his last physical, but he didn't want to tell anyone. He made me promise. So, I just told the kids. I know he hadn't told Charlie. Is Charlie there? I'd like to tell him myself!" Jenn thought about what Doug had said when he told Jenn about the cancer. "This could ruin things for Charlie and me, please don't tell anyone, please!"

Jenn started to cry when Charlie got on the phone.

"Hey Jenn, what's this Barb is talking about?" He listened as Jenn repeated the information the doctor had just given her.

"What cancer? Are you kidding me? He didn't mention it to me. No!" It seemed that this was Doug and Jenn's secret. But Charlie still tried to calm her down and said, "Listen, Jenn, we'll head over there right now."

Barb grabbed the car keys and headed toward the driveway with Charlie in tow.

"Charlie, what's going on here? Every time I talk with Jenn, there's some horrible new twist to Doug's condition. Did you know anything about cancer?"

Charlie turned to Barb and exclaimed, "Of course not!"

Barb shot Charlie a look and slowly asked him again. "Charlie, did you know anything about this?

"Barbara, I didn't know anything about any of this; please understand!" Charlie tried not to make eye contact with her.

Barb shot Charlie another glance from the driver's seat and shook her head.

"You better not be lying to me, Charles Henderson. If you are, you're in big trouble. I'll be so disappointed if you knew and didn't tell me. Furthermore, I don't think Doug's chances are very good at this point," she said.

Charlie turned away from Barb and stared out the window as they raced toward Hyannis to the hospital. Deep in thought, Charlie wasn't paying attention to the traffic or Barb's driving. Charlie thought about cancer and how it had changed the situation, but he couldn't believe Doug had only told his wife about his cancer. If it was so far along, it might complicate his recovery.

Barb glanced over at Charlie and patted his knee. She could tell he was worried. Now, she felt bad that she had snapped at him.

"Don't worry, this will all be all right soon, and Doug will be back home calling you to see if you want to go out fishing. Maybe this time, you can say okay."

"I hope so, dear, I hope so," Charlie whispered and shook his head.

When they got to the hospital, Barb parked the Porsche in the back lot in a space away from all the other cars. Charlie never liked parking his beautiful Porsche 911 near cars that might inadvertently bash it with a door or bumper. Charlie remembered parking his car in a restaurant parking lot and watching from a window inside as a car backed into the side of his other Porsche about three years ago. He ran out of the restaurant and shouted at the driver, but the guy just waved and drove away. From that point on, Charlie was very careful where he parked his cars.

They went to the side entrance of the new Mugar wing, which had been partially funded by a $5,000,000 donation by David Mugar in 2002. He also gave millions of dollars to support the Boston Pops Orchestra and the 4th of July concert held every year with fireworks on the Charles River. David's father was the founder of the Star Market supermarket chain, so he had plenty of money to donate. Charlie and David had known each other for many years and worked together on several philanthropic endeavors.

Barb took Charlie's hand and led him toward the elevators. Once on the fifth floor, Charlie appreciated the momentary distraction of the incredible view that overlooked Hyannis Harbor. You could see all the tour boats, the ferries for Nantucket and the Vineyard, and all the private crafts that dotted every inch of the harbor. From this vantage point, you could see the beautiful beach cottages and large homes along the shoreline, as well as the Kennedy Memorial and the Veterans Memorial. It was a nice view for the patients and their visitors. But Charlie could not appreciate the scenery when his mind drifted back to the real reason they were at the hospital.

They headed toward Doug's room. Barb stopped and put her hand on Charlie's arm and gave him a warning.

"Just listen to Jenn, and don't say a damn word about anything! I don't know what you know or what you might have heard from Doug – just don't say a word!"

They were shocked at what they saw as they entered Doug's room. Jenn sat next to his bed, holding his hand. Doug was pale and appeared lifeless.

Jenn came over, hugged Barbara, then turned to Charlie.

"Charlie, did you know about this? Did he tell you?" Jenn looked at Charlie.

"No, Jenn, I didn't know. This is all news to me," Charlie shook his head.

"I knew about the diagnosis, but he didn't tell me the severity of it. I hope you do not mind, but I can't believe Doug wouldn't have told someone. It isn't like him to keep secrets! He didn't tell me, so that could only leave Charlie," Jenn said.

Barb didn't know what to say to her friend. This was a terrible way to learn about Doug's cancer, and Barb struggled to find the right words.

"Jenn, I'm so sorry. I don't think Charlie knew."

"Dr. Moran said they want to take Doug out of the coma," Jenn said. "He thinks it would be easier to treat the cancer if he's out of the coma. The head wound is stable for now."

Barb sat down with Jenn and said, "You know we are here for you, whatever happens. The doctors will do their best. The hospital has an excellent oncology department."

Jenn and Barb held hands while Charlie paced the room. He eventually sat next to Doug and looked at him. Then he leaned forward and whispered, "Hang in there, Doug, you'll be okay, I promise."

Chapter Twenty

The next day, Barb and Charlie joined Jenn in Doug's room. Doug's daughters were in the café getting coffee when Barb and Charlie arrived.

Doug was out of the coma, but didn't look much better. He looked worse. His eyes were shut tightly, almost like they were glued shut. His color was a light gray except for the bright white bandages wrapped around his head. He had transfusion portals inserted into both of his forearms. And he was lying back down, which made him look worse than when he was sitting up. Currently, the doctors were only using the left portal, but they had used both to transfer clean blood into Doug just the day before. The blood with the leukemia cancer cells was being removed from Doug's system, and new, clean blood was being transfused into his system. Hopefully, this would stop the cancer from spreading until Doug was healthy enough for radiation or chemotherapy.

Charlie was over at the bed holding Doug's hand when he felt a rather violent squeeze, and to his surprise, he jumped back a little.

Jenn turned toward him and said, "What's the matter, Charlie?"

"He just squeezed my hand!' Charlie exclaimed and stepped back.

"Hi, sweetie, it's Jenn. Can you hear me?" Jenn stepped in front of Charlie, grabbed Doug's hand, and said, "Are you okay?"

"Help me, please help me." Doug whispered and managed to squeeze Jenn's hand.

Jenn was startled for a moment and then said to Doug, "We're all here to help you, don't worry."

"We're helping you get better, Dougie. We're all here to help you get better." Charlie leaned over the other side of the bed, reached down, and held Doug's face in his hands.

Doug turned his face away from Charlie toward Jenn and then took his last breath. The alarms went off simultaneously: heart, lungs, and blood pressure. Doug had succumbed to respiratory and heart function death, known as congestive heart failure. His entire respiratory system had shut down. In a flurry of activity, nurses and the doctors who were "on call" rushed in to try to revive him, but he was gone. They called the time of death and quietly gave Jenn their condolences as they left the room to give her some privacy.

"Doug, I love you. Doug, you're going to be okay. Doug, please stay with us. Please don't leave me, Doug." But Doug was gone and wouldn't be coming back. Jenn sat by his bedside, holding his hand. After what felt like an eternity, she put her head on his chest and wept.

Charlie and Barb sat quietly by Doug's side. Barb was sobbing while Charlie wiped the tears from his face.

"I'm glad you were here for him at the end," Jenn said to Charlie and Barb through her tears.

Charlie started to say something, but Barb interrupted and said, "Jenn, we're so sorry. We hoped for the best, and we thought Doug would turn the corner; we're just so sorry."

Jenn got up, gave them both a big hug, and went out to find her daughters.

"What a sad day this is; we've lost a friend, and Jenn lost her husband and best friend all at once." Charlie appeared to deflate with grief. "So sad."

Barb walked out of the room to find Jenn and her daughters, to let them know that she and Charlie would do anything to help her in this time of need. She found them getting off the elevator. Jenn was holding Emily's hand and pulling her toward Doug's room. Emily was sobbing. Hannah was behind her mother and sister but pushed in front of them as they got to the room.

"Dad, no, he can't be gone; Dad – stop, please stop!" Hannah wailed. As the family gathered around Doug's bed, Barb motioned for Charlie to leave the room.

"They need to be alone with Doug now. It's their time to be with him," Barb said as she led Charlie to the elevators.

When they got home, Charlie made himself a martini and poured a glass of wine for Barb. He then left Barb alone on the veranda and went to his study to call Billy Flynn to give him the bad news.

"Aw shit, Charlie, I'm sorry to hear that. Doug was a great guy. We're gonna miss him, I tell ya." Even though Billy was a tough guy, he had a soft spot for Doug and Charlie. They had all been through so much together and had such big plans for the future. Doug's death was going to make things a little more complicated.

Charlie said thanks and then realized he had a couple of questions for Billy.

"First, are you all set with Felix regarding the issues we discussed yesterday? And secondly, have you told Felix that nothing else matters except getting the money?"

"Felix is all set, no worries. And yes, I did tell him that the movement of this money is his top priority. I will double-check on it and get back to you tomorrow."

"Thanks, Billy, thanks a lot." Charlie finished his martini and stared out at the ocean with a faraway look in his eye. He thought, "This thing with Doug is awful, and I hope he will rest in peace. He was such a great guy and a wonderful friend. I'll miss him – for sure!"

Chapter Twenty-One

Matt Davis had spent the last few days at Cape Cod Hospital talking with all of the doctors who dealt with Douglas Wood. Unfortunately, it took an inordinate amount of time to see them all because of their alternating schedules and on-call status. Eventually, Detective Davis was able to speak with each of them, and the message he gleaned from everyone was that it is "highly unusual" for anyone to fall backward after an event unless they bumped into something that would provide some level of rebound force. "Nearly impossible" was what each doctor had said. In addition, there was no evidence that Doug Wood had any type of medical trauma that would have caused him to fall – no heart attack, aneurysm, or brain trauma. He certainly didn't throw himself backward as an attempted suicide – plus, there was no note.

As Matt walked down one of the long corridors at the hospital toward the exits, he overheard two nurses talking. The first said, "What a shame about Mr. Wood. I thought he had a great chance to recover."

Matt stepped in front of them and introduced himself.

"I'm Detective Davis from the Barnstable Police Department." Matt held up his badge and asked, "What's going on with Mr. Wood? Did something happen to him?"

"Yes," the older nurse started to say, then caught herself and said HIPAA regulations do not allow us to speak about the medical condition of our patients. But his wife and daughters are here, you could speak with them in his room."

"Thanks for the suggestion."

Matt turned toward the elevators and thanked them both. When Matt returned to his car, he looked up a name on his cell phone and called the number listed – Danny Rider, the Chief's administrator over at Barnstable HQ.

"Hey Danny, do me a favor and look up Douglas Wood over in Osterville on Eel River Road. I need to know his bio and if he's ever had any action with the Barnstable Police Department… or any other police department for that matter."

Danny was able to check the "book" on Douglas Wood through a system used by police to do deep background checks on just about anyone, anyplace. The system, known as the National Crime Information Center (NCIC), has extensive personal data on every citizen in the United States, whether they were involved in a criminal act or not. The average citizen would be very surprised at how much data is stored on the NCIC about them and is available only to law enforcement from this system.

"Nothing at all except a bunch of speeding tickets – he owns a Ferrari, no kidding," said Danny.

Matt found that hard to believe since most people have done something to get themselves flagged by some police department, somewhere, or sometimes. Even Danny thought it was funny that nothing more serious was available for Douglas Wood. The guy must have lived a very sheltered life to avoid any crime-related actions over his lifetime. Just some traffic tickets.

"Sure, he was a big dog in the banking industry, and he has a trail of buys and sells of big houses and boats here on the Cape and Islands and in and around the greater Boston area. He also has some huge bank accounts, mostly in the Boston area. But not even a parking ticket when he was in college," Danny said to Matt. "Pretty unusual stuff."

"Oh, all right, send it over to me, and I'll take a look tonight. I appreciate the help; thanks! Give my best to Debbie and the kids." Matt hung up and ran his hand through his dark, wavy hair. He was getting a strong feeling about Doug Wood's accident, but he just couldn't pinpoint it. He just knew that something wasn't right. He drove back to headquarters slowly, almost preoccupied with his thoughts.

Ginny Jensen was waiting for him when Matt got back to his office. Officially, Danny Rider was the person you'd go to if you had questions about any external factors regarding a case you were working on. Ginny worked for Danny, but she was generally in the background. She was a data mining guru; she could find anything about anybody. She used background checks, family information, social media, and access to NCIC to find details of someone's life. In addition, Ginny was great at ferreting out information that only showed up on the dark web – stuff that might not be admissible in court but was helpful as background information. So, she spent a lot of her time each day interfacing with the detectives.

"Hey Matt, we got something on your guy Doug Wood." Ginny smiled at Matt, happy to be able to give him some information about his case. "We searched for his passport and found that he went down to the Caymans six times in the last year. He chartered a jet for each trip. A Gulfstream IV – costs him about $5,000 each way. Might be nothing, but a banking executive who makes multiple trips to a place like the Cayman Islands in the same year does make you wonder a little bit, right?"

Matt considered it for a minute and them said "Oh, I think so, Ginny. Very suspicious, I think so. Thanks for the info." Ginny turned and started back to her office.

Matt shrugged his shoulders and thought, "That's an expensive way to get down to the Caymans, but it's convenient and pretty private too. I wonder if there were any big deposits at any of the Cayman banks while he was on the island. Or was he like most other people, just on vacation with the family?"

Matt turned toward the hall and followed Ginny into her office.

"Hey Ginny, can Danny get the passenger list for any of those flights?"

She stopped and turned back to him.

"No need, Matt, we already got that info for you. He was down there with two other guys from work, the CEO of the bank, Mr. Charles Henderson, and another guy by the name of Billy Flynn, who was the head of the bank's security. They were both there with him each time." Ginny added, "Not too unusual, though – maybe just getting away from their busy lives in Boston. You know, play some golf, raise a little hell, chase some skirts, and pretend that you're not 60 but 20 again."

Matt laughed, "Hmm, maybe… But traveling down there that frequently with that kind of income, I'd expect one of them to buy a vacation house on the island." Matt thought for a minute and then said, "Ginny, would you be able to do a little more looking into Charles Henderson?"

Ginny sat down at her desk, tapped on her keyboard, and then turned to Matt.

"Nope, nothing bad on Charles Henderson either – look, clean as a whistle just like that Doug Wood guy – nothing except his passport indicates that Mr. Henderson was on those same visits to the Caymans over the last couple of years. Nothing else unusual!"

"How about Billy Flynn?" Matt asked.

"For sure, he's got some dirty spots on his file, mostly when he was younger. He did have a run-in with the FBI back in 1999, something about counterfeiting, but that was all cleared up the same year. I did find that he was dishonorably discharged from the Army for stealing and selling Army office equipment. Maybe he's not as squeaky clean as his records seem to indicate," said Ginny.

Matt thought back to the brief phone conversation he had with Billy Flynn a few days earlier.

"You know, Ginny, when I spoke to Mr. Flynn on the phone, he sounded a little nervous when I asked him if he'd been down to Doug's house on the 28th. Although he seems clean enough, between that conversation and the trips to the Caymans, he raises a red flag."

Matt made a mental note to ask him again and put him into the suspect category for now. What Matt didn't know and what Billy didn't tell him was that Billy had spent 5 years in the Walpole State

Prison now known as Cedar Junction Prison, for forgery and stealing client funds.

"There could be something more there. I'll keep looking into the banks in the Caymans," Ginny smiled and got back to work.

"Thanks, Ginny." Matt wanted to see if he could talk with Officer Thomas about his perspective on the accident and what he thought happened. He also decided he'd take a ride over to the fire station in Osterville to talk with the two EMTs and the paramedic on-site the day of the accident.

First, Matt called Officer Thomas and invited him to meet for lunch at the diner down the street. While they sat inside and ate their lunches, Matt started to ask questions.

"Hey Reid, can you tell me whatever additional details you may remember about that Eel River call the other day? Did you see anything unusual in the house, specifically the library, anything out of place, you know, something that looked funny?"

He took a minute to finish chewing his sandwich and then looked up at Matt and said, "There was a shit-ton of blood, but there usually is with that type of accident, a head injury– right?"

"But did anything seem contrived? Did it look like the body was moved? Did anyone touch anything before you got there? Was Mrs. Wood nervous, or was she distraught?" Matt was trying to get any sense of surprise that the on-duty officer might have had while he was at the scene.

"Sorry, Matt, it looked like it was a straightforward accident as far as I could tell. Nothing out of place and nothing suspicious either."

"Mrs. Wood told us that her husband had some things to do in the morning, which is why he didn't drive up to Hingham with her to visit his daughter and granddaughter. I asked her what he was doing at home, but she said she didn't know." Matt paused and said, "Funny, I have no reason to think she's lying… why would she? She was a little puzzled about her husband's behavior. Funny, eh? He stays home rather than go with his wife to visit his daughter and his new granddaughter. He must have had a good reason, but it seems odd that his wife didn't ask him why he couldn't join her. That's very unusual… unless he had something to hide from her!" Matt was going to keep Jenn on his active list even if she had an excuse for not being at home. The spouse is always suspected of being involved in anything to do with their partner. He'd also keep Billy Flynn on the list for obvious reasons.

Matt asked Reid a couple more questions, then he thanked Reid for his time, and they both left the diner. Matt walked quickly to his car, got in, waved to Reid then headed over to the Osterville Fire Rescue station to have the same conversation with the EMTs and paramedics who were the first responders at the scene of the accident. After talking with each of them Matt still felt something was out of place. Something just wasn't right. However, there didn't seem to be any additional information that would lead Matt to believe that the accident was not an accident. Although the scene appeared normal, the case wasn't. Matt thought to himself that something didn't fit – something didn't feel right to him.

Chapter Twenty-Two

Alison had stayed up all night going over the most recent data. There were a few anomalies, but that aside, she had some intriguing data points that indicated some servers could not see anything after midnight. That explained why some handshakes failed from midnight to 2:00 AM. She had no idea why these servers were disconnecting from the majority of servers that made up the Nest, but at least she had some valid data points that might help explain the issue of failed handshakes. Alison decided she would need some additional assistance with the tech stuff.

"Agnes, can you get me the head of the IT department, please, uhm, what's his name, Michael Ross? Please get him down here pronto – I mean, tell him now, not later! I want him in front of me in five minutes, or he'll be kissing my ass!" Alison paused, then trying to sound a bit cheerier, shouted, "Thanks, Agnes!"

Michael Ross was one of the youngest IT directors in the Federal Reserve System. He was only 30 years old and probably one of the brightest IT guys in Boston. His undergraduate degree was from MIT in computer science, and his graduate degree was from Harvard, also in computer science and artificial intelligence (AI). His first job was at IBM in the AI Lab, working on the Watson Project, in support of the next generation of AI servers. He developed and deployed server nests for IBM clients worldwide. He wasn't just computer smart; he was off-scale smart, and that intelligence had allowed him to walk into the Federal Reserve System and take the senior IT position without having to compete for the job. He could have gone to any of the financial giants or big Boston-based technology start-ups. Still, he chose the Federal Reserve Bank of Boston because his uncle, Warren, had worked for them his entire career and told Michael that he'd be overjoyed to have him there when the time was right. Well, it turned out that Michael wanted to return to Boston after a stint in California working at Google and he remembered his uncle's words, "You'll be proud to be at the Fed in Boston."

Alison had met him briefly a few weeks ago when she was introduced to the bank's management team and liked him a lot. Michael was bright but down to earth; none of that IT bullshit. A real straight-shooter who could explain complicated things in simple ways. Alison thought he would be a real help to her and she felt a certain attraction to him just from that initial meeting.

Michael arrived and leaned into Alison's office with a massive smile on his face.

"Hey Alison, how's the nicest girl at Fed Boston?" Michael was a little flirty with Alison. She didn't seem to mind. He felt attracted to her too, but tried to remember that she was a colleague. He wasn't sure why she wanted to see him, but he was happy to swing by her office.

"Hi, Michael. Thanks for coming down. I've got a couple of questions for you. Do you mind sitting down?"

"Sure, what's up? Hey, nice candy dish; mind if I try one?"

"Help yourself. They're out there for the taking," Alison said.

Michael reached into the dish and grabbed a Werther's Caramel Toffee and a single large peppermint Life Saver. He held both up and said, "For later, right?"

Alison smiled and turned on the two giant displays behind her desk. She swung around with her back to Michael, typed in her username and password, and activated the fingerprint reader with her thumb. With a smile, she turned back to Michael and asked if there were any new intrusion detectors she'd have to learn.

"No, you passed Alison. Maybe a sonic voice print someday, but for now, that's it." He smiled back at Alison, "And please call me Michael – all my friends do."

"Okay, Michael," Alison said with a smile.

"So, what's this all about, Alison? Find anything new?" Michael then frowned at her, "Wow, you look tired. How long were you here yesterday?"

"I never left, Michael. I've been here all night. But never mind that, take a look at these." She turned back to the two enormous screens and loaded the scatter diagram that showed the up times of all the servers in the local Fed's nest. Michael immediately saw the locked ones – there were five.

"What the hell? Why are those down?"

Alison turned back toward Michael.

"Exactly. Why the hell are those servers down, Michael?"

Michael was already on his phone with the server support group, asking them to run the numbers on S5, S12, S55, S239, and S431. "No, I want it right now, please. Yes, I'll hold." Then he looked over at Alison, who was laughing.

"Big man on campus, Michael! You say jump, and they ask how high. Right?" They both laughed.

Michael refocused on his phone call.

"Really, can you see the clocks? All of them? Okay then, dump the memory and reboot them one at a time. Thanks, and call me back once you can see everything." Michael turned to Alison and relayed the information that they would find out why the servers failed and why their backup servers hadn't taken over for them. Then they would rebuild each of them so they would not crash again.

"I'm more interested in how five random servers would stop working around the same time in the same building without any warning. This kind of failure is not normal, and I'm curious if it has anything to do with those failing handshakes we've seen over at Treasury – oops!" Alison said, covering her mouth and shaking her head.

"Michael, you're not supposed to know that. It's one of those Treasury secrets I shouldn't be talking about. I'm not sure you are covered." She was referring to the Level 4 clearance that Michael would need to be able to hear about things like the handshake problems at Treasury. Level 4 information was only available to the top echelon of government employees, and Alison wasn't sure if Michael qualified.

"Your secrets are safe with me – I promise," Michael said as he raised his hand. Then he smiled and answered his phone. Alison leaned forward to listen, so Michael put it on the speakerphone.

"So, Jim, you have no idea why they went down, but each server was on bypass at about the same time." Jim Clark was the server specialist for the Fed Boston IT group and was a no-nonsense guy with a giant brain. If Jim didn't have an answer, there probably wasn't one. Michael asked about the clocks.

"No, they were all clicking with Denver at the time," Jim answered. Denver was the time source for the Fed systems; the nuclear clocks in Denver kept all servers on accurate time. Always. If a system failed, there was usually a clock synchronization problem, but in this case, there wasn't.

"Jim, what about the RAM stacks? Did they unclip? Any backplane issues? How about the application itself; did it wander off the reservation or shut down? Any worms? Did you find anything like that yet? Any visible problems?"

Jim told Michael he would look into it a bit more and keep him updated.

Michael hung up and turned his attention back to Alison, who was still leaning toward him and twirling a piece of hair around her finger. It was a habit she displayed when she was preoccupied. He wished he had an answer for her.

"Listen, only a few things bring servers down or take them out of the nest. Jimmy is very good at his job; he'll find out what it was, and we'll take care of it."

Alison smiled but then she frowned and said, "I'm worried about these handshakes that keep failing. The numbers are growing and might eventually get to a critical mass where we have to shut down everything to keep the regional banks from failing. If that happens, we're out of business, at least until we find a workaround or the solution."

Michael nodded again. He knew this could become a potential disaster.

"Michael, listen, I shouldn't have mentioned anything about the handshakes. Please keep that to yourself. I'd be in 'deep yogurt' if Treasury finds out that I breached our confidence levels."

"No worries, Alison, I promise I won't tell a soul. And if it makes you feel any better, I have a Level 4 clearance here and across the whole system, including a separate DARPA clearance." Between level 4 and the military clearance from the Defense Advanced Research Projects Agency, Michael was set.

"Thanks for sharing that, Michael; it's all good then," she smiled.

Alison thought to herself that she had better be more conscientious of what she says in the future to anyone here at the Fed, to Agnes, and even to Michael. Her assignment was highly classified, even the President was in the loop. And so, she had better not give too much information, or she might accidentally compromise the whole investigation. She thanked Michael for his assistance as he got up, walked to the door, turned, waved, and smiled as he headed back to his office.

The next thing Alison had to do was unravel the communication between all the servers. She wanted to learn how they all interacted within the nest. Also, it would be helpful to learn how they interacted as individual servers connecting between two or more points, like to a member bank or another federal district.

There were a lot of intricacies within this network, and she needed a better understanding of how it operates. She hoped Michael and Jim Clark could help her rather than her having to try to drive over to MIT again – "That was a mistake, for sure," she thought. The more she knew about the network, the easier it would be to see the inconsistencies and discover the whereabouts of any ghost accounts. This was beginning to look like a bigger problem than she initially thought it was.

Alison made a mental note to call Michael in the morning to see if he had any additional suggestions. For now, how about a nice bath and a glass of wine back in her hotel? Yes, that sounded pretty good she thought. Of course, after giving her mom a quick call.

On the call, Alison told her mom about Michael and how he went to both MIT and Harvard. She may have even mentioned that he was pretty cute too.

Alison's mom let out a loud breath.

"Finally, Alison, finally a man in your life! Now I can stop worrying about you."

Chapter Twenty-Three

Dr. Rick Spencer picked up his phone and called the Medical Examiner, Jack Fernald, to let him know that Doug Wood had passed away last night. Dr. Moran and Dr. Spencer had spent some time trying to sort out what had happened to Doug. The lack of answers convinced them that another expert set of eyes might provide a new point of view to help unravel the mystery of Doug Wood's untimely death. That's why they reached out to Dr. Fernald again.

"We're still unsure of the cause of the accident in terms of the fall Mr. Wood took and exactly how that could have happened. I know his wife would certainly like to know what happened too. It certainly is a strange case. I'll check my schedule and make some time to come over there this week," Dr. Fernald replied.

"Sure, I'll arrange it with the ME here at the hospital. This week is good for us, and I know Mr. Wood's wife wants to have the funeral soon. Thanks, see you then."

Rick was not happy to make these calls. Death was brutal for any family, and having someone examine a body for a specific cause of death made families even more upset. However, Rick felt that enough questions surrounded his patient and that he wanted as much input as possible. He then called the hospital's ME, Brad Miller.

"Hi Brad, it's Rick Spencer. Would you mind if we have Dr. Fernald from the MME Massachusetts Medical Examiner's office assist you with the autopsy of Douglas Wood? He is already familiar with the case, and I think the extra set of eyes could be useful." Rick listened and hoped that Brad wouldn't mind the additional input. He knew it was a territorial thing so he hoped it would be OK to have Dr. Fernald visiting in Dr. Miller's autopsy room. Also, if the investigation changed from an accident to something intentional, the Massachusetts Medical Examiner would most likely take the lead position. Then the autopsy would be the responsibility of the MME.

Luckily, Brad was amenable to the idea, so Rick hung up and breathed a sigh of relief. This went better than he anticipated.

Rick's last call was to Dr. Steve Moran, Doug's primary care physician, to fill him in on the details. It would be important to let Doug's widow know what they were doing.

"Hi Steve, I arranged to have Dr. Fernald attend the autopsy. He'll be assisting Brad Miller, the ME on the hospital team. I'm sure they'll be able to connect the dots for us," he said. "Can you reach out to Mrs. Wood and get those formalities taken care of?"

Dr. Moran agreed and immediately called Jenn Wood to let her know how sorry he was for her loss and explained that Dr. Fernald would be coming over to the hospital to assist with the autopsy in hopes of discovering how the accident had occurred.

"Thank you, Dr. Moran," Jenn said. "Thank you for all your help with Doug, and thank you for arranging everything for the autopsy. I'm sure you'll let me know what they find out."

"Of course, Mrs. Wood. I'll always keep you up to date," Dr. Moran replied.

Dr. Moran decided the next best step would be to organize a meeting with everyone involved; Dr. Rick Spencer and Dr. Brad Miller both agreed to meet at the hospital. He also contacted Detective Matt Davis because he wanted to ensure everything was covered if the autopsy proved that the death was not accidental. He made the necessary calls and then went back to his other work. "This was a tough day for everyone," he thought.

The next day everyone arrived at the conference room on the third floor – Dr. Spencer entered first and ensured that lunch was set up. Detective Davis walked in at about the same time. Dr. Miller then arrived with Dr. Fernald, who drove over from Falmouth, and Dr. Moran, Doug Wood's primary care physician, arrived a couple of minutes later.

Rick Spencer greeted everyone and thanked them for coming in. "I want to make sure we're all on the same page in terms of a valid explanation for the fall that Mr. Wood took. We must determine how a backward fall might have occurred and under what circumstances.

"As you all know, the injuries were significant enough to cause severe bleeding, which was a partial cause of death. We will assess the brain hemorrhage, see if the hematoma was also a cause of death, and confirm that the fall was ultimately the reason for the trauma. In addition, we want to assess the actual damage to the brain from the fall, as well as evaluate the damage to Mr. Wood's system as a result of the excessive bleeding." He looked around the room for reactions before continuing. The other doctors nodded their heads.

"The cause of death needs to be confirmed from the inception of the accident to the death here at the hospital. Dr. Kosta, head of our ER, will join us after lunch to describe what he saw when Mr. Wood was admitted. Also, Detective Davis has a statement from the two EMTs and the paramedic who were all on-site the day of the accident."

He turned toward Matt and said, "Detective Davis, would you please read each of those statements?"

"Sure," he said.

"The statement from the EMTs reads as follows: 'We arrived at 1100 Eel River Road at approximately 5:25 PM on July 28th, having left the Osterville Station on Main Street at approximately 5:19 PM. Officer Thomas pulled into the driveway just behind us. The four of us entered the house and found the patient in the library. He was on his back, unconscious, and his head and neck were sitting in a sizable pool of blood. His wife was in the room, and two other people were also in the room, Charles Henderson and his wife Barbara, both neighbors and friends of the family. We checked his pulse, which was faint, and his pupils, which were reactive. We looked at the head wound, put on three large bandages to stop the bleeding, and then wrapped the head. We then lifted the patient onto our stretcher, brought him outside to the ambulance, and put him inside it. His wife and the other woman joined him for the ride to the hospital, and Officer Thomas followed in his car. Once at the ER, we were met by the intake team, including Dr. Nick Kosta. At that time, we turned the patient over to the ER team and filled out our intake paperwork. Once that was completed, we went back to our vehicle and returned to the Osterville station."

"Thanks, Officer Davis – sorry, I mean Detective Davis. Thanks for taking the time to read the statement and for joining us today. Do you have any questions or other comments for us?"

"Not really, but I guess I'd like more insight about why you've called this meeting regarding Mr. Wood and his cause of death. What are your concerns about the autopsy? Do you already have some evidence that supports an option that something else happened? That this accident may not have been an accident. Anything at all?"

"Well, we do," said Rick Spencer. He glanced at Dr. Moran and added, "We're not sure how the accident could have happened, how Mr. Wood hit his head."

"You mean how he fell backward?" the detective asked.

"Well, yes, it is very unusual," said Rick. "Most of the time, when someone falls, no matter the reason, they fall forward instinctively as a protective reaction. So, it's very unusual for someone to fall backward, like in this case, unless he walked into something and essentially bounced off it, like a door or a wall – something that's an immovable object. We know that Mr. Wood did not contact anything before he fell. Additionally, we know that a person could fall back if they were pushed backward with enough force, let's say."

"Do you think someone pushed Mr. Wood?" asked Matt.

"We don't know, but we've got two very seasoned medical examiners who will be looking at the body tomorrow during the autopsy to determine how and why Mr. Wood fell backward and the relationship between that fall and his death."

"Would you mind if I return here tomorrow to observe and see what Dr. Fernald and Dr. Miller find out during the autopsy?"

Rick looked around the room for any dissent.

"No, we don't mind if you join us tomorrow. It might be helpful for you to observe and discuss the findings right then and there."

"Please join us," Dr. Fernald added. "The autopsy is scheduled for 9:00 a.m. in Theatre 5 on the basement level."

"Thank you, Dr. Spencer. I'll be there," said Detective Davis. "I have no other comments or questions, so if you don't mind, I'll excuse myself – and again, thank you for inviting me, and thanks for lunch."

"You're welcome, Detective Davis, and see you tomorrow."

As Detective Davis got up to leave the room and reached for the door, he turned back toward Rick Spencer, who was beginning to sit down again, and asked another question.

"If Mr. Wood fell backward because someone pushed him, would there be any specific marks or tell-tale signs?"

"Sometimes yes, and sometimes no." Dr. Fernald answered. "Let's see what, if anything, Dr. Miller and I uncover tomorrow. I don't want to get ahead of the autopsy and what we might discover. Thanks for your understanding and patience, Detective Davis – see you tomorrow."

Dr. Fernald nodded and smiled at Matt Davis as the detective left, then turned back to the others sitting with him.

"This is a little more complicated than I initially thought. There may be a good chance, as Detective Davis said, that Mr. Wood was pushed. Maybe it was accidental, or maybe it was on purpose. We need to find out and let him know tomorrow, one way or the other." Everyone nodded in agreement, and then each doctor got up from the conference room table and began filing out of the conference room and back to their own offices. Rick asked Dr. Fernald how he liked having his office over near Otis Air Force Base versus working from Boston.

"Oh, I loved working in the Boston office, but I'd rather be closer to home and not have that long Boston commute," Dr. Fernald said.

They said their goodbyes, and Dr. Fernald headed out of the hospital to his car, then started driving out of the hospital parking lot. A moment later, he almost drove into Matt Davis, who was running toward his car.

"Hey, Dr. Fernald, just one last question!" Matt shouted. Jack Fernald stopped and rolled his window down. Matt leaned into the window and asked, "If you find any defensive wounds in the autopsy or if you see any marks on the shoulders that indicate that Mr. Wood was shoved backward, would you be willing to ask Brad Miller to change his ER report?"

Dr. Fernald nodded his head yes, and Matt Davis smiled and said, "Thank you."

Chapter Twenty-Four

Matt was sure the autopsy would come up with new information about the accident. Just the fact that they were revisiting the possible cause of death made him more than a little curious about Mr. and Mrs. Wood. Who are they, how do they know the Hendersons, and who are the Hendersons? He decided to make an appointment with Ginny to find out if she had any additional information about these two families.

"Hi Ginny, are you busy right now? I was wondering what more you might have found about Doug Wood. Unfortunately, he died yesterday, and the hospital is doing an autopsy tomorrow."

"Sorry to hear that. Stop by my office, and we'll see what we can find out!" she said.

He hung up and turned his car onto Phinney's Lane toward the police headquarters. Matt pulled into a parking spot next to the front door of the Barnstable Police Department and hurried down the hallway to the double doors where Danny Rider and Ginny Jensen had their offices. No surprise, she had four computer displays hanging on her wall, two on her desk in front of her laptop, and a docking station. Matt was always amused at the amount of computer power she had at her fingertips. Ginny did more than detective work with these monitors – she even helped Matt find an online date once! It didn't work out; the girl was well over 6' tall, while Matt only reached 5'9". Unfortunately, he couldn't get over the height difference, but Ginny had been happy to assist.

"Hi Ginny, what have you got for me?" Matt smiled as he walked into her office and sat on one of the chairs in front of her desk. "I've got to tell you, I'm a bit confused about this guy Doug Wood. The docs are telling me that it's very unusual for someone to fall backward when suffering a stroke or something else; they reactively fall forward or to the side. Maybe he tripped on something or other. Or perhaps he was pushed, and if he was pushed, then we have a case to get involved in since the other person must have fled the scene and isn't talking. The information you and Danny shared about the Cayman trips was helpful, but I need to know more about these folks."

"Okay, let's take a closer look at Mr. and Mrs. Wood," Ginny said as she opened her system, which had a direct online link to NCIC. The only data that came back was from years ago, a high school prank where Douglas Wood was the target, and the other kids in his class had stolen his car and filled it with popcorn. His parents pressed charges, but the police got them to drop the charges the next day. There was nothing on his wife Jennifer, either. Ginny learned that Doug had worked for Fidelity and then became the Chief Financial Officer at First National Bank of Boston, later renamed BankBoston, then after the merger, FleetBoston and when he retired five years ago it was from the latest merger with Bank of America. She also found that the couple had two daughters, one married, and both living off Cape.

Ginny took a look at Charles Henderson and his wife, Barbara. She found even less about them. There were no criminal charges or events with either of the Hendersons. There was lots of travel outside the United States, including travel with the Woods. She found that Charles Henderson was the retired President of First National Bank of Boston, BankBoston, and then FleetBoston. He also retired five years ago from Bank of America. Barbara did some charity work. The couple did not have any children. Mrs. Henderson had one brother, a neurosurgeon at the Mayo Clinic in Minneapolis.

"Matt, these folks are squeaky clean – not so much as, well, not so much as anything. Let's take a look at social media, shall we?" Ginny booted up another computer screen with Facebook, Instagram and LinkedIn.

"Wow," Matt said when he saw all the screens light up with information about Doug, Jenn, Charlie, and Barb. "These guys are something! Bankers, socialites, philanthropists, Wellesley, Newton – graduated from great schools. Country clubs, and yacht clubs around Boston, and down here, they're all members of the Wianno Beach and Golf Club, the Hyannisport Club, and the Wianno Yacht Club. Wow, huh?"

"Now, Detective Davis, you know that a lot of these people in Osterville, Oyster Harbors, and Cotuit have similar bios. They have lots of money - that's why they all stay here for the summer in those big houses by the ocean. Then they all travel to their winter homes on Fisher Island, Jupiter Island, or Palm Beach. No worries, Detective, no worries."

"Right, Ginny – let me know if you find anything unusual with any of them. I'll be upstairs for now."

"Sure, Matt, I'm happy to help!" she said with a smile.

Matt Davis headed to his office, sat as his desk and opened his laptop to Google Chrome, typed First National Bank of Boston, and then did a global search. He was hoping to see any references to Douglas Wood or Charles Henderson. The first line that came back was the history of the First National Bank of Boston from 1784 until it ceased operations in 1999 when Fleet Bank of Rhode Island acquired it. Matt read a few sentences and left the page after seeing that both Douglas Wood and Charles Henderson had senior positions with the bank through all of the mergers and acquisitions – BayBank, Fleet Bank, and finally, Bank of America. He couldn't find any unusual references to either person, so he continued to read each of their bios.

After about an hour of heads-down reading without a single piece of usable information about either of them, he thought, "Fuck this noise. I'll be here all day – I think I'll let Ginny take another shot at this stuff!" He started to log off his laptop but stopped. Instead, he logged onto NCIC, and then typed IRS. When he entered the

IRS website through NCIC, he typed in "Douglas Wood – audit." He couldn't remember if Ginny or Danny mentioned that they had searched any of the IRS files so he had decided to take a quick look himself. Much to his surprise, he received four pages listing tax years from 1975 to the present when the IRS had audited Douglas Wood for various tax issues. In every case, it seemed like Mr. Wood was using some type of "tax dodge" that the IRS was questioning. However, in every case, the audit was dismissed due to a lack of evidence. Matt thought, "Strange, it almost looks like Mr. Wood knows more about IRS policy and procedures than the IRS does."

Next, he typed in Charles Henderson's audit on the IRS website, and, low and behold, he found about the same number of pages listing audits for about twenty years starting in 1976.

"Of course… it looks like Henderson uses the same tricks Wood uses starting at about the same year," Matt mumbled to himself. "Must be nice having such a sneaky accountant on the payroll and as a friend. There's more to this than meets the eye. I wonder what's going on here?"

Matt turned his attention to their travel documents. Sure enough, just as Ginny predicted, he saw through a passport search that the Hendersons and the Woods did extensive traveling together. Looking deeper, he found that Doug Wood and Charles Henderson had made almost thirty different trips to the Grand Cayman Islands and Europe. "Wonder what that's all about," Matt thought to himself. He'd connect back with Ginny to see what she thought about all this travel. Still, something just didn't seem right to Matt.

Matt decided to take a look at some of the banks down in the Cayman Islands to see if he could figure out which ones were actually safe havens for money laundering. He found that, by most accounts, all the banks in the Grand Caymans were highly secretive regarding their clients, not unlike the Swiss banks. Something didn't sit right with him about these frequent island visits. "I gotta talk with Ginny about these trips," Matt thought.

Chapter Twenty-Five

Alison couldn't sleep, so she wandered down to the hotel lobby, grabbed a copy of the Boston Globe, then sat in one of those comfy leather couches next to the entrance to the dining room. Same old news, mostly sports stuff, Red Sox trades, a new wide receiver for the Patriots, someone on the Bruins was injured; the usual stuff. After pushing through all the sports, Alison started to read about the city budget and what the mayor would or would not support. Then Alison noticed in the column to the right, a mention of the First National Bank of Boston.

"Well, that's quite an antique," she thought and smiled. That bank was gone twice – once swallowed by Fleet Bank and then swallowed again by Bank of America. But she read further and found that the notice was about Douglas Wood, who had worked for the First National Bank of Boston, and had died in an accident at his home on Cape Cod after his retirement. Alison thought it was a shame that someone died so soon after retiring. Then she remembered that she'd read a brief note in the paper a few weeks ago about this same Doug Wood guy having some type of accident and being in the hospital on Cape Cod. This link to the banking industry was interesting, so she filed the update of Douglas Wood's death again in the back of her brain for possible future reference.

Alison called Michael Ross after breakfast to get an update regarding the server failures affecting some of the in-region handshakes she had discovered earlier in the week. She was concerned that the handshake problem was being caused by something outside the Fed, but she was very reluctant to make her concerns public. No need to create a situation and sound the alarms unless and until there was more data and she could accurately say what the server problem was. At this point, Alison still didn't know what was causing the issue, so she certainly didn't know how to fix it. She'd need more time, and she'd need Michael's help. She gathered her things from the couch then dialed Michael's number on her cell phone.

"Hi, Michael, good morning. I hope you're okay! Do you think you'll have some time today for me? I'd like to get on top of this server problem."

Michael replied that he'd be in his office later if she wanted to stop by. Maybe around 10:00 am, he said. She thanked him and then hung up.

Next, she called Agnes to let her know that she was running a few minutes late and was just leaving the hotel. As Alison walked down Atlantic Avenue toward the Fed Bank building, she was of course, thinking about the servers. Still, she couldn't help but enjoy the beautiful morning sky over her left shoulder as she looked out toward the Boston Harbor. She could even see the reflection of some large planes approaching and departing from Logan Airport in East Boston.

When Alison and Agnes sat down to discuss the most recent failed handshakes, Alison told Agnes she planned on meeting with Michael Ross that morning.

"Can you get me a complete list of this week's handshake failures so that Michael can try to match them with any server failures?" she asked Agnes.

"I'm already on it!" Agnes said with a smile. "I'll have it for you in a couple of minutes. Let me know if you need anything else. I'm glad you're working on this with Michael; he's a great guy, isn't he?"

Agnes' words were ringing in Alison's ears when she knocked and entered Michael Ross' office a little after 11:30. Michael had just taken a bite of half of his Subway sandwich: an Italian BMT with salami, pepperoni, and ham, plus all the fixings.

"You want half of this?" He held up the sandwich and smiled at Alison. "It's delicious."

"Take a breath, don't choke on that, huh?" Alison shook her head.

Michael shrugged and kept chewing.

"Didn't your mom ever tell you to take little bites?" She smiled and let Michael finish chewing, then said, "Looks good – how is it?"

"Give it a try; you'll like it." Michael handed Alison the other half of his sub sandwich. "Want some chips?" He passed the half-empty bag of potato chips over to Alison, who was just taking her first bite of the sandwich.

"Thanks for sharing your lunch with me, Michael. I wasn't expecting that."

Michael smiled at her and said, "You know, if you want, we can share dinner sometime."

"Why, Michael, are you asking me out on a date?" She looked at him with those beautiful blue eyes and blinked twice. "You are, aren't you?"

Michael got flustered for a moment and started to turn a brighter shade of red, his cheeks were warm, and he began to stutter a little bit. Alison was amused and thought Michael was being so cute.

"Well, what the hell? I guess I am asking you out on a date - I think. So, would you want to go out to dinner with me sometime?" Michael looked right into her blue eyes and couldn't help himself. "Boy, she is something," he thought.

"I think I would like to go out with you for dinner - out on a date. Yes, I would. Thank you so much." Alison smiled again and blushed a little bit as she nodded to Michael.

"Great so when would you like to go out? I'm free every night."

"Any time you like Michael, anytime you like."

They decided they'd meet up the next night at 6:00 pm. However, the moment of fun passed quickly, and Alison was back to asking Michael if he had been able to identify any additional servers at banks in the district that failed to complete and acknowledge a handshake with the Fed. She handed him the list that Agnes had compiled earlier that day. Michael said he would have a matching list for her by end-of-week. In the meantime, he would give her specific dates when any of the clustered servers in the nest did not complete their handshakes out to the regional banks.

The first report Michael sent to Alison later that day contained sixty examples of incomplete handshakes. The second report went back a whole year and included almost two hundred cases in which servers were briefly offline and did not complete handshakes. Alison started to feel sick when she thought of how big a problem this could be in the future since it was already looking like a huge problem. Even worse, it seemed that the failed handshakes were not new but had been occurring for the past few years. Why didn't anyone notice this?

As Alison reviewed each handshake failure, she noticed some shadows in and around the failing server handshakes. It was reminiscent of those ghost accounts that grew out of the Bernie Madoff Ponzi scheme, where he was lifting money away from client accounts behind shadows and dropping the money into ghost accounts with the same IP address the client accounts sat on. The difference was that the money was flooding the ghost accounts and draining the client accounts drop by drop. When Bernie finished his IT accounting magic, he had drained approximately $65 billion away from his client accounts without anyone knowing what had happened or why.

After doing some more digging, Alison grabbed her phone and called Michael. "I think someone has been taking money away from the regional clients and the Fed, and it looks like it's been going on for some time. Can you come over here, please!"

The next thing she knew, Michael was standing in Alison's office with a quizzical look on his face and out of breath.

"Hey, what's going on?" he asked.

"I don't know, but I've found some old failed handshakes because I typed in the wrong dates – you know, back ten or more years ago, and I can't see where those handshakes went. I found some shadows and several ghost accounts in and around the servers that had failed handshakes. It looks like money might have been moved through the ghost accounts just before an acknowledgment was sent back through to confirm the transaction. A sort of fake acknowledgment, but one that covers up the money movement. This looks like it might be a major problem!"

"Hey Alison, I'm not sure I understand what's wrong. Could you please start at the beginning?"

"Sure, right, okay. So, I've been looking for incomplete handshakes here in District One because the Fed called us and told us they noticed some issues. The client banks never completed their handshake, but on the Fed's end, they appear complete with what now looks like a false acknowledgment. So, one of the servers here would reach out to one of the regional banks with a handful of new or confirmed transactions. The regional bank responded to most of the transactions but for some reason, would drop or lose a few of them. They just disappeared! Then a false acknowledgment was sent back to the regional bank and Fed Boston, making the transaction look like it had been completed, but it hadn't. The funds in those specific transactions were diverted out of the Fed System. The transaction showed as complete, so everything looked okay when in reality, money was missing. This happened infrequently, so the Fed didn't get too rattled about it. They just cleared the handshake and re-sent it. But over the last year or so, incomplete handshakes were getting more frequent, and larger amounts of transactional data began to get lost. So, the Fed started screaming about the data loss and asked Treasury to look into it for them."

She took a deep breath, frowned at Michael, and continued. "We've been seeing 'shadows' which are images that surround a ghost account and keep the ghost account invisible, at least invisible to us. But the hacker can see past the shadow into the heart of a server and manipulate any of the server data, including handshakes."

"But why you, Alison?" Michael asked. "What's your MO? Why did they send you up here, and what can you do to find out what's causing these handshake failures, huh?"

"Well, first of all, I'm charming, right?"

"Oh, you're right – cute and smart – what a great combination!"

"Well, thank you, Michael! Although, not surprisingly, it takes more than just being cute to do my job. I will let you know, off the record, that my skills helped uncover the ghost accounts that Bernie Madoff used to wash money away from his clients.

"Bernie Madoff was quietly clipping 1 to 5 percent of every inbound transaction; millions of dollars a month were being redirected to these unseen ghost accounts. This was all done in a relatively short period, under three years. At that time, it was unheard of for someone to be able to create these ghost accounts that would essentially act as a landing strip for criminals who had figured out how to divert data… data that controlled the money.

"Here it is in a nutshell," Alison continued to explain, "transactional handshakes are being opened. Funds are being removed at a rate of up to 5 percent per transaction. This is growing in the number of occurrences. It looks like this diversion has been going on for several years, slowly increasing each year. A lot of money has gone missing in this Fed region. I've been charged with discovering who is involved with this crime and helping to capture the perpetrators."

"Shit. This is hard to believe," Michael said quizzically. "Are you sure you've witnessed these handshake issues? I mean, I can see there are problems with the handshakes, but in particular, can you see the diversion of funds into ghost accounts? This is unbelievable. I'm shocked that we never came across any of this stuff, never!" Michael was starting to sound a little embarrassed maybe even a little guilty.

Alison waved her left hand and said, "Michael, for Christ's sake, this isn't your mistake! It's not your fault that you didn't notice any of these events. This is my background. I'm trained to look for these clouds sitting at the edge of these accounts. But can you do me a big favor and keep this under wraps for a while? It's a classified issue at this point here at the Fed and over at Treasury too."

"Sure, I will, Alison. My lips are sealed."

"Thanks, Michael."

They exchanged a glance as each of them thought about the ramifications of how big a scandal this could become if it ever got out. They knew they had to stop it.

Michael smiled again and said, "Hey Alison, let's not wait until tomorrow; let's get dinner tonight. This is starting to sound like a big problem, and I'm getting nervous that I should be doing something more about this – right now!"

"Turning a date into a work dinner?" Before Michael could start protesting, she added, "I'm kidding! Tonight is fine – where would you like to go, Michael?"

"Do you like seafood?" Michael asked.

Alison's eyes lit up, so Michael suggested dinner at the No Name Restaurant on the Fish Pier over at the Seaport area. Seating at the No Name was family style, and the fish was the freshest in Boston. Michael thought that the No Name would be a comfortable environment for a first date. Sitting at a long table with ten other people you don't know would be fun, he thought.

"Look, Alison, the Fish Pier and the No Name have been around for a long time. All the fishing boats dock and unload right next to the No Name. Some of the fishermen go there for dinner, so it has to be good," said Michael. "I'll swing by and pick you up around 5:00. How's that sound?"

"Great," said Alison, and then she smiled that beautiful smile of hers.

Chapter Twenty-Six

Alison spent the rest of that day looking over the list of failed handshakes and identifying which servers, past or present, were unable to complete their transactions. Then she dumped the list onto an Excel file, saved it to her thumb drive, and printed a copy for Michael. While reviewing the failures, she noticed some were tagged to an older, non-server system labeled SV31, which was replaced in 1988 by the first official Fed Boston server. The Feds brought in a newer server with up-to-date technology in late 2009. It was called SV2010-31. The new server contained all the transactions that took place over the life of the server, including the transactions of its predecessor, system SV31. What Alison discovered was that hundreds of ghost accounts had spawned from the original system, SV31, which seemed to imply that someone or something had been hacking the systems for a while. That meant that someone had been stealing funds from member banks or directly from Fed Boston for a while. A closer look at these ghost accounts would provide a detailed roadmap of all transactions between the member banks and Fed Boston, so she could see the transactions that went through correctly and those that failed.

Michael could help her look at all the failed transactions on any server. She dumped several additional server failures and associated lost transactions onto another Excel spreadsheet and printed it for Michael. Then she took a peek at some of the ghost accounts that surrounded the older servers, which implied that they may have been the original targets that were breached first. There weren't many, but just enough to catch Alison's attention.

She glanced at the clock on the wall and realized it was already 5:00 PM. Time had a way of slipping by when she was hot on the trail. She logged off her systems and grabbed her coat and purse. When she looked up, Michael was standing in her doorway with a big smile on his face.

"Hi Michael, hungry?"

"I'm starving; how about you?"

"Sure, I can eat. Let's go."

The restaurant was in a building at the end of the famous Boston Fish Pier, and yes, many of the local fishermen tied up their boats in the evening and unloaded their catch of the day. The service was as good that day as it was when the restaurant opened in 1917. The Federal Reserve Bank building was near the restaurant, so they walked arm in arm, slightly skipping their way down Dorchester Avenue toward the Seaport District. Once in the Seaport District, they walked past the giant building known as the World Trade pier, then turned left onto the Boston Fish Pier and continued to the end of the dock to the No Name Restaurant. The original owner who started the restaurant didn't give it a name, so it became a restaurant with no name, which stuck over the years. As always, it was crowded but, not so much that they didn't mind waiting a little while. It gave them a chance to talk a little bit.

Alison and Michael greatly admired each other, but there seemed to be more, an attraction that went beyond just work. Truth be known, Michael had a little bit of a crush on Alison, partly because she had those piercing blue eyes and was pretty, but also because she was astute. Michael liked women who were educated in areas he was unfamiliar with, and he appreciated women who liked him for the same reason. They worked well together and enjoyed each other's company.

The restaurant was busy, but Michael got them a table pretty quickly. He had made a reservation back at the bank and used the name Thomas Crown, like in the movie "The Thomas Crown Affair" starring Steve McQueen and Faye Dunaway. When Alison heard the hostess call for Thomas Crown and watched Michael wave to her, she giggled under her breath. The table was right up near the front, with a beautiful panoramic sight of the harbor, including a view of Logan Airport to the east. They could see the jets descending across the harbor and landing.

"Wow, Mr. Crown, this is perfect, and what a great view! I'm starving."

"Me too," said Michael, as he started laughing. "What do you feel like, Alison? Do you want to start with a glass of wine?"

"I'd love one."

Michael asked the waiter to bring over two glasses of Pinot Noir. It was one of Alison's favorite red wines, and Michael also liked Pinot Noir, particularly the ones from the Russian River Valley out in Sonoma County California.

The waiter returned with the wine, and Michael ordered a large shrimp cocktail as an appetizer to share. They were in no rush to order dinner, so they sat back and enjoyed their wine, the shrimp, and the beautiful view. The seating was perfect; it was a table with at least ten other diners sitting with them, so the conversations flying around the table were never dull. It also provided Michael with the added delight of being able to look at Alison when she focused on someone else sitting near her. Kind of "sneaking a peek," as Michael would say.

"So, Michael, I have some spreadsheets highlighting the failures of handshakes on a bunch of the early servers and systems. Not many, but enough to make me curious. Now some of the failures are showing up on several different servers. In many cases, when the failure occurs and the handshake is incomplete, there is an account shadow that makes me think a ghost account was built and used to deflect some of the funds of select transactions. As I said, there are not so many that you'd notice. However, since I went way back in time, I came across several failures and corresponding ghost accounts. I think it's contagious and growing, and I think the Fed needs to do something about it as soon as possible."

"What do you need from me, Alison? Just let me know, and it's yours!"

"Thanks, Michael. Well, I need the equipment tags for these servers when they first went online, any dates or times that they were offline, and lastly, when they were replaced. Your service schedule will tell me when they were vulnerable, which may indicate when some transactions were altered and funds were moved to the ghost accounts."

"All right then, I'll have everything to you by Friday, if not sooner. Now do you want to order some dinner."

Alison decided to have the fisherman's platter with scrod, shrimp, and scallops. Michael asked Alison if she liked Calamari. Her eyes lit up at the thought, so he ordered some to have with their dinners, like a second appetizer. Then he requested the broiled filet of sole for himself. After the waiter took their order, he brought them another glass of wine.

They ate their dinner around good conversations, talking about family and friends. Alison told Michael about her mother, how her parents divorced when she was thirteen, how her mother calls Alison every night to check in with her, and how she always asks her if there is a man in her life.

Michael's folks lived in Washington, D.C. His Dad was a lobbyist, and his mother taught a couple of classes at Georgetown. So, when Michael heard that Alison was a Georgetown graduate, he immediately asked if she knew his mother.

"Oh, I don't know, Michael. It's a pretty big school, right?"

"So what? You might have taken a class with her at some point. She taught some undergraduate finance classes and a few graduate classes in economics. She used her maiden name, Brady, like the quarterback from the Patriots. Ever heard of him, Tom Brady?"

"Oh my God, Michael, I had two classes with Professor Brady. Was that your mother? One in my freshman year and one in my sophomore year! This is unbelievable, isn't it?"

"See, I told you she might have been teaching when you were there!

What a riot! I'll have to tell her about you. Did you do well in her classes?" Michael was grinning from ear to ear. "Never mind, I'll ask her if she remembers you. I bet she does. Yeah, I'll tell her, you know Alison, the pretty one with the beautiful blue eyes. She'll remember." Michael smiled.

Alison blushed at the compliment, then leaned forward and kissed him on the cheek. She said, "Michael, I was face down in my textbooks when I sat in your mom's classes. I never looked up. I'm sure she won't remember me.".

"But enough about me, Michael, how did you get up here to Boston? I would have thought you'd stay close to home and get a job in D.C."

"It's a long story, Alison. I'll share it with you sometime, okay?"

"Michael, we've got lots of time, so why not start at the beginning?"

Alison smiled at Michael, so he shrugged, smiled back, and started with something that surprised Alison.

"I wanted to get away from my parents. They were both overbearing overachievers. My dad was a big deal with Lockheed Martin, first as their government attorney and then as the aerospace industry lobbyist. I hardly ever saw him. You know, dinners and meetings and lots of travel. We grew apart naturally, and it wasn't much better with my mom." It was unusual how comfortable Michael felt telling his story to Alison. She leaned in and listened attentively.

"She already had a Ph.D. in economics but returned to school for some post-doctoral studies. She was always over at Georgetown, so I was one of those latch-key kids. I'll tell you; I looked after myself and my younger brother since I was fourteen." Michael sighed and took a sip of wine. "I'll be brutally honest with you, Alison; I couldn't wait to get the hell out of D.C. So I got into MIT with a scholarship and stayed here after graduation to attend Harvard. After that, I went to work for IBM down in Purchase, New York. After two years in New York, I did a short stint with Google in California, then decided to come back to Boston. I found this job with the Federal Reserve, and the rest is history. I was pretty young to be running an entire IT group, but I was very familiar with all the new technologies, and that's what the Fed was looking for… I guess I was pretty lucky."

"Well, I'm pretty lucky that you're here and willing to help with this ghost hunting that I'm doing." She meant that. Alison was enjoying Michael not just as a colleague but maybe something more.

"Hey, dinner was great, and if you walk me back to my hotel, I'll buy you an after-dinner drink." Alison smiled, and her beautiful blue eyes lit up the whole room.

Michael was already standing and offered Alison his hand. "I'm happy to walk you back to your hotel, and you don't have to buy me anything."

The walk back to Alison's hotel took a little longer than expected because they would stop and embrace and share a kiss from time to time. Once they finally arrived at the hotel, Alison could only focus on her wonderful notions about her potential new beau. Michael just stared into Alison's beautiful blue eyes and thought how lucky he was to know such a lovely young woman. They were both in that magical transitional phase from acquaintances to friends to maybe something more.

Alison led Michael to the same couch she had sat on the other day when she had sipped her Mai-Tai and noticed the lack of romantic prospects in the hotel bar. That seemed so long ago now. They ordered two glasses of sherry. The waiter brought them some mixed nuts, and they both dug into them as if they hadn't had dinner two hours earlier.

"Man, these are great, and the sherry tastes refreshing. But, you know, I'm happy we met for dinner tonight. It's always nice to get out with someone since I spend so much time chasing those funny ghosts at the Fed these days. Plus, I enjoy your company, Michael. You're very pleasant to be with." Alison smiled at Michael as she relaxed on the big couch.

"Thanks. It has been nice getting to know you better. I think we should do this more often, Alison, Don't you?"

"Good idea!" Alison leaned forward, kissed Michael on the cheek, and then sat back. Michael, ever the gentleman, thanked Alison again for the company and reminded her that he'd have the additional server information for her by early next week.

"Thank you. I appreciate all your help with this." Then she got up, took a few steps toward the elevator, turned quickly back, and planted another kiss on Michael's cheek. "See ya, Michael, and thank you again for everything."

Michael smiled and watched as the elevator doors closed behind Alison. "What just happened?" he thought to himself.

Then Michael turned and walked back to the Fed. He made his way through the nearly empty lobby and headed for the parking garage, but he stopped and took the express elevator to his floor instead. The computer screens in his office were all asleep but still powered up, so he tapped on the keyboard spacebar and logged into his primary server inside the nest.

In a minute he was inside the server nest and running through the test apps that allowed him complete access to any of the Fed servers, their client servers, and all banking partners in the United States.

His first inquiry was to ask for all server errors starting from day one: the first time a server was installed at the Federal Reserve. Before having servers, each district had a room full of IBM mainframe computers that provided server-like functions but were not dedicated to specific applications like servers are today. So, by going to the first server installs, he could see all transactions across all of the Fed systems and any moments when transactions failed. Based on the information he had sent Alison, he estimated that the timeline would be from late 1998, when the first servers arrived, to the present. With almost 6,000 servers active, he thought there might be five unspooled transactions that failed per server per month. That would equal roughly 60 errors on each server every year, or 360,000 errors yearly for all of the Fed servers. He thought that it sounded like a lot, but he knew that ninety-nine percent of these errors were explainable and never got a second look by his audit counterparts in IT. So, it was only about 3,600 handshake issues or data transmission problems per year for all of the Federal Reserve System.

"Not too bad," Michael thought, "Not too bad at all."

It was at that moment that Michael realized what Alison had already discovered, that any one of those failures may be caused by external influence. In other words, it might be due to hacking from the outside, with criminal intent.

Just then, Jim Clark walked into Michael's office with a puzzled look on his face.

"Hey man, what's up? Why are you here so late?" he asked.

Michael explained that he'd had dinner with a friend and decided to come back in to run some tests that someone had asked him about.

"Is this for that girl from the Treasury? Oh, you had dinner with her, right? So, what are you – her knight in shining armor?" Jim grinned at Michael. Michael started to reply, but Jim quickly said, "Hey man, just kidding. Just teasing you, no harm, no foul."

Michael smiled at Jim and said, "Bite me."

Jim smiled back and asked if he could help with anything.

"No. But can you tell me how I can see the failed transactions across all the old mainframes before 1998?"

"Well, we can see if that data is still around in the archives." Jimmy frowned at him and said, "If it is, I can build you a spreadsheet highlighting the failures and the surrounding data loss. Give me a day, and I'll see what we can find." He was already at Michael's door when he turned around and said, "You know, she's a real looker, that Treasury girl. Good hunting…"

Michael smiled and gave Jim a quick nod. He'd have to tell Alison that she had another admirer at the Fed.

Jim got the gist of the relationship between Alison and Michael the same way he got the gist of how important these queries about the servers were starting to become. He was ready with some answers when Michael called him the following morning, but Jim had some questions of his own.

"Hey Michael, you know I've dumped all the servers, and I have all the errors categorized, including failed handshakes. I've also dumped all the images of the previous system's 'pre-server' back to 1977. Some very odd, random errors continue to repeat several times each month. I've got them clicking off time based on that other atomic clock located at the Naval Observatory in D.C. It looks like somebody was fussing with the clocks and the error matches. Like they opened the handshake, closed it a nano-second later, opened it for about a minute, then closed it twice, so it looked like it wasn't open the second time. Are you thinking what I'm thinking?" He paused to let it sink in.

"That's right, buddy. Somebody is hiding something in the server systems and not telling the member banks or us. They seem to have a full minute or two with the system's doors fully unlocked, meaning they could remove data or funds around. This smells very fishy, Michael, very fishy." Jim had a worried look on his face after he had explained his concerns.

Chapter Twenty-Seven

The autopsy went well with little or no surprises. Most autopsies are like that – no surprises, pretty standard. However, there were a couple of things that Jack Fernald and Brad Miller couldn't explain, and Matt Davis had questions for both of the Medical Examiners. They sat in a conference room just outside the autopsy suites in the Cape Cod Hospital. The room also served as a place where patients' families could meet with the hospital's medical examiner.

"Guys, I'm not sure you explained the bruising on the shoulders in such a way that there is any other scenario besides someone pushing Mr. Wood. If someone pushed Mr. Wood hard enough to have him fall backward, even if it was a surprise, wouldn't it leave a small bruise on Mr. Wood's shoulders? How else would those two bruises on his shoulders have happened?"

"Well, Detective Davis, the bruising could have happened independent of the accident," Jack Fernald spoke up and nodded his head. "It's very possible that Mr. Wood could have bumped into something someplace else earlier in the day... it is possible."

"But Dr. Fernald, isn't it also possible that Mr. Wood may have been pushed with enough force to tip him off balance so that he fell backward? Wouldn't a firm grip on his shoulders cause some bruising at the points of contact on each shoulder?"

"Detective Davis, I'm required to look at all the possibilities, and I cannot rule out the scenario you're suggesting. It's possible that Mr. Wood was pushed and fell backward, but it's also possible that the bruising on his shoulders was caused by something entirely different."

"But Doctor Fernald, tell me, which is the most likely cause of the shoulder bruising under these circumstances? Someone grabbed him by the shoulders, maybe shook him, and then pushed him backward, which caused him to fall. Or maybe he accidentally bruised his shoulders on the day of the accident, and he somehow fell backward and hit his head. Doctor, I think it's obvious that someone pushed him backward – maybe intentionally, maybe not!" Matt Davis felt the doctors could agree with him, which would turn an accident scene into a crime scene. He was sure that something more had happened to Doug Wood than they initially thought, and he knew the doctors probably felt the same way.

"Detective Davis, we do not disagree with you. We believe that it is possible that the bruising on Mr. Wood's shoulders resulted from someone grabbing him, shaking him, then pushing him backward with enough force that he bruised, then fell directly backward and hit his head. But we are also of the mind that those bruises could have happened due to some other type of contact with Mr. Wood's shoulders." Jack Fernald looked at his colleagues for any additional input they might add.

"We think we need to gather additional information to confirm how the shoulder bruising occurred one way or the other," added Brad Miller. "And Detective Davis, this is where we think you can help us determine how the bruising occurred."

"Doctor, how can I help you?"

"We'd like it if you could look into what other activity may have happened surrounding the accident. For example, family or friends visiting the day of or the day before might shed some light on things, wouldn't you think?" The others nodded and looked toward Matt.

"Fine with me. Let me get to it and see what other information I can gather for you. I'll reach out to both of you if I find anything new. Thanks for letting me be part of this, and thanks for your help." As Matt stood to leave, he turned around in their direction and asked them one last question.

"If someone shook Mr. Wood by his shoulders and then pushed him, wouldn't there be some type of bruising on the backside of his shoulder blades where an index finger squeezed with the thumb? Sort of like a vice. Wouldn't the index finger leave a bruise on his back? Did it?"

"Well, Detective Davis," Dr. Fernald answered for both doctors, "We did find a little comparative bruising on the back of his shoulder blades, consistent with being squeezed with the thumb and index finger, but not consistent with the angle of the fall. Meaning, if you were to grab me by the shoulders using your index fingers and thumbs, unless there was equal pressure in both hands, the likelihood that my body would fall backward in a straight line, in symmetry, would be minimized."

"I'm not sure I fully understand you, Dr. Fernald."

"Well, Detective, it would be like holding an open handkerchief by the two upper corners and trying to make it fall in the same symmetrical shape from top to bottom. It would probably not hit the two bottom corners at the same moment and certainly not in a straight line, would it?"

Matt thought about it for a moment, then said, "Well, probably not, but then again, it could. So yes, it could fall in symmetry, just as Mr. Wood could have fallen backward symmetrical to the position he was standing in before being shaken and then pushed. Right? Couldn't he?"

Dr. Fernald again answered for both of them and said, "Well, I suppose he could." Then he turned to Dr. Miller and said, "It seems unlikely, but I suppose he could have fallen in symmetry. Why don't we check the back of Mr. Wood's shoulders again to see if there are any other bruises which could have been caused by someone squeezing the shoulder blades using both thumbs and the index fingers together? Maybe there are signs of shaking Mr. Wood while holding his shoulders tightly between the thumbs and the index fingers."

They agreed to take another look since Doug's body was still in the hospital morgue and said they'd all get back in touch later that day.

Chapter Twenty-Eight

Matt Davis left the meeting with only one thing in mind: this would be a problematic case no matter who was right about the pushing or shaking. So, he exited the hospital and headed directly to his newest case. There was a shooting in Marstons Mills, another village in the Town of Barnstable, in which one man - the jilted husband- shot another man to death because the other man was having an affair with the jilted man's wife.

When Matt pulled into the driveway of the victim's house and got out of his patrol car, he noticed that Officer Thomas was standing on the front lawn talking with the shooter's wife, Melanie. He waved at Officer Thomas, went over to them, and introduced himself to the wife. She shook his hand and said, "I'm Melanie."

"Sorry to interrupt, but I have a couple of questions for you, Melanie. First, when did your husband realize you were having an affair with his best friend, Bobby?"

Melanie started to cry and said she didn't know that her husband knew that she was cheating until he shot Bobby, and then she figured he knew.

"Well, how do you suppose your husband found this out? Did you tell him about your affair with Bobby?"

"Well, hell no, Officer, I mean Detective, I didn't tell him anything.

Really, why would I? It was a secret!"

"I don't know, ma'am. I'm just asking you if you told your husband, you were screwing around with his best friend. Did he see you or follow you? Did Bobby tell him, or did someone else tell him? Did anyone else know about your affair? Is Bobby married? Did his wife tell your husband about the affair? How did your husband find out about you cheating on him?

Melanie assured Detective Davis that she had not told her husband anything. She then went on to explain that her friend, Elise, had covered for her a few times when her husband was looking for her.

"But she would never tell my husband–she's my best friend!" she exclaimed.

Matt and Officer Thomas looked at each other knowingly. They each jotted a few notes, took Elise's contact information from Melanie, and turned to go.

"Thank you, ma'am. I'm sure this is a difficult time for you. Please don't leave the Cape unless you check in with me first. Here's my card."

"Yes, sir!" Melanie started to cry again.

As they finished questioning Melanie, the crime scene investigators started packing up and taking down the police tape. Finally, they told her she could return to her house, and if she wanted to visit her husband at the jail, she'd have to call either Officer Thomas or Detective Davis.

"Hey, are you still working on that accident case over in Osterville?" Officer Thomas asked Matt as they walked to their patrol cars park in the street.

"Yes, in fact, the guy just died this week, and I was just at a meeting with the doctors to review the autopsy. There was bruising on the shoulders, but they don't think it means someone shoved Mr. Wood. They said the bruising could have happened earlier, like the day before. I'm not sure of that, and I asked them to double-check to see if there was any bruising on the back of the shoulders. Like if someone grabbed him hard, shook him, and pushed him backward, right?"

"Matt, when I first got to the Woods' house and saw Mr. Wood lying there in a pool of blood, I couldn't figure out how he fell. I thought it seemed unusual. I played high school football, and you never saw anyone fall backward unless they ran into somebody and bounced off, like one of those giant linemen, or unless they got shoved and pushed backward. Never."

"Listen, Reid, I want to go back over to see Mrs. Wood this afternoon. Would you care to join me? If so, please call her and set up a meeting for us."

"Thanks, Matt. You know I want to be a detective someday, so the more time I can spend with any of you guys, the better off I am. What time works for you?"

"Any time that works for Mrs. Wood will be all right for us. Thanks," said Matt. Officer Thomas waved back at Detective Davis and then got into his cruiser.

Chapter Twenty-Nine

It was interesting, but not surprising, for Matt to speak with Melanie about cheating on her husband with his best friend. There was little to no remorse in her voice, and she certainly wasn't going to blame herself for Bobby's death. Melanie was, in a very real sense, a co-conspirator in the death of her boyfriend, but her actions were one step removed and considerably displaced from the crime.

Matt then thought about Jenn and how removed she seemed to be from the fall that Doug took. It was not beyond belief that Jenn could have hurt Doug in a rage by shoving him backward. Maybe an argument over the same issue that Melanie and her husband had fought about – maybe Doug was seeing another woman, and Jenn found out. It was conceivable that Jenn could have shoved her husband to the floor, deleted the security video files, left the house, and then just driven around for a few hours to make a believable alibi. Not the least bit remorseful, just like Melanie.

Matt stopped by Captain Pierce's office to have a chat about the shooting crime and Matt's thoughts regarding the possible murder of Doug Wood. But first, Matt wanted to call Ginny and get her perspective on Jenn.

"Hi Ginny, hope all is well with the nicest computer guru in the precinct."

"Oh, Matt, you're the best. Thanks, I'm great. How about you?"

"I'm fine, but I have some questions for you about the Wood case, specifically about Mrs. Wood. Do you have a couple of minutes?"

"Sure, Matt, shoot."

"Listen, Ginny, I don't know about Mrs. Wood. She's been notably vague about the accident and about why Doug stayed home that day. She's insistent that she does not know why Doug remained on the Cape that day and does not know who he was meeting with, if he was. But she insists that the visit to Hingham was pre-scheduled for both of them. That's a little odd, don't you think?"

Ginny considered what Matt said and then replied, "It could be Matt. Yes, if she is so connected with her husband, then the chances are pretty good that he would have told her why he wasn't going to join her for the trip to Hingham. I don't think he could have neglected to tell her about this. You know, if he ignored answering her when she said to him, 'How come you can't join me today, Doug?' I'm guessing she would have pushed him for an answer, right? No pun intended, right!"

Matt smiled then nodded his head and said to Ginny, "Yes, I think he would have had to answer her for sure. So how come she couldn't answer me – huh? How come she didn't know what Doug was doing that morning? And what about the surveillance videotapes? She could have erased them, couldn't she?" Matt asked.

"Sure, Matt, she definitely could have done that." Ginny nodded her head.

Matt agreed with Ginny and told her that he was going to check on Jenn's car computer to see where her vehicle was on Tuesday. That would shed some light on her possible involvement and, at the same time, her possible guilt.

"What are you gonna do about this, Matt? Are you gonna speak with Mrs. Wood again, or will you look into her car telemetry first?" Ginny asked.

Matt thought for a moment, then said, "I'll check out the car first. Make sure it was in Hingham for sure." Matt smiled, thanked Ginny for her help, and said he'd get back to her this afternoon after he had the car checked out.

"Bye, Matt," Ginny said.

Matt smiled and said goodbye.

The next call Matt made was to the vehicle tracking office at the Barnstable Police Department to see if they could tell him where Jenn's car was last Tuesday. They were very helpful and told Matt that they would check the plate number against the vehicle identification pool for Massachusetts and see if they could track the vehicle for last Monday, Tuesday, and Wednesday. The administrator told Matt they would probably be back in touch with him by the end of the day.

Next, he called Bill Pierce to see if Bill had a few minutes to share with Matt. Bill said to stop by anytime today, and he would fit Matt into his schedule. Matt thanked Bill and headed for the police department.

Matt parked in a shady spot under a big oak tree, walked into the building, and took the elevator to the third floor, where Bill Pierce's office was. He waved at Bill's secretary and walked straight into the office. Bill was on the phone, but motioned for Matt to take a seat right in front of his desk. Matt could hear the conversation, at least Bill's side, and could tell that Bill was speaking with his wife. He said that Matt was in his office, then he smiled, nodded, and said goodbye. He smiled as he turned toward Matt.

"What's going on? How's the investigation with the Wood accident?"

Matt cleared his throat and told Bill that the doctors thought it might not have been an accident, that someone could have shoved Doug Wood backward, which caused him to fall and hit his head. He added that he was a little suspicious of Doug's wife, Jenn. He told Bill that Jenn had been vague regarding her not knowing why Doug had not accompanied her up to Hingham. What was so important that he couldn't join her?

"Listen, Captain, I was surprised that Mrs. Wood could not even guess why her husband stayed home last Tuesday. She sounded a lot like that woman here in Hyannis whose husband killed her boyfriend in a jealous rage. Maybe Mrs. Wood thought he was cheating on her, stayed home, got into a huge argument with her husband, and shoved him, causing his head trauma. I don't know, but I'm just thinking she might be a suspect in all of this."

Bill looked over at Matt and said, "Have you reached out to the vehicle tracking guys to see if her car was home in the morning or someplace other than Hingham?"

"I just called them, Bill. They'll have something for me this afternoon. I'll let you know what they find out. In the meantime, I've got some other banking matters to look over. You know, those two guys, Wood and Henderson, were putting a lot of cash deposits into the offshore banks in the Grand Caymans. I've got someone looking at that as well. I'll let you know what I find out."

Then Matt got up and headed across the hall to the elevators. When the elevator stopped on the second floor, he hurried over to his office, where he saw Tim Stanton from the vehicle tracking office waiting for him. Matt waved Tim into his office and shook his hand.

"Have a seat, Tim. Any luck? Were you able to trace her car? Did it show up in Hingham, or was it in Osterville?"

Tim held out a piece of paper for Matt to look at and said, "Well, Matt, the car did show up in Hingham, so we're pretty sure that Mrs. Wood did visit her daughter just like she said. But, we also queried the telemetry systems to see if any cars were on Eel Road the morning of the 28th. Guess what? We spotted a car at her street address that arrived around 9:00 a.m. and didn't leave until after 11:00 a.m. We're trying to track the owner, but it's a bit cloudy at this point. If we can track the owner, I'll update you. We might have to use the satellite, but we will if we have to. But as far as I can tell, we can't get the chip info from the car. Probably because someone removed the chip earlier in the day. And remember, the visual satellite is only good to track a license plate if there is a direct angle to the back of the car. And we don't have that capability, so we may be out of luck, I think. Sorry!"

"You mean there was someone near the house, like in the driveway or parked out front? Hell, Tim, I'd like to know who that was as soon as possible," said Matt.

Tim got up from his chair, nodded at Matt, and headed out the door. Matt just sat there for a minute and ran his fingers through his hair. "This is getting more suspicious, minute by minute, he thought. I will have to let Ginny know."

Chapter Thirty

Officer Thomas arranged another visit for Detective Davis with Mrs. Wood for that afternoon. Officer Thomas mentioned how sorry he was for her loss and that he and Detective Davis had a couple of questions they'd like to ask as a follow-up to their previous discussion. He wondered if she was available that afternoon.

"Sure, about 3:00 is fine with me," she said.

"Thank you, Mrs. Wood. We'll see you at 3:00, then."

After Officer Thomas told Matt the time they were going to meet with Mrs. Wood, Detective Davis called Ginny Jensen. He hoped she had uncovered additional information about Mr. Wood, his wife Jennifer, or their friends or family. Ginny told him she'd be happy to have him come to her office to discuss what she had found, so Matt went right over.

"Hey Ginny, give me some good news. Have you found anything that leads you to believe that this accident with Mr. Wood was not an accident? You know, the docs think the bruises on his shoulders could have happened a day or two before the incident, so they can't be sure that the bruises are a result of someone grabbing Mr. Wood's shoulders and shaking him or pushing him. Kind of strange, right?"

"Listen, Matt, the family information is clean, as is the information about Mr. Wood's friends. I've found nothing else that gives me a reason to believe anyone hurt Mr. Wood in such a manner. So, let's start looking somewhere else, or maybe we should go back to thinking it was an accident."

"Fine, Ginny, you win! We'll move on from the family. But let's start looking elsewhere because I still think this may not have been an accident." Ginny smiled and gave Detective Davis a little shot to the arm. Matt turned and smiled at her, then said again, "The thought that this was an accident is difficult to fathom. I just have a feeling there is a piece of information we haven't found yet."

"If there is anything suspicious about any of the players, I promise I'll find it in the next few days," said Ginny.

"Thanks, Ginny. I hope we can find something before the captain puts this into the cold file." Matt realized he had some other cases that needed his attention, so maybe putting this one down for a little while would be a blessing, but something about it just bothered him.

"Matt, listen to me," Ginny replied, "this one is different, and it may just take a little longer for you, but I know you'll get to the bottom of it sooner or later."

Matt shook his head, walked out into the hallway, and headed upstairs to his office. But then he turned around because he remembered he hadn't told Ginny about the car that was at the Wood's house from 9:00 to 11:00 the day of the accident. Ginny was amazed and told Matt to call the tracing folks again to see if they had already identified the owner of the car. Matt smiled and said he would call them again and let her know as soon as he had any new information regarding the car.

Once in his office, he turned on his laptop, logged onto the NCIC computers in Denver, and typed in the names Douglas Wood + Charles Henderson and Jennifer Wood + Barbara Henderson. The results were unsurprising; none of the data linked any of them to any type of untoward or illegal activities. Next, Matt expanded the connections to people with two degrees of separation from them. The list grew significantly but didn't seem to connect to anyone who was the least bit suspicious except the names of William (Billy) Flynn and Felix Brown. Billy was an ex-employee of Bank of America.

Felix was an independent computer specialist who had worked as an IBM Fellow specializing in network analysis and AI systems. Both had worked with Doug Wood and Charlie Henderson in the past. Billy Flynn had been at each bank that Wood and Henderson had worked at and was still involved with Bank of America, not as an employee but as a security consultant. Felix Brown was a computer consultant who had done quite a bit of work for Billy Flynn as well as for Charlie Henderson and Doug Wood. It was pretty clear that Billy Flynn was the go-to security guy for the Bank of America, so Matt thought he'd reach out to Mr. Flynn to see what and who he knew and what he thought about Doug's accident. He looked up the contact information for Mr. Flynn, then picked up his phone and called him at his office number. He'd look into Felix Brown later.

"Mr. Flynn, this is Detective Matt Davis from the Barnstable Police Department on Cape Cod; we spoke a few days ago. Do you have a few minutes to talk with me about Douglas Wood?"

"Sure, I do, detective. How can I assist?"

"Do you know Doug Wood from Osterville?"

"Yes, I have worked with him in the past."

"Can you tell me where you know him from and what your relationship with him is?"

"Well, I worked with him at the bank."

"How well did you know him? What was your relationship?"

"I worked at BankBoston and he was the Chief Financial Officer. I also worked with him at Fleet Bank after they acquired First National Bank. I know him personally and professionally. Why are you asking me about Doug Wood?"

"I'm sorry to tell you this, but Doug Wood died earlier today and we have some questions about the cause of death."

"I know about that. He fell at his house, what a shame. Why are you asking me about it?" Billy said with a bit of a defensive tone.

Matt paused and decided to push just a little more.

"We have reason to believe that it may not have been an accident. How did you hear about Doug Wood?"

"His friend, Charlie Henderson, called me. We all worked together. Charlie called me to let me know what happened. Charlie and Doug are good friends and have worked together at the bank for years. Yes, they were very close. This is a real shame." There was a pause in the conversation, as each man thought about what to say next.

"If there's nothing else…" Billy started to say.

"Do you know any reason why someone would want to hurt Doug Wood?" Matt decided to just get it out there, to see if Billy would give him anything.

Billy Flynn thought for a moment and then said, "Doug Wood was a very respected and well-liked senior manager at the bank. I can't think of anyone who might want to hurt him, let alone cause his death." There was a slight tone of resentment in Billy's response. "And having said that, I don't believe anyone, including his friends or co-workers, would have wanted any harm to come to him. I think this was a terrible accident, and that's it."

"I'm sorry, Mr. Flynn; I'm sure Mr. Wood was well-liked. I'm just trying to get to the bottom of his death. Please call me if you think of anything else or hear anything."

"I sure will, Detective."

"Thanks, Mr. Flynn." Matt hung up and just rubbed his forehead. He felt like that guy knew something but wasn't talking – nothing, nada. Each time Matt spoke to him, something about his tone rubbed Matt the wrong way.

Next, he called Felix Brown, who was also in the Boston area. He introduced himself and told him that he was investigating the accident that ultimately caused Mr. Wood's death. Felix said he had heard about Mr. Wood's death and was sorry that Mr. Wood had passed away. His answer was the same as Billy's. No, he didn't know anything about the accident and certainly didn't know anyone who might wish to harm Mr. Wood.

Matt Davis thought for a minute and asked Felix if he knew why Mr. Wood had been down to the Caymans with Charlie Henderson and Billy Flynn.

"Oh, I don't know, they must have been down there for some relaxation, you know, golf, sunshine, and maybe just a venue change," Felix explained.

Matt smiled to himself, thanked Felix, and ended the call.

Matt started to dial Ginny's extension, but then hung up. He decided that this would be better in person. It was always harder to explain a hunch over the phone. He grabbed his coat and headed toward the stairs. But first, he called Tim Stanton over at the Traffic Office.

Chapter Thirty-One

Matt went down the stairs, turned left toward the administration office, and into Ginny's office. He was anxious to get more information, not only about Billy Flynn but, more importantly, what happened to Doug Wood. Ultimately, he couldn't shake the feeling that something else was happening.

"Can you take another look at this guy, Billy Flynn, for me?" he asked Ginny. "He was employed at the same banks as Doug Wood and Charlie Henderson. He's a private security consultant to the bank now. I'd like to see more of his data, if you don't mind. Also, can you please look up that guy Felix Brown again? Thanks."

"Sure, give me a few minutes, would you? But any news from Tim Stanton?

"No news, he said the tracking chip had been disabled on the car. Can you believe that? He'll see if there is another way to confirm tracking." Ginny just shook her head.

Matt said, "I'll be back in ten – want some coffee?"

"No thanks, but thanks."

He walked down to the cafeteria, grabbed a cup of coffee, took a few sips then headed back to Ginny's office. On the way, he bumped into his boss, Bill Pierce. Matt smiled and said hello to Bill, then experienced a pleasant flashback. Bill Pierce was the person who hired Matt Davis almost twenty years ago as a street cop. Getting a street sense in and around Hyannis was a great starting point. He had an opportunity to get to know all the villages of Barnstable and learn more about crime on the Cape. This included the drugs, guns, and domestic violence issues that had developed over the years. Matt would never forget how Captain Pierce had helped him with the interminable quantities of paperwork after each patrol night. It was endless, and Bill's assistance was greatly appreciated. As Matt's mentor, Bill also helped him with gun work on the range. Bill had excellent shooting skills and had placed second in the All-County Pistol Competition several times. He guided Matt and improved his shooting skills to rival his own. Most of all, Bill was a friend, and when there was an opportunity to ride, shoot, or work together, Bill would always reach out to Matt.

Bill was the one in the department who encouraged Matt to take the detective exam, and when he passed, Bill was elated to have Matt join the team. Over the years, they became very close friends and always shared stories, beer, and off-time. They were both from the area; Bill was born and raised in Hyannis, and Matt grew up in the next village, Centerville. It was a friendship that would last a lifetime, both in and out of the precinct.

"Hey Matt, have you got a minute?"

"Sure, I'm just waiting for Ginny to finish a new report. What's up, Bill?" They walked back over to the cafeteria. Bill grabbed a coffee and then sat down across the table from Matt.

"I was just wondering how that shooting case in Centerville is going. Any idea what happened there? I heard that you and Officer Thomas have pinned down the victim as the boyfriend and that the husband killed the victim in a jealous rage – right?"

"That's right. We interviewed the wife a couple of times. She confirmed she was having a fling with the victim. She also confirmed that her husband caught them in bed, and before the victim could reach his car, the husband grabbed his gun and shot the boyfriend right in the driveway. The wife was standing on the front porch and watched it all happen. Two neighbors were outside and witnessed the whole thing. Ouch, right? That was a bit of a knee-jerk reaction by the husband, but all's fair in love and whatever, right?"

Bill thought about it. "It's probably what any husband would do if he caught his spouse cheating. Remember that Lorena Bobbitt woman, the wife who cut her cheating husband's 'pickle' off? Geez, I still squirm thinking about that." Matt and Bill shared a grimace.

"Speaking of wives, how's Bev? Is she still directing from the corner?"

"She's good. We were just talking about having you over for dinner some night." Bill smiled at his friend.

"I'd love that. Just to wrap things up on that case, Bill. The trial is set for two months from now, and the DA thinks it's an open-and-shut case for murder two. I'll have to testify with Officer Thomas, and I'll keep you updated."

Bill and Matt each took a sip of coffee. Bill then said, "Sounds good. Just one more thing – how about that guy over in Osterville who fell and cut his head open? How is he doing?"

"Doug Wood," Matt answered, "Well, Bill, he died from complications from the head wound, and I just found out that he had cancer on top of it all. Anyway, the autopsy was a little inconclusive in that the ME thought Mr. Wood could have tripped and fallen, or someone could have pushed him. There were some marks on his shoulders, but nothing conclusively indicating that he was shoved. We're still going back and forth over the cause of death, a full week after the accident. I have a feeling there's more to this case than we know yet. I'll get back to you if I can get anything positive from the doctors regarding the cause of death."

"Matt, you should be careful with these guys from Osterville. They all have deep pockets and connections back to Boston and with the FBI. On the other hand, your hunches usually are right. So go ahead and keep investigating but be careful. Keep me in the loop every step of the way." Bill smiled and then changed the subject.

"Remember, let's schedule dinner at my place this week. Don't forget to let us know what works for you, and let me know if you want to bring somebody."

Bill winked at Matt and waved goodbye as he headed toward his office on the fourth floor. Matt turned around and headed for Ginny's office.

That's when Bill turned around and said, "Hell, Matt, why don't we just ask Ginny to come along to dinner at our house? She's really nice, you know."

Matt smiled, nodded at Captain Pierce, and walked into Ginny's office.

Chapter Thirty-Two

When Matt walked into Ginny's office, he looked at her with a new appreciation. Maybe Bill was right; he should ask Ginny to join them for dinner. That would be a lot of fun, and she's a true friend. He always enjoyed her company. Her face lit up when she saw him.

"Hey Ginny, any luck with our guys?"

"Matt, I did find something you might find interesting."

"Tell me..."

Matt sat down at Ginny's desk in front of all her displays and watched Ginny log into NCIC.

"Matt, this guy, Doug Wood, is a mover and shaker in the accounting world. He's never done anything illegal that I could find. He is considered one of the smartest guys on the planet when it comes to sum-of-the-years-digits, double-declining-balance, LIFO, FIFO, and all those other ways to depreciate assets. He has been on the Board of Advisors of the Financial Accounting Standards Board and was twice the FASB liaison to the IRS. He also sat on the Board of Directors of Ernst & Young and several Fortune 500 companies, including Booz Allen Hamilton, and Bain and Company. This guy is an accounting legend."

"So, what you're saying, Ginny, is that Doug Wood's character is unimpeachable and that no one would want to harm him?"

"That's right, Matt. This guy is as clean as a whistle, except for those few speeding tickets in his Ferrari. And who knows, if you owned a Ferrari, I guess you'd get some tickets, right?"

Matt just sat for a minute, almost disappointed that Ginny hadn't discovered something more nefarious about Doug Wood.

"Well, thanks, Ginny. I wanted to make sure no one had something in for him. I'm still just a bit confused. If nobody pushed him and he didn't walk into something and rebound, then he must have fallen backward, but the docs tell me that's almost impossible. So, I'm stumped. As you know, I don't like to be in this position, so if you find anything else, please let me know. What about his friends? Anything new there? And thanks again for all this." Matt waved his hands in a circle and smiled.

Ginny put her hand up and said, "I already took a closer look at Charlie Henderson, and he came up clean as a whistle as well. Nothing unusual, nothing criminal, and nothing with his family either. I mean nothing. But then I decided to run him with Doug Wood inclusive, as a closed hyphenated search, and look what comes up."

Matt looked up at the big display right in front of Ginny's desk and said, "What the hell are those, Ginny?"

"I don't know, Matt, but they look like some sort of bank account transactions that bumped into a bunch of other transactions, and then they all disappeared like they never existed. I didn't see any identifiers or transaction IDs when they disappeared. They just went poof! That's highly unusual for a server to lose a transaction, especially today. Something funny about this, Matt – particularly since these show up under the specific Henderson/Wood inquiry. Let me do some more digging around this and see if I can find anything else about your guys."

"Okay, Ginny, but before you do that digging around, would you mind telling me if you found anything else about these other two guys, Bill Flynn and Felix Brown?"

Well," Ginny said, "Flynn is tightly coupled with Charlie Henderson and Doug Wood. As I mentioned, he was the Chief of Security for all the banks these guys worked for and moved right along with them.

Matt nodded and said, "I just spoke briefly with him today. He's in business for himself and seems to know more about what happened than you would expect – a close friend of both guys in and out of the workplace. But I think there's something he's not telling me. I think he knows more than he's saying about Doug and Charlie. If Charlie and Doug are up to something, this guy Billy Flynn is part of it."

"Well, and so is this guy, Felix Brown. He was a big deal at IBM. He worked on developing the Systems Network Architecture, SNA, the communications environment for all IBM hardware. Then he worked on the Watson project, IBM's Artificial Intelligence Program, until he had a falling out with IBM. Something about lifting packet data out of transactions and shifting the contents to a different location. Kind of odd, I think. I don't know exactly what that means, but it sounds like the Feds were brought in, and then everything evaporated with him and IBM," Ginny said.

Matt thanked Ginny, smiled at her, and left her office. Standing in the hall, he thought about what Bill Pierce had just said about asking Ginny to dinner next week. After a minute of reflection, Matt decided to mention it to Ginny.

She was a good friend aside from being a good police administrator, particularly if you needed to know something about crime data, computers, or anything else. In addition, Matt always thought she was an attractive young woman with one of the prettiest smiles he'd ever seen. And beyond her good looks and data retrieval skills, she was a genuinely kind person, patient, very caring, and a great friend.

Maybe he should ask her to dinner over at Captain Pierce's house rather than leaving it to Captain Pierce or his wife. She'd certainly have a good time with them, particularly if Bill invited his neighbors, Smokey and Terri. That would make it even more fun because Terri is a great person and an easy conversationalist, and her husband, Smokey, is one of the funniest people Matt has ever met. He points that long finger at you and says, "Hey, I missed you, whatever your name is." He was one of those guys with natural comedic timing – and dry humor too!

"Hell," Matt thought, "maybe I'll just mention it to Ginny right now. Might as well get it on her calendar rather than wait for Bill to ask her." His first thought was to call her when he returned to his office, but then he shook his head and slapped himself on the face. "Don't call her, you dope. Walk right over to her office and ask her in person." He argued with himself and then decided just to do it!

Matt strolled back to Ginny's office and leaned into the open door. "Hi Ginny, I have another question for you."

"Sure, Matt. What's up?"

"Okay, so I'm just wondering if you're free Saturday and if you'd like to join Bill, Bev, and me for dinner over at Bill's house? He was gonna ask you, but since I was already here, I thought I would. You know Bill Pierce pretty well, and you'll like his wife, Bev. What do you think, Ginny?"

"Well, I guess it would be all right. Sure, that would be fun. What can I bring, what would you like?"

"Oh, I don't know, why don't you surprise us?" Ginny had a big smile on her face, and so did Matt. "I'll get you his address, or I can pick you up if you'd like, say around 5:30. Does that sound good for you, Ginny? You're still over in Sandwich by the beach, right?"

"Sounds great, and yes, I'm still in that little house near Town Neck Beach. See you around 5:30 on Saturday."

Matt smiled and waved goodbye. When he returned to his office, he called Bill Pierce to tell him that he had already asked Ginny to join them for dinner Saturday night. Bill was delighted and decided to call his wife to tell her that Ginny was also coming to dinner. He knew that Bev would be happy to hear that Ginny would be joining them.

Matt's next call was to Charlie Henderson, but there was no answer at his house. So, he left a short voice message asking Mr. Henderson to call him back when he had a few minutes. Finally, Matt called Reid Thomas' cell phone and got him in his patrol car.

"Hey Reid, I was wondering if you had heard anything about the fingerprints yet? You know, I can't shake the feeling from our conversation the other day that someone Doug trusted was in that room with him. Maybe someone got into an argument with Mr. Wood, shoved him, and then realized what he'd done and ran."

"Right, Matt, there were four fresh sets of fingerprints: Mr. Wood,

Mrs. Wood, and both of the Hendersons. And then there was another set of prints equally fresh, from the same time frame. We don't have a match yet, but we will soon enough!"

"Okay, so we know that Henderson has been over there. I wonder how recently they've been in that study – I mean, library. I know that the victim couldn't have fallen backward, hit his head, and just lay there until his wife came home without somebody wondering where the hell he was. So, let's cut through all the shit and see what we have on Wood's friends and people he worked with who live around the Cape. I don't care if it's someone out on Race Point; I need a suspect because now I'm thinking that something other than an accident occurred. And I think that it might be someone close to Doug Wood. Maybe a family member or maybe one of his friends!"

Chapter Thirty-Three

Charlie Henderson had spent almost half an hour looking through Doug's desk, his file cabinets, and his personal computer, but he couldn't find what he was looking for. He'd run out of time and had to rejoin Jenn and Barb in the kitchen, otherwise one of them would have come looking for him, and he didn't want to get caught snooping around Doug's office. It just wouldn't look right. So now he'd have to figure out another way to get back into the house and look upstairs at Doug's other desk in that spare bedroom next to the master suite. The information had to be somewhere, and he didn't want to get Billy Flynn involved if he didn't have to.

Charlie walked out of Doug's office and across the oriental rug that covered the wide plank mahogany floor. He then entered the spacious white kitchen, which also looked out onto the Eel River. Jenn and Barb were putting plates of shrimp and pasta on the trestle table in the breakfast area next to the windows. Charlie had a moment of regret as he joined the ladies for dinner. "Doug should be here," he thought. What a shame.

After finishing their dinner, they took a glass of wine out to the terrace. The chairs were set in a row facing out to the river, and the view was beautiful.

"I don't know what I'm going to do without him," Jenn said. "Just look at that boat. He loved that boat. We had such fun on it." Barb and Charlie nodded. The Bonanza III rocked gently at the dock beyond the sweeping lawn. Doug's big Post 56 Convertible was secured to the extended pier, and a smaller boat, a twenty-foot Regal center console runabout named Rendezvous, was tied up to the other side of the dock. Both boats had been untouched.

Jenn said, "Hey, I have an idea; let's get another glass of wine and go out to the boats and sit on the big one. Doug would love to see us doing that, wouldn't he?"

Charlie agreed, so he, Barb, and Jenn got some more wine and then walked across the lawn and down the pier to the big boat, the Bonanza. Each one stepped up and over the side of the deck, then down the steps to the cockpit. There were four seats and a captain's chair. They each chose a spot and put their wine in front of them on an individual table that was screwed onto the teak floor.

Charlie looked across the cockpit at Jenn while she poured each of them some more wine and asked her, "Jenn, are there any other things we need to review and help you with before the funeral? How can we be there for you and the girls?"

"Thanks, Charlie. We're all set for now. I am so grateful for your help and friendship. I know you miss Doug, too."

Charlie nodded his head and said, "Jenn, if you don't mind, I would like to stop by tomorrow to check Doug's study for those documents having to do with the accounts we all shared. I have to change the ownership from Doug to you. Doug had a set of spreadsheets detailing each account, and I don't have a copy of it on my computer. Do you suppose I could take a look tomorrow?"

"Of course, you can stop by anytime. I have to meet with the Priest tomorrow, so I might not be home when you get here."

Charlie said, "Oh, okay, if you don't mind, I'll stop by tomorrow morning. How should I get in if you're gone?"

Jenn replied, "Charlie, you can use the code key for the garage. I'll give it to you when you leave."

They sat in silence, each immersed in their own thoughts as they watched the setting sun. The sky turned from orange to pink, the swallows were flying over the river, catching bugs. It was a special but solemn moment for the three remaining friends.

Barb said, "Now, let's clean up and let Jenn get some rest." So, they stood up, walked back down the pier, and went back into the house just as the colors changed on the Eel River.

Barb turned to see the sun setting and said to Charlie and Jenn, "What a beautiful sunset. I bet Doug did that for us, you know, to let us know he's fine and happy to see us together again."

Charlie and Jenn nodded their heads in agreement.

They walked into the kitchen, and Jenn went to the keyboard on the wall next to the door leading to the garage and handed Charlie a copy of the code, which was etched on a brass tag. "Use this one; it will unlock the whole security system and give you access through the garage entrance."

"Charlie, just leave it – don't bother Jenn with this now," Barb interjected. But Charlie shook his head, indicating that he needed to find the account info immediately. Barb just shrugged her shoulders.

Chapter Thirty-Four

The next morning, Charlie pulled into the driveway, got out of his car, and walked up to the center garage door. When he put in the keycode Jenn had given him, the door opened and the lights came on. He walked into the garage, staring at the bright red Ferrari sitting alone in the left bay of the garage. Doug had always wanted a Ferrari but thought it was much too expensive. Charlie talked him into it when they got their stock and bonus payments from the Bay Bank acquisition. Charlie even went with Doug to the Ferrari dealership on Route 1 in Norwood to be sure Doug bought the car. It was a beautiful, bright red Ferrari Superamerica with a powerful 540HP V12 engine under the hood. Doug ordered a manual transmission and had fun shifting it up and down the shift gate while revving the engine up to 8000 RPMs. The noise was deafening, and the car flew like a jet plane.

Charlie's only advice to Doug was to drive carefully and set aside a few thousand dollars to pay for speeding tickets. Doug lost the car a few times when cops would watch him go past them at twice the posted speed limit. Most times, it was just a regular speeding ticket, but more than once, Doug traveled on Interstate 95 and found himself doing 125 to 130 MPH as he passed a parked state police car. It took a few minutes for the policeman to catch him, but twice they towed the vehicle, leaving Doug to call Jenn to pick him up at the State Police barracks. Charlie remembered the day Doug called him to say he would be late to the office. The police caught him speeding in the tunnel on the Mass Turnpike. They said he was doing around 100 MPH in the tunnel when the speed limit was 50 MPH and strictly enforced. He earned himself more than a ticket; this time, it included a mandatory court date. Doug, of course, had all of this expunged from his file - because he could.

Doug loved the car so much, and Charlie understood because it brought Doug something he didn't have as an accountant – freedom. Charlie reached out and touched the Ferrari as he headed toward the door leading into the house and smiled as he thought about Doug and his adventures.

Once Charlie unlocked the door to the house using the keycode, he shut it behind him and walked through the kitchen. He glanced out the back of the house toward the river and the terrace where they had just had drinks the night before. The two boats were gently bobbing at the dock.

Charlie walked to the other side of the house, past the library where Doug fell and hit his head. He decided to avoid that room and entered Doug's office from the other hallway. The office had a large bay window, also looking out onto the river. Doug had placed his desk to look directly out at his boat. Charlie made one final sweep of the office in case he missed anything the night before. Finding nothing, he moved on to the guest bedroom. This room had two computers, a second desk, and a credenza. The computer on the desk was for Jenn, and Doug used the one on the credenza. There were also a couple of lateral file cabinets.

Charlie sat down at the desk, turned around, opened one of the file drawers in the credenza, and looked through all of the files to see if he could identify any that might have bank account information. Next, he looked through the other file drawer in the credenza and searched both lateral file cabinets, but could not find what he was looking for.

"Damn, they must be here someplace, but where?" he muttered to himself.

He got up from the desk, walked to the back of the bedroom near the French doors that led to a small deck, swung the doors wide open, and looked out toward the river. He stared at the boats.

"That's where Doug put the files: out on the boat! Probably at the navigation station inside the main cabin of the big boat, Bonanza. No one would think to look there." Charlie said.

Charlie closed the French doors and hurried down to the key hooks on the wall next to the kitchen desk. He grabbed the boat keys for Bonanza III and headed out of the kitchen slider with determination. Charlie went over to the stern of the boat, quickly stepped into the cockpit with its beautiful teak deck, then moved to the cabin door on the starboard side, unlocked it, and entered the main cabin. In the corner up against the bulkhead was a navigation station which included a table with several built-in desk drawers. He opened the top drawer and saw some old US Coast Guard navigation charts. Charlie thought, "Wow, I bet Doug hadn't used these for years since navigation had moved from paper to radar and computers."

When he lifted the folded charts, he immediately saw two red folders. Charlie opened the first one, checked the contents, then opened the second folder. He smiled, got up from the desk, pushed the chair back under the navigation table, walked out the starboard side door, and locked it. He retraced his steps down the pier and into the kitchen and left a thank-you note for Jenn. He checked that the doors were locked and started walking toward his car when he noticed a car parked across the street in front of a neighbor's driveway. Charlie was a little surprised that a neighbor would let a visitor park out on the street since Eel River Road was private, and the residents were a bit "upper crust" and all that stuff. Then he noticed someone leaning on the driver's side door of his Porsche. Charlie quickened his steps toward his car.

Before Charlie could speak, the fellow said, "Afternoon, Mr. Henderson. I'm Detective Matt Davis from the Barnstable Police Department; I left you a message yesterday. Mind if I ask you a few questions?"

"Not at all. How can I help the Barnstable Police Department, Detective?"

"Well, two things, Mr. Henderson. One, what are you doing here at Mr. Wood's house this morning? It doesn't seem like anyone else is here. And two, where were you on Tuesday the 28th when Mr. Wood had his accident?" Matt asked.

"Well, I'll answer your second question first. I was over at the Hyannisport Club playing golf, and when I finished, I stayed and had a couple of beers before heading home. Why?"

"I'll tell you why after you tell me why you're here at Mr. Wood's house right now," Matt said.

"Sure, officer. Doug, I mean, Mr. Wood and I had some investments pooled together, and he kept the books on them. I wanted to collect the files, so I could have someone manage them for Jenn and me." Charlie waved the two red folders so Officer Davis could see them. "I asked Jenn, sorry, Mrs. Wood, if I could stop by today, and she gave me the door lock combinations. She knows I'm here."

"Pooled investments," Matt said, "what does that mean?"

"Well, we made some investments in a variety of REITs."

"What's a REIT?" Matt asked.

"They're Real Estate Investment Trusts which include a variety of real estate investments held in a single fund. In addition, we had some fixed-income positions with various investment funds – so-called passive investments. We each put a certain amount of money into single accounts with different investment firms, and Doug kept all the records," Charlie explained.

"You mean you mixed your money? How does that work?"

"Well, Doug and I would each put a certain amount of money into the same investment – let's say a million each. The fund manager looked at it as a single investment of two million dollars from our Limited Liability Partnership, not as two investments coming from two separate sources."

"Why would you do that? I don't understand the benefit of doing that, and it sounds like a lot of record keeping too."

"The pooled investment is a larger amount – two million dollars, so we get a better price on shares of stock or whatever the investment vehicle might be. If you can buy a larger amount, it's less cost per share, and you cut the fees in half." Charlie was calm and relaxed but started to wonder why Detective Davis had such an interest in the investments. He put his hands in his pockets. He was hoping that Detective Davis would stop leaning on his car.

"Okay, so you pooled your money to buy investments, and Mr. Wood took care of the bookkeeping for both of you. So, you're looking for the ledger of accounts or something."

"Well, it's not an old-fashioned ledger anymore. It's a computer file, so I've been looking at Doug's computers. Would you mind?" Charlie nodded his head at the Porsche.

"Oh, sure." Matt took his hand off the car and stood up straight. "You found what you're looking for since you have those papers in your hand, right?"

"No. Actually, these are not the account records. They're just a map of where to find the accounts in Doug's cloud-based storage service. I'll have to call them to get a printout of all the funds and their locations with each investment firm. It's a giant pain in the ass, but Doug was pretty careful and didn't want the account records just hanging around."

"So, you were just picking up some paperwork here today. Would you mind if I confirm that you had Mrs. Wood's approval to come over? And I'd like to confirm that you were at Hyannisport Club Tuesday morning."

"Oh no, not at all, Detective go ahead. I think you'll find everything is in order and that I was over in Hyannis last week when Doug hurt himself."

"Right. Mr. Henderson. Do you know William Flynn? What is his relationship to Mr. Wood and you?"

"Billy Flynn was our Chief of Operations and Head of Bank Security at the First National Bank of Boston. He continued to hold those positions after the first merger with Bay Bank and maintained those positions through the merger with Fleet Bank and Bank of America. He is now an independent consultant specializing in bank fraud and funds theft. But why do you ask?"

"Is there any chance that Billy Flynn might have been here on the Cape with Doug on the day of the accident?"

"I don't know, but I really doubt that Billy would have been here on the Cape without telling me." Now Charlie was wary and starting to become annoyed and a little concerned. This line of questioning seemed inappropriate, and he wasn't sure where it was going or why.

"I'm sorry for all the questions, Mr. Henderson. I'm only wondering out loud if you knew anyone who may have had reason to be in touch with Mr. Wood the morning of his accident."

"Sorry, Detective, I don't know of anyone who would have reason to be visiting with Doug. Why don't you ask his wife?" Charlie frowned at Matt. "Is that all? Can I go now, or do you need something else from me?"

"No, we're all set for the time being, Mr. Henderson. If I need anything else, I'll be in touch, and again, thank you for your cooperation. I'm sorry for your loss. You can go now."

Matt waited for Charlie to drive away before he got into his car. Sitting down, he paused before starting the car and thought, "What's going on here? Charlie Henderson seemed a bit touchy and defensive. I wonder if he saw me follow him over here to the Woods' house. I wonder what all this investment stuff is really about. And who is this guy, Billy Flynn? What's his real involvement with Doug Wood and, for that matter, with Charlie Henderson? Charlie didn't mention the Cayman Island trips the three of them took together at all. I'll have to look closely at all three of these guys because something just doesn't feel right." Matt started up his cruiser and headed back to the station. But after a minute or two, he decided to stop in Hyannisport for a chat with the golf pro or maybe the club manager.

When Matt got to Hyannisport, he turned onto Irving Street, drove up to the top of the hill, and turned into the front gate of the country club. He parked his car facing the sound and was presented with a beautiful view of the ninth hole coming up toward the clubhouse and an equally stunning view of the back nine running down the hill toward the marshlands that tied the course to the ocean.

"What a spectacular view," Matt said to no one in particular. "How can you even concentrate on your golf game with this beautiful scenery?"

He got out of the cruiser, walked across the parking lot to the main entrance of the Hyannisport Club, and followed the hallway down to a stairway that led to the Pro Shop. Ricky Jones, the assistant professional, was sitting at the counter reading Golf Magazine and didn't look up until Matt cleared his throat.

"Can I help you, sir?" He said while pushing the magazine off to his left.

"Hi, I'm Detective Matt Davis from the Barnstable Police Department," Matt said as he flashed his badge. "I have a couple of questions about one of your members. Was Charles Henderson on the course last week? Specifically last Tuesday?"

"Let me take a look at my computer. Yes, he was out here Tuesday, the 28th. In the morning. I think he had a 10:00 a.m. tee time, probably got here around 9:30, and might have taken around four hours to play 18 holes, maybe a bit longer if he stopped for lunch at the turn."

Detective Davis asked if Ricky could see in the records whether Charlie had stopped for a drink or anything during the day.

"Looks like he was here around lunch, but he didn't use his charge for it. And yes, he did have a beer after his round, at about 3:00."

Matt began to ask if he could have paid cash for his lunch, but Ricky had anticipated that question and said, "Oh, someone else may have put his lunch on their tab. No cash is used here."

Matt thanked the assistant, left the pro shop, and returned to his cruiser. On the way back, he pulled his cell phone out, called Ginny, and asked her to check with Verizon regarding Mr. Henderson's phone. "And don't forget to tell them we have a warrant for the phone records."

She called him back five minutes later and said, "No, it was on all the time he was there, it was active the entire time on Tuesday. Within a half mile of the clubhouse."

"Thanks, Ginny," Matt said.

It seemed like Charlie Henderson was telling the truth about being on the golf course, having lunch at the turn, and drinking a beer after golf last Tuesday. Matt still felt there was something off, though.

Chapter Thirty-Five

Alison had considered telling her mother that she'd finally had a date with one of the guys from the Fed, but then she thought better of it. The questions would never end if she told her mom about the date. Plus, she needed to spend some more time looking at the server data to see if she could confirm that the breaches were intentional.

The first set of reports that Michael gave Alison told her exactly when the hack occurred and on which server it had occurred, but he could not explain precisely how or why it happened. So, she picked up the phone, gave Michael a call, and asked him if he'd come across anything that might indicate how the servers were being hacked and, more importantly, for what reason.

Michael, up until now, had just speculated as to why someone would try to hack the Federal Reserve Bank. He surmised that it was probably to gain access to the money transfers occurring every second between the Fed and any of their client banks. Gaining access to a Fed server would allow the hacker to modify the handshake and possibly move some of the restricted data and the money elsewhere. With the handshake data available, the hacker might be able to alter transfer values and locations, thus enabling electronic theft of federal monies or client monies. Either way, if the handshakes were violated and the data passed outside the Fed's network, it might be possible for someone to redirect funds to ghost accounts and ghost accounts are invisible. Michael used to think that it was nearly impossible to hack into any of the Fed's servers. But now he was sure that someone or something was hacking into the servers at the Fed in Boston, and it was a big enough deal that Treasury had sent one of their senior analysts up to the Federal Reserve Bank of Boston to find out how it was happening and who was doing it. He hoped Alison could answer these questions.

Michael assumed now that if you saw ghost accounts, you could probably find someone trying to steal from the Federal Reserve System, a position Alison had already surmised. Alison was a step or two ahead of Michael, and he knew it. She started to see data proofs that confirmed ghost accounts in and around all of the Fed's servers and some of the client servers, too! She had even seen some ghost accounts as far back as 1998 sitting on some of the Fed's client systems, including many of the larger banks in New York and New England.

"What the hell has been going on all this time...I thought we were impenetrable?" Michael thought to himself. "I guess we're not."

Alison finally had some proof that all of the Fed's systems, including client systems, had been hacked and breached. The timeline went as far back as the 1990s and moved forward as recently as yesterday. The Boston Federal Reserve Bank was responsible for the first district (District One) in the Federal Reserve System; eleven more districts made up the whole organization. The incomplete handshakes were examples of hacks to both the sending and receiving servers. The specific transactions represented data being moved to and from the Federal Reserve System. Each incomplete handshake meant data loss for the Fed or the Fed's client, and each data loss could represent a potential loss of funds.

As Alison read the list of incomplete handshakes Michael had sent her, she was dumbfounded – the list was massive. The document count started with 25 incomplete handshakes in Boston in 1998 and spiked with 3,846 incomplete handshakes around the country this year. Worse, there were even more predicted based on next year's projections of transactions. Alison had to get to the bottom of this sooner rather than later, or the whole system might crumble. So, she picked up the phone and called Michael.

"Hey, Michael, can you come down here for a minute? There's something I need to talk with you about. Thanks."

A few minutes later, Michael pushed open Alison's door and said, "Hi, Alison. Did you want some dinner company tonight – is that it?"

Alison smiled and shook her head. "Not right now, Michael. Let's talk business for a minute, can we? I need you to confirm that each of these individual servers failed over the last five years, so I can position this data loss to the Treasury. It's time the Treasury knew what happened here so they can take the appropriate action."

"Hold on a minute, Alison. Are you thinking you might try to push the blame onto the Fed's IT service group and me? Because that's not fair. We had a lock on the failures as soon as you started your investigation. And by the way, is that the real reason you showed up here, to spy on us and point the finger at us?" Michael felt threatened and couldn't believe what she was indicating. "You know, we didn't see the handshake problem until this year, and we thought we fixed it with the new server patches and some help from the folks over at Breaker Corporation, the virus scan software specialists. They have a prototype piece of anti-hacking software we've been running since the end of last year, and it's doing a damn good job keeping everybody out of our servers, so it wasn't a break-in we knew anything about." Michael took a deep breath. His face had flushed, and he was not pleased.

"Michael, first of all, I'm not accusing you or your team of missing anything. You and your guys are doing a fantastic job guarding the servers, the nest, the network, and the Fed's systems. No, I'm just looking at the facts and seeing that the servers are getting hacked. The Fed has almost 4,000 incomplete handshakes per year, meaning somebody is siphoning a bunch of small, almost undetectable amounts of money from various funds daily." Alison tried to reassure him with a smile. Then, she gently said, "I'm on your side, Michael, and I want to find out who these bastards are and shut them down."

"Maybe I did overreact and jump to conclusions," Michael looked at Alison sheepishly. Finally, he shrugged and said, "Sorry, let's get back to work. It looks like we have a lot to do." He got up to leave her office, but Alison leaned over her desk to keep him for a moment.

"Michael, I've already told them you're doing a great job helping me. I couldn't do any of this without you."

"Thanks, Alison, I'm sorry I got a little defensive, but you know, IT always takes the blame for everything. Any issue and they say, 'Oh, and it's IT's fault, they screwed up.' I'm just tired of being blamed for every problem."

Alison said she was not trying to pin this on anyone at the Fed in Boston, but she wanted to know all the details about these ghost accounts and ultimately the people who create them.

Chapter Thirty-Six

Matt picked Ginny up at her house in Sandwich around 5:30 Saturday night. She lived right on the beach on North Shore Boulevard in a house her grandparents built in the 1930s, shortly after her grandfather retired from the Sandwich Police Department. Ginny's parents gave her the house when they moved into an assisted living facility in East Sandwich. The only condition was that Ginny maintain the home in good condition as well as visit her folks weekly. She did both.

Matt knocked on the screen door of the classic Cape Cod-style shingled house. Ginny answered the door and asked him to come in for a minute. She grabbed her coat and walked back through the living room, where she had offered Matt a seat. Her living room looked out through a large picture window right onto Cape Cod Bay.

Matt just stared out the window and finally said, "Wow, what a gorgeous view!"

"Want to see the rest of the house?" Ginny said.

"Sure," Matt said. Ginny walked him around the house, and Matt again noted how each window had the same gorgeous view looking right out at the ocean. Ginny brought Matt back to the living room and handed him a glass of wine.

"Is the wine okay, Matt? I hope you don't mind the ice, but I forgot to chill the bottle." Ginny smiled.

Matt nodded with a smile as he looked into her eyes. Ginny was wearing a nice pair of dark pants and a grey top that matched her coloring.

"You look great, Ginny; you clean up nice. I mean, it's just that you look so different at the office." He smiled. Ginny usually had her hair tied back in a ponytail and wore glasses. Her hair was down, and she had curled it a little, so it sat right on her shoulders and was a little springy. Tonight, she was wearing contacts, and it changed her look. Matt was intrigued.

"Thanks, Matt! You look pretty spiffy yourself. Thanks for inviting me over to Captain Pierce's for dinner. I'm looking forward to seeing Bev."

Matt and Ginny talked a bit about Sandwich and the beach erosion that seemed to plague that area ever since the canal was built. She regaled Matt with stories her grandfather told her about the original canal. It was privately owned by a young Harvard graduate by the name of Belmont, whose family owned the Belmont Race Track in New York. He had built the canal as a toll canal. But it was narrow and only allowed passage one way at a time. That aside, it did allow ships to avoid going around the outer Cape, so a lot of time and money was saved by the shipping companies who used the canal. Unfortunately for the Belmont family, it eventually failed as an investment for them. Eventually, the Army Corps of Engineers successfully rebuilt it as the wider and safer two-way canal that continues operating today.

Ginny remembered coming to the beach when her grandparents lived here and commented that there was a lot more sand than there is now.

"What nice memories you must have had growing up on this beach," Matt said.

"I've always loved this place, and I'm so thankful my parents left it to me to watch over it."

They finished their wine and left the glasses in the kitchen sink. Ginny offered her arm, and Matt looped his arm around hers. They walked down the front walk to Matt's car.

"Wow, Matt, I didn't know you still drove a Corvette. I guess I've only seen you driving your police car – this one is beautiful."

"Thanks, Ginny. I love Corvettes. It's my second one, and I enjoy it in contrast to the Ford Taurus I've been driving for the last six years. Someone stole the first Corvette, and when we found it, it was totaled. I guess the guy who stole it couldn't handle all the horsepower. Anyway, Corvettes are a lot of fun to drive and good for the ego."

"Oh, I don't think you have any ego issues, Matt. Even though you're one of our younger detectives with a senior rank, you don't seem to let it get to your head."

"Well, Ginny, you know it's very competitive at Barnstable, and there's a ton of other great officers and detectives who are on the fast track too. But thank you for the compliment. I'm glad you decided to come over to Bill's house with me tonight."

"Thank you very much." Ginny touched Matt's arm again and then smiled and said, "I'm thrilled you suggested it."

After a twenty-minute drive to Barnstable, they pulled into Captain Pierce's driveway. He lived over in Cummaquid Heights, a private golf course community. The Cummaquid Golf Club was one of the oldest golf courses on the Cape. Bill and Bev Pierce moved here after Bill became a Captain. Captain Pierce was an avid golfer, and his house was right on the tenth fairway. He could walk over to the clubhouse, meet his foursome, and start their round of golf on the first hole. Other times they would meet on the tenth tee right near Bill's backyard and play the back nine first. The course was always in beautiful shape, and the grass on the tenth fairway was much greener than the lawn in his backyard. He'd asked the greens crew how they kept the fairways and greens so healthy, but all they said was, "Water, water, and more water." However, he kept track of what they did, and it included much more TLC than just watering.

From time to time, when he was sitting in his backyard, he would collect some mistakenly hit golf balls. Other times he would gather them when he was cutting his lawn. Either way, there were always several golf balls in his backyard because most golfers tend to hit the ball off to the right into someone's backyard. Many golfers leave them there because they don't want to enter anyone's yard without permission. In fact, members were forbidden to cross past the out-of-bounds markers onto anyone's property to retrieve or hit a golf ball. The rules of golf state that if a golfer should hit their ball out of bounds, they are to return to the position of their last shot and try it again with a penalty of one stroke added to their score. So, they would have to go back to the tenth tee and start again with a two already on their scorecard. Some homeowners who lived right on the course joked that they should put signs on the edge of their property reading, "YOU'RE OUT OF BOUNDS," "GO BACK TO THE TEE – AND NOW YOU'RE HITTING THREE," or "HEY – TAKE A LESSON!"

Some of the members were decent golfers while others were terrible. Bill Pierce was an excellent golfer, having played varsity golf in high school and all four years on the golf team at Boston College. He was runner-up at the NCAA Division I All-American tournament two years in a row. He also considered playing in the Massachusetts State Amateur Championship. Unfortunately, his police academy starting date was the same week in August, so he skipped the golf tournament in favor of becoming a police officer.

Matt parked the car and went around to open the door for Ginny, which Bill Pierce and his wife observed through the front door. Ginny took Matt's arm and strolled up the front walk together. Ginny gave Matt's arm a gentle squeeze, and they smiled at Bill as he opened the door for them.

"Well, Ginny, that Matt Davis is quite the gentleman, right?" Ginny smiled, hugged Bill, then gave Bev a big hug and a kiss on the cheek and said how happy she was to be there.

Matt leaned toward Bill and asked, "Are Smokey and Terri coming over tonight?"

"Sorry, Matt, they're away on a cruise for the week, but don't worry, they'll be back. When they are, we'll have you and Ginny back over."

"Oh, too bad," Matt said. "Ginny, you'll like them a lot. Smokey is a real hoot, with lots of great stories. And his wife, Terri, is so sweet. She's patient while Smokey tells his stories – he's met all kinds of people."

Dinner and drinks were served on the back deck, offering a great view of Bill's backyard and the tenth fairway with the tee down to the left and the green slightly uphill to the right. And wouldn't you know it? Midway through dinner, a young golfer sliced his tee shot into Bill's backyard about twenty feet from the deck! Bill jumped up, ran out to where the ball landed, picked it up, and threw it back into the middle of the fairway.

"That was a great tee shot," Bill said as he got back to the table, "That guy will never know he hit his ball out of bounds. Everybody chuckled and waved at the golfer when he approached his ball in the fairway.

"I have enough found balls like that one, so I throw some of them back once in a while. He'll be talking about what a great tee shot he had for the next week or so." Bill smiled.

"You know, I have a funny golf story to tell you." Bill loved to tell stories, and he had an endless supply. "When I was in college, we played at many courses around New England. Once, while playing a course in Connecticut, we stopped after nine holes to have a quick lunch. We sat on the back deck of the clubhouse, which looked out onto a tough little par three with a tee shot down a steep hill and over a big pond. It was about two hundred yards from the tee to the green, and the water went right up to the edge of the green. Visually it was daunting."

"So, we're watching this foursome teeing off, and the first three golfers hit the green or were just off the green onto the apron. The last guy hits his tee shot into the pond. Now, you're supposed to go down to the edge of the water to a designated drop area and drop your ball, hitting three. But he decides to hit from the tee again and hits his tee shot into the pond again. Two more times he hits his tee shot into the water! We can hear the other guys in his group start laughing. They must have talked him into going down to the drop area, and so now he's hitting seven even though it's only a par three. He hits this one into the water as well. Now he's lying nine and hitting his tenth shot, which he tops, and it rolls into the pond." Matt and Ginny were leaning in at this point of the story. Bill's wife just smiled – she had heard this story a few times before.

"At this point, everyone on the deck is chuckling while his group is laughing their asses off. So now the guy takes his golf bag and throws it into the pond – splash! Then, he turns away from the drop area, marches back toward the clubhouse, passing under the deck where our seats are, and presumably heads for the parking lot.

"A few minutes later, we're still talking about this poor bastard, here he comes marching back toward the pond, pants rolled up to his knees, and he goes into the pond to retrieve his golf bag and clubs. We all think, "Ah-ha, it's not his last round of golf." But then we see him unzip a pocket on the golf bag, grab his car keys, throw the golf bag back into the pond, and head toward the parking lot. We stopped laughing when he walked under our table. True story," Bill said. Matt and Ginny laughed as Bill poured everyone another drink. Bev got up to clear the table, and Ginny jumped up to help her.

"Wow, golf sounds like a lot of fun – huh?" Matt said to his boss.

Bev served some Drambuie with the dessert – a key lime pie. It was a very relaxing and enjoyable evening on Pierce's deck. After a few hours, Matt said something about needing to head along.

Ginny thanked Bev for a delicious dinner, saying, "It was nice to see you again, Bev, and thank you again for such a wonderful evening. I hope to see you soon."

Matt gave Bill a hug and a handshake and thanked him for inviting them to dinner. "This was a blast, Bill. Oh, thanks, Bev, this was awesome, as usual. See you both again soon."

Then he and Ginny headed out the front door and turned to wave goodnight. Matt offered Ginny his arm, and they walked together to the driveway, where Matt got the door for Ginny. He then walked over to the driver's side, opened the driver's door and slid into the Corvette.

"Hey Ginny, want to stop for a drink before we get you back home?"

"Sure, Matt. We can go over to the Mattakeese Wharf Restaurant and Bar in Barnstable. It's right on the water and on the way back to Sandwich. Not too far from my place."

"Good thinking, Ginny that's a great spot."

Matt pulled into the parking lot at Mattakeese Wharf. He remembered being there last year on a date. They went for dinner, and there was only valet parking. Matt didn't want the valet to drive his car, so he did something he'd never done before: he showed his shield to the valet and told him he was on a case and needed his car left next to the front door. When they got inside, his date thought he was so funny!

Matt planned on doing the same thing tonight, but before he could pull his shield out, the valet smiled and said, "I remember you. Are you on a case again tonight?"

Matt said he was and left the Corvette right at the front door. Ginny looked at Matt and shook her head with a smile as she walked up the front steps and held the door open for Matt.

"I bet there's a story there," Ginny said.

Matt just grinned back at her and led her into the bar section of the restaurant, where they found a quiet table near the windows. The restaurant had a fantastic nautical theme, from the blue carpets to the captain's chairs at each table. Even better, their table sat next to the windows looking out onto Barnstable Harbor and beyond. Matt ordered a Sam Adams Summer Ale, and Ginny ordered a 'Kim Crawford Sauvignon Blanc'. The sun had just started to set. Through the windows, you could see the sun beginning to dip down just behind the storage buildings over at Barnstable Marine Service. It was so beautiful to watch the sunset from their table, and as an extra, they could see the giant whale-watching boat returning to its dock right next to them.

"Evening whale watches at sunset are beautiful. I'd love to do that sometime – would you?" Matt said to Ginny.

"Sure," Ginny answered. "I haven't been out on one of those in a few years. They're great fun."

She smiled at Matt and he immediately smiled back at her. They were relaxed and talked about everything under the sun as they finished their drinks and got ready to leave.

As Matt pulled into Ginny's driveway, he said, "Ginny, this has been a great evening. I hope you had as much fun as I did."

"It was a wonderful evening. I'd love to do it again sometime."

Ginny smiled, leaned over, and kissed Matt on the cheek. Then, she got out of the car, smiled at Matt, thanked him again, and headed into her house. Matt stayed in the driveway to make sure she got inside safely, then backed out, honked his horn, and headed back toward 6A.

Chapter Thirty-Seven

Charlie and Barb sat on the back terrace, having coffee and tea, enjoying the day. As Barb got up and deadheaded some of the flowers along the edge of the patio, Charlie looked out at the ocean view to watch the Woods Hole ferry pass by. It almost seemed surreal to him that his best friend had passed away.

Finally, Charlie got up, put his hand on Barb's shoulder, and asked, "Have you talked with Jenn today? How is she doing?"

"I just called her this morning. She seems to be doing fine, but she's worried about the girls. I don't know if it's set in yet that Doug is gone. I think the funeral will be hard, but it will also give her some closure." Barb sighed, "It doesn't seem real to me either." Barbara worried about her best friend. Losing Doug was so hard on Jenn; they had been married for over 30 years and were so happy together.

"I know, I feel the same way," Charlie said. "I've got to give Billy Flynn a call. I'll be right back."

Charlie headed into his office and closed the door behind him. Charlie's office was on the back left side of the house and had a fantastic view of the swimming pool and across the back lawn that ran out toward Nantucket Sound and the ocean. While Charlie called Billy Flynn, Barb gathered up the flowers and went into the kitchen to make herself another cup of tea. She sat in front of the windows that looked out toward the lush, green lawn bordered by the blue hydrangeas and beyond to the bright blue Atlantic Ocean called Nantucket Sound. The kitchen was in the back center of the house and had access to a large patio that ran across the back of the house. Many mornings, Charlie and Barb would take their coffee or tea outside to enjoy the sound of the waves and feel good about the beautiful view.

"Charlie was right to buy this house," Barb thought. They had some arguments at the time. Barb liked the two-family house they owned in Dennis and saw no reason to sell it. But Charlie was insistent so she finally gave in. Then she reminisced about the wonderful times they had together with Doug and Jenn for dinner and drinks. They always enjoyed sitting on the back patio looking at the Atlantic Ocean. What a beautiful place to live, and what a great place to share with friends and family. Barb thought to herself she was going to miss Doug and Jenn over in this setting. What a horrible thing to lose, a friend, a husband.

Meanwhile, Charlie gave Billy a call and said he wanted to see him as soon as possible. Billy suggested they could meet up in Hingham or Cohasset.

"Thanks, Billy. Let's make it Cohasset, the same place as last time. Later today would be great."

Later that morning, Charlie hit the road to meet Billy. It was a quick ride over the Sagamore Bridge and up Route 3, about an hour to Lenny's Grille. When Charlie got there, Billy was already sitting at a table near the back of the dining room.

"Hi Charlie, what's up? Are you okay? You look like shit."

Charlie thumbed through the menu, trying to avoid Billy's next question.

"I'm good Billy, but I need to get past all this shit and get to the fundamentals. Remember, we need to be smart about the fundamentals." Charlie was referring to the money they had put into the banks down in the Grand Caymans. He was also referring to the plan to move the money out of those banks and put it into the private bank at the Swiss Post Offices. Moving money from place to place was dangerous, but at the same time, it was an important fundamental that would ensure no one would be a suspect and no one would get caught with the money. Charlie insisted that everyone on the team, including Billy Flynn, remember that the fundamentals always came first.

"I know, Charlie. I've been back and forth with the guys on the island and our computer guy. They all say that there is no way anyone could see into any of our ghost transactions. They're certain. But, just so we're all on the same page, I brought in a second computer guy who worked with us a few years ago. He's really good, and he's very cool about being quiet about everything. I'll let you know what he thinks after he takes a look at the accounts. But I'm telling you, there is no way anyone can see the transactions, no way! And remember, they tell me that we can see anyone who gets close to those accounts, long before anyone could ever see us. We're safe, Charlie; we're impregnable."

A voice echoed in Charlie's head; it was Doug saying "Don't let anybody else know anything about what we're doing, just in case they can't be quiet. And don't forget if you can see something, someone else may be able to see it as well." At the time, Charlie thought Doug was overreacting, but now he wasn't so sure. Charlie hardly ever got nervous, but with all the things going on at the same time – Doug's passing, and the cops in Barnstable asking lots of questions, Charlie was getting a little bit nervous, maybe even a little bit twitchy too.

"Listen, Billy, that all sounds great, but I am concerned that someone else might have gained access to our accounts. They could have looked at the account folders and may even be trying to crack into them. We just can't let that happen. There's too much at stake here."

"I know, Charlie. I'll take care of it. Believe me, I understand how important it is that no one ever finds out."

They ordered lunch, and Billy gave Charlie back the updated spreadsheets outlining which funds were ready to be moved and which were on a 90-day hold. These were the spreadsheets he sent to Billy after he found the folders on Doug's boat. Charlie was very interested in the funds that were ready to be moved because those would become liquid immediately. Then he could take them over to

Europe, where everything was safer and much more invisible.

"Thanks, Billy. I've always trusted your judgment. I am confident that you have the right people on the team. Happy about that. I just sometimes overthink things, and then I get worried. It's just an old habit, remember?"

When Billy walked Charlie to his car, he reassured Charlie that he didn't have to worry and that he'd call him tomorrow with an update.

"Thanks, Billy, you know I really do appreciate your help with all this, and I won't forget it." Charlie got into his new Porsche Panamera and headed back to Route 3. Then he called Barb to let her know he was on his way home.

He thought about what Billy had said and grimaced. "If Billy only knew what was going on, he wouldn't be so confident," Charlie said out loud. He smiled and thanked Doug for his help by winking and saying, "Hey, Dougie, you're the best, and I'll always love you." Then Charlie laughed and shook his head. He missed Doug a lot and wished he was here right now.

Later that day, Charlie got a call from Billy Flynn, who reported that the new computer guy was on the job. The computer guy said there was nothing out of the ordinary with the accounts at this stage in the process of blending them into a single large account and moving it over to Europe. Charlie was pleased and told Billy he was earning his stripes this week.

"Thanks, Billy. I appreciate your help," said Charlie. Then he hung up the phone and went back into the kitchen to see if Barb had checked in with Jenn.

Chapter Thirty-Eight

Michael called Alison from his car, which was interesting because Michael never used his phone in the car unless it was an emergency. Michael had a bit of a problem once while trying to use his cell phone and ended up crashing into the side of another car while driving into Cambridge on his way to MIT. The phone slipped out of his hand and fell on the floor. Michael fished around and finally got his hand on the phone just as he ran into the car in the lane to his right. Both cars spun, and the driver in the other vehicle was seriously hurt (a broken leg and some facial lacerations). Michael was shaken by the whole thing and vowed never to use a handheld phone while driving again. But this was a bit of an emergency, or so he thought.

"Alison, I found something last night. It may be the link you're looking for. I located some recent transactions from the Bank of America here in Boston. I know they acquired FleetBoston a few years ago. Anyway, some of the transactions follow a dull, less clear pattern that includes several failed handshakes, where in some cases, the data failed to cross back over to the Fed, and it looks like some money from those transactions may have gone out of sync. That's right – lost. I can't see where the money went, but I can certainly get to it once I locate the packet codes and reverse the transactions. This is exactly what Jim Clark had warned me about. Don't do anything until I get there."

Michael ran from the Fed parking lot down the two flights of stairs rather than waiting for the lobby elevators.

"Come with me, Alison – let me show you what I'm talking about," he said as he pushed Alison's office door open. He took her hand, directed her to the basement elevators, and hit the up arrow five or six times until the doors opened. He turned to Alison with a grimace and said, "These elevators are so slow – hurry the fuck up!"

Alison started to say something, but Michael put his hand up.

"Sorry, Alison, sorry about that."

Michael rarely used harsh language, only if he was excited, surprised, or upset. They stopped at the fourth floor, and Michael grabbed Alison's hand again and pulled her down the hallway toward the IT department. They went into the door that led to Michael's office, turned the corner, and rushed inside. He sat at his desk, and in less than fifteen seconds, all four computer displays popped on.

Michael's typing speed was close to 100 words per minute with zero errors, and as his friend Joe used to say, the difference between an average programmer and a great programmer was just typing speed. Michael had the four screens all focused on a series of folders that the system filled with transactions from the day before the transaction, the day of the transaction, and the day after the transaction. This allowed the Fed to see any disparities with the handshakes and point to the source of the problem. Each of the failed handshakes pointed to ghost accounts Michael could not open until he sent a phishing expedition – a group of synthetic emails targeted to disrupt the stability and security of an account, typically someone's email. But in this case, the objective of the phishing expedition was to see if the ghost account would reply to Michael's computer. If it did, Michael could trace the email acknowledgment and, maybe, see where the ghost account lived.

He turned to Alison and said, "One of the ghost accounts replied late last night, and I have it located someplace down on the Cayman Islands! And you know what happens on the Caymans, right?"

"Do you think you can give me the island location or an address?" asked Alison.

Michael clicked on his laptop computer, and the screen displayed Seline Bank & Trust LTD, Shedden Road, Georgetown, Grand Cayman Island. Michael turned toward Alison and smiled.

"That's where the money is, Alison, right there."

"Are you sure it's there?" Alison asked.

"Sure, as shit, unless they moved it after it landed there," Michael shot back. "This is where those early failed handshakes are pointing, and I bet we can find some more if you give me a minute." He tapped on the keyboard and said, "Bingo, more replies back from the Grand Cayman Islands. There must be several separate accounts down there that they've been using to hide the stolen money.

"Alison, this is criminal! Someone is stealing money from the Federal Reserve System and depositing it in bank accounts on the Grand Cayman Islands. Just look at all the ghost accounts replying to my phish, and they're all coming from the same bank on the Grand Caymans: the Seline Bank & Trust LTD. This is not a coincidence!"

"Michael, can you give me the other side of these transactions? Who sent the money down there, and which banks? Who's doing this, and how much are they taking?" Alison was very calm on the outside, but very excited by this new information. She had gotten up from her chair and was pacing around Michael's office.

"You know, if we can map your email replies to our list of failed handshakes, we'd have a pretty good look at where the ghost accounts were set up and maybe, just maybe, a look at who set them up," she said.

"Alison, look over here." Michael pointed to one of his screens. "These are the accounts, and this is the amount of money in each account. It looks to me like there is over $800 million if you add all the accounts together, maybe $850 million." He let out a slow, soft whistle. "Alison, someone has stolen almost $850 million from the Fed and our client banks here in District One. And it looks like these all took place in 2006, 2007, and 2008. This is unbelievable – right?"

"Michael, don't say a fucking word about this until I have a chance to call my team back at Treasury. They'll need to get feet on the ground at that bank in the Grand Caymans, and they'll need to speak with any of the banks involved up here. And don't forget, my job is only to find this shit and inform my team, I'm not supposed to take action, so be careful!" She ran her hand through her hair and repeated, "No action! So please keep this all under wraps for now."

"Now, who's using bad language?" Michael smiled at her to calm her down. "No worries, Alison, I'm just happy that we found some of the connections, and with some luck, we can find out who's got all the money. I just hope it's still sitting in that bank in the Grand Caymans and hasn't gone elsewhere. Let's get some dinner; I'm starving."

Alison agreed that all of this excitement made them both hungry, but she insisted it was her treat.

"Fine, Alison! In that case, I could use a beer too."

They walked to the nearby steakhouse and asked for a table in the corner. Dinner was wonderful, and the conversation ran around the ghost accounts that Michael had cracked into with his phishing expeditions and how grateful Alison was for his assistance. After dinner, Alison asked Michael if he'd like to come over to the hotel again for a drink. The hotel lobby was dimly lit and looked elegant, with the tiled marble floors and colorful Persian rugs. They sat on the leather couch and ordered a couple of Sambucas. Michael felt good that he could help Alison, and he enjoyed that she appreciated him. Then Alison surprised him and asked Michael if he'd like to come up to her room. He smiled, leaned forward, and gave Alison a full kiss on the lips. At that moment, the second part of their relationship began to blossom.

Chapter Thirty-Nine

Ginny called Matt to tell him about her newest findings the minute she understood what she had discovered. But Matt kept talking over her, trying to get her to tell him the information faster than she could speak.

Finally, Ginny just blurted out, "Shut up, Matt, and let me tell you what I found out this morning!"

Silence at the other end of the phone signaled that Matt had gotten the point.

"I did a deeper passport dive and review and found that Doug Wood and Charlie Henderson have been to the Grand Caymans more than we thought! More than six times in the last year and over ten times in the last few years. They were also down there a few times more recently with their wives and additional trips with William Flynn. And Mr. Wood was down there twice in the last two months." Ginny added, "Kind of makes you wonder how much was vacation and how much was business, and what kind of business. I wonder if Mr. Henderson and Mr. Flynn have anything to say, and what Mrs. Henderson and Mrs. Wood would say if we called them."

"Hell, that's a lot of trips to the same place in a very short period. You think there's some funny business going on in the Grand Caymans, Ginny?" Matt asked the question in his head out loud.

"I don't know, Matt, but that's a lot of visits to a place that's not just known for beaches. I wonder how much banking they were doing down there and why."

Matt was also very curious about why they would spend so much time in the Grand Caymans when he fully knew they both had houses in Bermuda and St. Martin's.

"Good question. I'll ask Mrs. Wood this afternoon when I meet with her if she knows why Doug and Charlie Henderson made so many trips to the Grand Caymans." Matt nodded even though Ginny couldn't see him. Then, he made a note on his phone to ask Charlie Henderson the same question the next time they spoke, which would be real soon.

"Yes, Matt, that's a great question, and I'd love to know what Mrs. Wood is going to say. Wish I could be a fly on the wall, but please, give me a call the minute you're out of there," Ginny said.

"Sure, Ginny. I'll call you from the road after I'm done at the Woods' house. I promise."

Ginny hung up her phone and turned back to look at her computer screens and typed her search through NCIC with a parallel search running on Treasury to see if anyone, anyplace, was looking at the Woods, the Hendersons, or this guy, William Flynn. What she found was something much more important than seeing the number of trips they had taken to the islands over the past few years. The NCIC indicated that the Treasury was making similar inquiries about Doug Wood, Charles Henderson, and William Flynn related to a bank called Seline in the Grand Caymans. She printed this information, shoved it into her purse, and headed for the exit.

When she saw Matt in the lobby, she shook her head and said, "Let me walk out to your car with you. Let's go to your car for a minute, could we?"

When they got out of the station and over to Matt's car, Ginny gave Matt the printout from her purse.

"What's this?" he asked, but then held his hand up in front of Ginny and kept reading the printout. Then Matt asked Ginny again what was going on.

She told Matt that some guys from the Treasury Department were tracking accounts that matched up to the same timeframe when Wood, Henderson, and Flynn were visiting the Caymans.

"It looks like they're pretty certain from their notes that Henderson, Wood, and Flynn were dumping money into various accounts, large amounts of money," Ginny said. Then she grabbed the printout, stuffed it into her purse, and said, "Matt, I'll keep this in a safe place for you. Come see me when you get back."

Matt was astounded that Ginny could get all that specific account information from U.S. Treasury data she had found and searched just a few minutes ago. "Wow," he thought, "this is really big."

Matt let out a big sigh, and then as if to himself, he said, "I'm getting an awful feeling about this whole thing with Douglas Wood. It's too much of a coincidence. When I get back, I think I'm gonna ask Bill Pierce to call the Feds to find out what's happening. I'm not sure what they're really up to, and I'm not sure what any of this means now."

"Matt, don't worry. This is good because now we have more information than we had last week or yesterday, for that matter."

Matt got into his car, waved goodbye to Ginny.

Twenty minutes later, Matt was pulling into the Woods' driveway. He couldn't help thinking that this whole accident with Doug Wood had more to do with money than with anything else. Matt got out of his car and walked over to Officer Thomas' car as he was getting out.

"Hi, Matt, good to see you," said Officer Thomas.

"Good to see you too, Reid," said Matt.

They both walked together down the front walk and met Mrs. Wood, who was just opening the front door. Matt stepped forward and reintroduced himself and Officer Thomas to Mrs. Wood, then they all stepped into the front hall and were led into the large, well-decorated living room. Mrs. Wood offered them a seat on a couch facing a large fireplace, and she sat in a wing chair next to the hearth. Matt thanked her for her time and said he had just a couple of final questions he'd like her to answer. To that, Jenn agreed.

As Matt began his questioning, he remembered that Jenn was a recent widow, but he had a certain amount of urgency in his questions.

"Mrs. Wood, you previously stated that you had no idea why your husband stayed home on the morning of the 28th. Do you still say that you have no idea why your husband stayed home, or have you remembered anything he may have said about that morning? Please let us know if there was anything unusual that your husband said as an excuse for his not joining you that morning up in Hingham."

Jenn said that there was nothing that Doug had said to explain why he wasn't going up to Hingham.

At that point, Matt said, "But, Mrs. Wood, it's hard to believe that you would not have gotten an answer from him other than he just couldn't."

"Well, Detective Davis, I didn't push him for an answer, and he didn't offer one. Sorry that I'm not more helpful."

Matt asked her if she knew anybody who might be planning to visit her husband that morning or anyone who had talked about visiting.

"No, I was not aware of anyone planning to see my husband that morning. Very few people visit my husband alone without being a dinner guest or without a spouse with them," Jenn said.

At that point, Matt had only one question left, but he wanted to be very delicate about asking it.

"So, Mrs. Wood, you're positive you weren't home that morning and maybe left for Hingham earlier in the afternoon?"

"Detective Davis, are you asking me if I was the one who pushed my husband down and then ran up to Hingham? Well, Detective, I resent that question and am done with your inquiry. Please, just leave my house – right now! I mean it. PLEASE LEAVE!"

Detective Davis put up his hands and said, "I'm sorry, Mrs. Wood, but I have to ask these questions. I have to know if you or somebody you know was here that morning. Maybe you saw someone on your way out? Maybe your husband mentioned something in passing that you've forgotten. And maybe you and Mr. Wood had some kind of argument that morning? I just need to know what happened and why."

'Well, now it certainly seems like you think something was wrong and that something else, something sinister, happened to my husband. But I didn't do anything. I wasn't here that morning."

Matt put up his hands again and shook his head.

"Mrs. Wood, I just found out that your husband, Mr. Henderson, and a guy named Billy Flynn have gone down to the Grand Caymans at least twelve times over the last couple of years. Do you know anything about that? And if so, please tell me what your husband was doing down there twice in the last two months."

"The next time you want to ask me any questions, I'll have my attorney with me. Now, please leave." Jenn shook her head and started to sob uncontrollably.

Matt and Officer Thomas left Mrs. Wood in the living room, found their way out to the front door, then left and met at their cars.

"Wow, Matt, she's pretty pissed at you!" said Officer Thomas.

"Oh yeah, she's not happy at all, is she?" said Matt. At that point, Matt shook his head and said, "Let's go, shall we? We can talk about this back at the station."

Matt was already sitting in the driver's seat when he remembered to call Ginny.

"Hell, Ginny, I just had to ask about all those flights. Right?"

"Sure, you did, and hopefully now you have her answer, right?"

"I guess she's not too happy with my questions. She said from now on, she'd only speak to me or anyone from the Barnstable Police with her lawyer present. Okay, I got her point."

Before he hung up, he asked Ginny if she'd like to join him for dinner. Maybe go back to the Mattakeese Wharf. When Ginny agreed, Matt said, "Great, I need to talk about this whole thing with someone who understands. I'll meet you downstairs, and we can take both cars over." So, they planned to meet in the station parking lot around 5:00 that afternoon.

When they met in the parking lot, Matt suggested that Ginny should drive in the lead position while he followed in his Corvette. She looked in her rear-view mirror a couple of times to make sure he was still following her, and each time she looked back, he waved. She sped along Phinney's Lane to the lights at Route 6A. As soon as the light turned green, she continued down Millway. She was in the restaurant parking lot and out of her car by the time Matt arrived.

"Wow, Ginny, you're in a bit of a hurry. What's up?"

She simply smiled and said, "I've always wanted to stay out in front of a Corvette. Kinda fun!" Matt laughed and nodded.

After they both ordered a glass of wine and some appetizers, Matt and Ginny continued to talk about the information Ginny had found that afternoon.

"Matt, it's hard to believe that Mrs. Wood didn't know why her husband stayed at home that day, and it's even harder to believe she wasn't a little bit surprised at the number of trips he took to the Grand Caymans. You know, Matt, you're right. There's something out of balance here."

Ginny looked around at the stunning views of Barnstable Harbor and the setting sun. The tables near the windows were always the most popular seats even more popular than the tables along the windows in the bar. Ginny nodded and looked out the windows towards Barnstable Marine Service then said, "You know, the guy that started that marina had a dude ranch here in town – horses, a stagecoach and lots of ten-gallon hats." Matt just smiled.

The following morning Matt called Bill Pierce to tell him about the latest information that Ginny found out from the NCIC database – that the United States Treasury and the Federal Reserve Bank in Boston have been watching Doug Wood's activities down in the Grand Caymans.

"Matt," said Bill, "tell Ginny that I want to see both of you in the conference room. Have Ginny set up a call for us with this guy Bill Flynn and while she's doing that, I'll get a warrant from the judge just in case Mr. Flynn doesn't want to talk with us. And if he doesn't want to chat with us today, I'll have the warrant, include a line asking him to join us down here in person. I'm always a fan of face-to-face meetings; they have a greater impact, don't you think?"

"Okay, Bill. Aren't you also interested in talking with the Treasury? They seem to be snooping around the same things we are. Maybe we should call them first?"

Bill said no, he'd call them later.

Around 1:00, the three met in the conference room.

"Let's find out more about all of this traveling down to the Grand Caymans and what the hell this guy William Flynn knows about it. I'm concerned that Mr. Wood was into something more than meets the eye. And I'm concerned that his death may not have been an accident," Bill said. He had a determined look on his face.

"Well, that's the first time I've heard Bill come right out and say that this may not have been an accident. That's good news for sure." Matt thought to himself.

The call to Billy Flynn went as well as could be expected, except that Billy Flynn stated he was unaware of the trips to the Grand Caymans that Doug Wood took, and that he had only gone down there for relaxation when he flew there. Bill Pierce asked him several more times about the twenty or so trips down there over the last few years, but Mr. Flynn stuck firmly to his story – just going down there for some relaxation.

Bill Pierce looked at Matt and Ginny as he told Billy Flynn that he would like him to make himself available to the Barnstable Police if needed. Billy Flynn agreed, and the call ended.

Chapter Forty

After the meeting with Charlie and the call from the Barnstable Police, Billy realized the urgency of moving forward with the plan to resolve all the financial issues. Nobody could get into any of Doug's accounts in the Grand Caymans, so Billy called Felix and told him to grab his computer and meet him in Cohasset at 4:00 pm. When Felix entered the restaurant, Billy was already sitting at a table in the back. Billy had Felix's favorite, a glass of Lafite Bordeaux, waiting when he arrived.

"Hope that's what you wanted, Felix – it's unbelievably expensive – what is it?"

"Oh, it's a wine the Rothschild family has been making in France since the last century, and some of them are really old and very good. They can run upwards of $10,000 per bottle for some years. This one is exceptional, thank you."

"Anything to make you happy, Felix. Now, what's going on with Doug's accounts? I can't even log in anymore."

"Billy, logging in is the least of our worries now. I just found out that the accounts have been red-flagged by someone in Treasury. They put network pylons around all the accounts, and if we try to do anything with them, they'll see us. We have to figure out a way under or around the pylons. It's the only way we can open the accounts and the only way to move the funds."

Billy leaned closer to Felix. He was no longer in a good mood.

"What the hell are you talking about with pylons and shit? Just fix it, or you'll be looking for a new job. We have to get all the funds out of the Caymans by the end of the week, no excuses."

Felix started to say something, but Billy put up his hand.

"By the end of the week, Felix, I'm not kidding around!" Billy was no longer interested in discussing wine. The amicable demeanor he had when they first sat down had disappeared. He glared at Felix.

"Listen, Billy, I'll find out what's going on and fix it." Felix tried to sound reassuring. "I promise," he added.

But Billy just stood up abruptly, knocking his chair against the back wall. Then, as he walked away, he turned and pointed his index finger at Felix.

"By the end of the week! And I mean it!" Then he was gone, leaving Felix alone at the table with his costly glass of wine.

Felix spent the next 12 hours searching for ways to bypass the pylons. Finally, he discovered that a phishing expedition (similar to the one Michael used) would prompt the pylons to self-identify, in which case Felix could evade their reach and gain access to each of Doug's accounts without detection. By 9:00 a.m. the next day, he was finished and called Billy.

"It's done, Billy. You can log into any of Doug's accounts freely, and nobody will see you. We dug a hole under the pylons and traveled directly to the accounts. Whoever put down those pylons around Doug's accounts will not be able to detect your activity. We sent each pylon an email. Each one responded and included their location on the network grid. We obtained the network address of each pylon and then redirected our account login access to be targeted under or around the pylon's address. Simple, eh?"

Felix was proud of his work and thought Billy might appreciate the effort, but Billy had no time for accolades. He just wanted it to succeed.

"Felix, I'm logging into account 24 right now, so no one better see me, or we'll be having a different kind of conversation. Understood?"

"No worries, Billy, everything's all right now. Just let me know when the accounts are all emptied, and I'll pull my software off the network." Unfortunately, Billy had already hung up, so Felix called him back to emphasize the importance of removing the software once the money was moved.

Then Felix finished setting the pylon addresses in his software for future reference and opened each of Doug's accounts to check the balances. This was the first time Felix had opened any of them, and he was surprised to see that each of the fifty accounts had an almost $16 million current balance. That was nearly $800 million in total. He whistled under his breath.

"Wow, this guy Doug has a lot of money here. No wonder they're worried about moving it as quickly as possible. I'd better get the tracking software started right now."

While Felix was finishing his work with Doug's accounts, Billy logged onto three additional accounts to ensure they were available. When he confirmed that they were, he made a call to Charlie Henderson to let him know that everything was now okay.

At the same time that Felix and Billy were accessing Doug's accounts at Seline Bank, an alert went off on Michael's computer, letting him know that someone was fooling around with his pylons. Michael stared at his screen, pinpointed the signal, and wondered, "What the hell is going on here?"

Chapter Forty-One

Dr. Spencer took another look at Doug's autopsy report, which included the MRIs and notes from Dr. Fernald and Dr. Miller, and decided to call Dr. Miller, the Pathologist at the hospital.

"Hi Brad, it's Rick Spencer. I have a couple of quick questions. Do you have a few minutes right now?" Dr. Spencer took the employee elevator from the 6th floor down to Dr. Miller's office and the autopsy suites. He hated coming down to this part of the hospital since it focused on patients dying. It represented all the failures of the rest of the hospital, which was focused on saving lives. As a neurosurgeon, this area conflicted with his duty to heal.

"Hi Brad, thanks for seeing me so quickly." Rick went over to Brad and shook his hand.

"Always good to see you, Rick. How's Bonnie and the kids?" asked Brad.

"They're great, thanks, and yours?"

"Everyone's fine, thanks, and we got some good news. My youngest just got into Yale, and I think he's planning to go pre-med."

"Wow, that's awesome. You know, I applied to Yale's undergraduate school, where my dad went, but they accepted someone else, and I had to attend Dartmouth instead. My Dad was furious, but I still got into Harvard Medical School, which is where my dad got his MD, so everything worked out fine. Plus, he was only a GP, and I'm a neurosurgeon, so I guess I had the last laugh." Rick smiled to himself, then returned to business.

"Can we talk about Doug Wood for a minute?"

"Sure, what's up?" Dr. Miller asked.

"I'm still a little confused by the autopsy report where you indicate that it was clear that Mr. Wood fell on his own and that he was not pushed backward or fell because he tripped on something or bounced off something. I know we talked about it, but are you positive he wasn't tripped or shoved, causing him to rebound and fall backward?"

Brad walked over to his desk and opened his computer. He scanned his files for a moment.

"Well, Rick, we reviewed his blood chemistry. Nothing medically could have caused the accident or caused him to faint or fall backward. The damage was consistent with a fall from an upright position to a prone position, and there was no bruising around the shoulders consistent with being pushed hard enough to invoke the fall. There was some question about alcohol or substances, but the blood chemistry, as I said earlier, was clear."

"Brad, tell me about the shoulders. Were you looking at them under those newer high-intensity, broad-spectrum lights that provide more accurate colors? That would be critical during a delayed autopsy like this. Did you see any shadows in and around the shoulder blades? Any temporary impressions you might not have seen with a scan?"

"We did have a bright light source, it might have been fluorescent, but I don't recall seeing any shadows around the front of the shoulders. I don't think we saw anything on the backside of the shoulders. No burst capillaries either. But listen, let's not talk about it. Let's go next door and take another look."

He led Rick down the hall to the autopsy suites. First, they stopped to put on gloves and masks, then they went across the hall. There were five autopsy stations with tables and overhead lights. Brad went to the table he and Dr. Fernald used for Doug's autopsy and got up on a ladder to verify the type of fluorescent tubes overhead.

"Hey, I was wrong…these are not the newer high-intensity, broad-spectrum lights. They're just regular fluorescents, the older ones."

"Well, Brad, let's use a table with the newest lighting and see what we can see – okay?"

Dr. Miller moved the stepladder to the next table and examined the labels on the lights to confirm that they were, in fact, the newest and brightest lights.

"Hey Rick, these are all good to go!" said Dr. Miller as he descended the ladder.

Dr. Spencer smiled and shrugged. He knew he was right and was anxious to see any additional clues regarding Doug Wood's injuries.

"I'm glad Mr. Wood's body is still here. The funeral home is scheduled to pick him up today," said Dr. Miller as he headed over to the refrigerator wall to retrieve the body.

He tilted the newer style of fluorescent tubes to the top of the autopsy table and focused them on Doug's shoulders. And when he brought the lights squarely onto the shoulder, both he and Dr. Spencer could see shadows on the front and back of both shoulders. There was also a tracing of shadows under the skin on the left pectoral area.

"No wonder we missed these; we didn't have enough light on him to see them. Damn! And if we had waited another day to look at him, he would have been cremated." Brad Miller shook his head and sighed, "Now that I've looked at his chest, I can see shadows from some mild blunt force trauma, just like the shoulders."

"I'm going to have to restate the cause, but if I had to guess right now, it might be that someone held Mr. Wood by the shoulders, shook him, and then pushed him backward. And those shadows on his left chest, well, maybe someone was poking him with their finger before they grabbed him by the shoulders. I might even say it's like when you're arguing with someone, and you poke them in the chest for emphasis. Maybe it was just that simple. Poke, grab, and push? Still likely an accident but with serious consequences."

Dr. Spencer looked over at his colleague. It was clear that Dr. Miller felt terrible about the possible error with the lighting.

"No worries, Brad, I'll reach out to that detective in Barnstable and let him know you took a second look at Doug Wood's body and maybe could conclude that he was pushed. You can tell him that you found some shadowing on and around his shoulders and chest. Just update your report, and I'll sign it with you. Let Dr. Fernald know what we found, and that should be that."

Dr. Miller took several pictures with a Leica camera from the credenza drawer in the autopsy suite and sent them to the hospital's online storage, as well as to his cloud storage, where a copy of the autopsy report was stored. He would update the statement this afternoon and send a copy to Dr. Spencer and Dr. Fernald at the Massachusetts Medical Examiner's Office in Falmouth.

"Hey Rick, thanks very much for your diligence here. This could have a material effect as to whether this was an accident or something else," said Dr. Miller.

"Thank you, Brad. Let's see what the Police Department has to say about this new information. Keep me in the loop!"

"Will do, Rick," said Dr. Miller. Dr. Spencer threw his mask into the disposal receptacle and headed out the autopsy suite doors. Once he had left, Dr. Miller looked at Doug's body. "I'm sorry," he said to Doug. "I don't usually make mistakes. I hope they find out who did this to you."

Chapter Forty-Two

The tension was high when Alison called Michael and asked him to join her in the conference room on the first floor. She said that her boss was here from D.C., and he wanted an explanation of the erroneous handshakes and why the Fed's servers were failing their security checks. Unfortunately, her boss was a stickler for details, and Alison didn't have answers for him. Michael said he'd be right down, but he wanted to grab his laptop and get Jim Clark on the line in case of any specific questions about security.

When Michael arrived at the conference room, Alison was sitting next to a guy who looked familiar. Michael thought they had met a couple of years ago when he was in D.C. at a security conference sponsored by the Treasury.

"Michael, this is Winston Glover, the Director of Security and Systems Support at Treasury." Alison's voice cracked a little bit during introductions. Michael went over and shook Winston's hand.

Winston Glover was in his mid-fifties, over six feet tall, a bit plump with a welcoming smile.

"Hi Michael, I think we met last year at Treasury's Security Conference, you were one of the guest speakers, right?" He shook Michael's hand with a firm grip.

"Oh yes. Hi Winston, good to see you again." Michael sat across the table from Winston and Alison, putting his laptop down. Winston smiled and started the discussion.

"I want to thank you for helping Alison, and to let you know we appreciate your efforts. The Treasury Department is working on a clear and secure operation here at Fed Boston to determine why the Fed's handshakes have been compromised and why this issue has persisted for so long. This operation that Alison is running has a high-security status. I know you carry crypto clearance, but I wanted to remind you that all your dealings with Treasury are strictly classified." Winston glanced at Alison as he spoke. Then he continued, "If we can't find out what's going on here in Boston, or if these hackers start to focus on additional Fed districts, we are looking at a financial virus that could have an enormous impact on the economy here and around the world."

"Winston, I understand, and I'm happy to say that we've got a good starting point, a point of reference from some failed handshakes we found when Alison uncovered the random ghost accounts. We identified the failed transactions as exchanges between the Fed and FleetBoston before the acquisition by Bank of America."

Michael continued, "They were able to interrupt the network packets for only a microsecond, but long enough to divert the funds away to an unidentifiable location. We were also able to locate the last deposit, which had been diverted into a Grand Cayman bank, by using a phishing expedition to get the accounts to respond. Red flags have been popping up all around the network pylons we installed for all the accounts MX15 through MX65 at Selene Bank."

Alison stared at Michael with her mouth wide open. "Are you kidding me?" Alison was in shock. "I can't believe you didn't tell me about these red flags."

"Now I think it's time to contact that bank and find out more about these accounts," said Winston.

"Here's the number at Selene Bank & Trust," Michael swung his computer screen toward Winston. "I already sent over the warrant."

Winston nodded and started dialing the number on the speakerphone in front of them. They waited a minute to connect. Then they heard a high-pitched tone, a series of clicks, and finally, a pleasant voice over the speakerphone.

"Good morning, this is Rachel at Seline Bank & Trust; how can I help you?"

"This is Winston Glover from the United States Treasury Department. Did you receive our fax that included a warrant?"

"Yes, sir, Mr. Glover. We received it this morning. How can I help you?" said the receptionist.

"Please connect me to your senior executive," Winston responded.

"Oh yes, sir, that would be James William Powell, just one minute, please."

Michael and Alison exchanged a look. Alison was still seething while they waited for a response. Winston Glover was all business.

"James Powell, Managing Director, Mr. Glover, we've received your federal warrant, so how can I help you?"

"Yes, thank you. Once again, this is Winston Glover, Director of Security and Systems Support at the US Treasury. Do you have a moment to chat with me, sir?"

"How can I help you, Mr. Glover?"

"We are interested in the registration cards for the following accounts, MX15 through MX65."

"Yes, Mr. Glover, may I ask what this is about?" James Powell seemed quite reserved, as one might expect, and unwilling to divulge information readily.

"Yes, of course." Winston was ready with a good answer. "We are testing our newest handshake software on our server platforms, and we want to follow the complete transactions from beginning to end. I'm at District One, the Federal Reserve Bank of Boston. We're watching some of the initial transactions and handshakes on the newer server platforms. We would appreciate it if you could release these account cards for the transactions that we are tracking."

"Just a moment, Mr. Glover. I can get that information for you while we're speaking." They waited in silence while James Powell clicked a few keys. "Oh, wait a moment, sir," James Powell interjected. "I'm seeing those accounts are no longer active. They have been closed since last night, Mr. Glover. I'm sorry, sir, but those accounts are closed and gone from this bank."

Alison threw her hands up and leaned toward Michael. "Where the hell did all that money go?" she whispered to Michael, who looked confused.

"Wait, do you have their telemetry?" Winston Glover asked. He was not amused. "Who closed those accounts, and where were the funds forwarded? You must keep that information, right?"

"I'm very sorry, Mr. Glover, that information is not available."

"Wait a minute, Mr. Powell, the United States Treasury is asking you where those account funds were sent when they were sent, and who asked for them to be moved. There must be a system in place to track this activity. I'm waiting, sir." Winston Glover let out a deep sigh as he rubbed his forehead.

"Again, I'm sorry, Mr. Glover, but we do not track that detail of information. The funds were cleared through the European Banking Clearing Center (EBCC), and all we did was release them from here to the new assigned account numbers. The Europeans did the rest. Please approach them for any additional information, and if we can be of further service, please feel free to contact me directly." Then Mr. Powell hung up.

"Fuck him!" said Alison. "He's just not willing to help us – just push it off to Europe, that's all. Fuck him!"

Alison was ripping mad. Michael felt slightly uncomfortable with her outburst, but Winston didn't even seem to notice. Michael thought that he must be used to it if he spent a lot of time with Alison in D.C.

"All right then, let's give them a call over at European Banking and see what they know." Winston turned to Michael and said, "Michael, can you give me their number at EBCC, please."

Michael looked it up and read it to Winston, who simultaneously dialed it.

"Good evening," another pleasant voice greeted them, "this is the European Banking Clearing Center. How can I assist?"

"Yes, thank you, this is Mr. Winston Glover calling from the United States Treasury Department. I want to speak with Sir Michael Notting, please."

"Yes, of course, just a moment, please."

Winston turned toward Michael and Alison and said, "He's a pushover. Plus, we were at the London School of Economics at the same time. Drank lots of warm beer together back then."

Sir Notting answered, and the two chatted for a moment. Winston finished with the small talk and then got to the point.

"We have some accounts that we're tracking from the Grand Caymans. Spoke with them, and they were less than helpful. I know; I should not have been surprised. So, they tagged the account numbers, sent them to you, and then clammed up in terms of who's account and where they went." Winston listened to Sir Michael for a moment and then responded, "Sure. MX15 through MX65. Please let me know if you can identify the owner and the destination you cleared them for."

"Listen, Win, we track the destination, obviously, but if they went to Switzerland, Brussels, Amsterdam, or any of the Eastern Banking centers, then they will not let you have any information at all. In that case, there's nothing we can do to help." Sir Michael then continued, "Let me get my Deputy General to see if there is any side information with the transactions, and if we have anything, which I'm very sorry, but I doubt. I'll ring you up. Give my best to the family."

Winston said his thanks and best wishes in return, and the call was over.

"Fuck this noise!" Alison glanced at Michael, then turned to Winston and said, "We need to know where the money is and who ordered it moved. Someone had control over these accounts and was aware that we were watching. I want to find them. They're taking millions of dollars away from the Fed and the Fed's member banks. And it's gonna get worse if we don't find them."

Winston agreed with Alison. This was a bigger problem than he had initially thought. "Listen, Alison, I will make another call tomorrow and see if Sir Michael has any additional telemetry for us. Now let's relax a little bit, maybe go get some dinner." He included Michael in his invitation.

They walked over to Legal Sea Foods, just around the corner on State Street, and took a table facing the Fed Building and beyond toward Boston Harbor. Winston loved going to Legal Sea Foods and had enjoyed their lobsters for as long as the restaurant had been in downtown Boston.

"Michael, I know you're running the same Gemini platform with the Solar Drift secure server software that we run. I also know it's near impossible to break into our servers, so I'm hoping we can find out how the handshakes are being breached." Winston said, "We need to know where the money goes, who's stealing it, and how they are doing it. The Treasury won't stop until we know and can stop them from doing anything else."

"Winston, let's see what we can do," Michael replied. "In the meantime, I've got a plan for circumventing Sir Michael and his team over at EBCC if you can help. I'd like to try it in the morning."

Winston agreed that this was a good idea, a good plan. They enjoyed their dinners and had the opportunity to discuss other topics.

"Let's meet up around 8:00 a.m. in the office dining room for a working breakfast. You good with that time, Alison?" Winston suggested.

"Sure, Winston."

They said their goodbyes, and Alison and Winston headed to the hotel. Michael returned to the Fed, where his car was parked in the underground lot.

Michael didn't go to the parking garage; instead, he turned toward the left bank of elevators in the Fed's lobby and headed up to his office. There was something he wanted to review and confirm before discussing anything else with Alison or Winston.

He decided he'd try to hack into the EBCC computers and see what he could see. If the Fed could be breached, why not the EBCC? He logged into his Fed Boston control server and then jumped over to the Swiss Post Office's website. Here, he forced his way into the backend server that ran the website. Once inside, he set up a ghost account and started to ping the security server that guarded the Swiss account numbers and account owners. This would give Michael a look at any computer that touched the accounts as they transitioned from one location to another, including inbound transactions from EBCC. Once there, he saw the origination at Bank of America and

Fed Boston. Then he tracked the passage over to Selene Bank & Trust in the Grand Caymans and saw the arrival of the money in Europe at EBCC. Next, he saw all fifty accounts landed in a single account in Brussels at the International Bank of Belgium. Finally, he saw when the accounts were moved to Switzerland to the private bank inside the Swiss Post Office. The bank within the post office was designed to provide customers with complete anonymity at the highest level, as is always expected in all Swiss banks. However, Michael was more than qualified to circumvent all the security measures in place at each stop along the way. Michael dumped all the account information onto his server and copied it to his iPhone for safekeeping. Then he made a couple of notes, which he also forwarded to his iPhone. Satisfied, he backed out of the Swiss systems, destroyed his ghost accounts, logged off the Fed Boston system, locked up, and went home.

Michael met Alison and Winston for breakfast at the Fed's private dining room on the top floor of the building. It had a million-dollar view of Boston Harbor and the coastline north and south of the city. Michael told Winston that if he looked down "that way," pointing south, he could see Cape Cod.

"I found the accounts," Michael said with a mouthful of pancakes. "They have landed in Switzerland at the Swiss Post Office's private banking center."

Before Michael could explain how he found out where the accounts had landed, Alison jumped at him. "Michael, were you planning to tell us this year?"

Winston cleared his throat, and Michael started to blush, but Alison didn't stop.

"You know, they have this thing called a telephone. Why don't you try it sometime? It makes it easy to communicate with people if you're not with them." She started to get up to leave, but Winston caught her wrist and shook his head no.

"Alison, please don't leave," Winston said. "Stay with us, we need to get to the bottom of this, and it sounds like Michael has some new information that will help us."

"Fine, I'll stay, but I'm pissed that Michael went off on his own without checking with me to make sure I concurred with his actions. Now the fact is, I do concur with his actions, so maybe I'm pissed because I didn't think of it myself." She began to smile and said, "So, Michael, what have you got for us?"

"Great. I'll meet you both in the conference room on the first floor and show you what I found," Michael replied.

When Alison and Winston arrived at the conference room, Michael had his laptop open, which displayed a series of transactions on the conference room screen.

"Alison, I'm sorry. Let me explain. I was walking in the parking garage when I thought if I could track the server packets instead of the account numbers, maybe, just maybe, I could follow the accounts to a final destination. Well, it worked! As I said, the accounts are now all located at the Swiss Post Office private banking center. You can see the transactions displayed here. Let's call them, shall we, Winston? Here's their number."

Winston dialed the number and was connected to the Swiss Post Office receptionist.

"Good morning. This is Winston Glover, the Director of Security and Systems Support at the United States Treasury. Did you receive our warrant this morning?"

"Oh, yes, sir, we did receive it, and I passed it on to our senior director, Haakon Graf," said the receptionist.

Winston thanked her and said, "Please connect me with Mr. Graf."

"Absolutely." There was a soft click, and then they heard a voice.

"This is Haakon Graf, Executive Director. How can I assist the United States Treasury this morning?"

"Oh, hello, this is Winston Glover, Director of Security and Systems Support. I'm with Alison Abrams of the Treasury and Michael Ross of the Federal Reserve Bank of Boston. We are tracking fifty named accounts that have been moved from the Selene Bank & Trust on the Grand Caymans to your private banking center. We watched them leave Selene, go through EBCC, through the International Bank of Brussels, and land at the Swiss Post Office. As you know, we're in the middle of an investigation involving these accounts and would like some information."

"I'd be happy to help as much as possible," Haakon replied. "Thank you for faxing me your court order this morning. This is very unusual, but I am happy to comply." Michael faxed the order directly to the Private Banking Group at the Swiss Post Office as soon as he tracked the server packets the previous night. The bank had confirmed receipt of the court order and forwarded it to the head of Private Banking. Usually, Swiss banks are very reluctant to share client account information with anyone. Still, in this case, the United States Treasury Department was seeking funds stolen from the United States, so the Swiss bank was happy to assist.

"We faxed you the fifty account numbers in question, including their parity numbers. Do you have the account information for us? Again, this is part of an ongoing investigation regarding questionable transfers from the United States to your bank," Winston said.

"All right, sir, let me get them for you." Haakon only took a few minutes to respond.

"They are all private accounts controlled by a limited partnership in the United States. The partnership is organized as an LLC in Delaware and has a post office box address in Wilmington. PO Box 2575. The partnership's name is Sutton Partners, LTD. The principal is Mr. Douglas Wood, who holds signature authority, along with Mrs. Douglas Wood, Mr. and Mrs. Charles Henderson, and Mr. William Flynn. That's all we have. I'm sorry we don't have any other information for you."

"Thank you, Haakon. You have been very accommodating." Winston nodded at Alison and Michael and then hung up the phone.

"This is exactly what we're looking for, but I just read that Douglas Wood died the other day," said Alison. "So, who are these other guys, Charles Henderson and William Flynn? We should find out about them before we take another step."

Winston nodded and looked at Michael as if to say, "Number, please." Michael found a William Flynn with an office in Boston over at 60 State Street, the old First National Bank Building, now a Bank of America Boston Office.

"What a coincidence," he said. He dialed the number, and Winston moved closer to the speakerphone. When the secretary answered the call, Winston introduced himself and asked for William Flynn.

"Hello, this is William Flynn. How can I help you?"

Winston introduced himself again and said he wanted to know about the accounts down in the Grand Caymans that moved over to Switzerland – the accounts belonging to Mr. and Mrs. Douglas Wood, which he had signature authority.

"And Mr. Flynn, who are you?" Winston added with emphasis.

Billy Flynn cleared his throat and said, "Listen, I don't know what you're talking about. I don't know anything about any accounts, and I don't have any knowledge of the Grand Caymans or Switzerland. You've got the wrong Billy Flynn!" Then Billy hung up the phone. Winston was shocked and then got mad. He just stared at Alison and Michael, shaking his head.

Chapter Forty-Three

"Listen, this has gone far enough! I want some answers from the doctors over at Cape Cod Hospital in terms of the cause of death, and I want some answers from these banking people about where the hell all this money came from," said Captain Pierce.

Matt and Ginny had told him everything they knew, all about what they had learned regarding the Caymans, the Treasury search, and questions about the cause of Doug Wood's death. The captain was still angry and frustrated that they hadn't gotten any new information from that guy, Billy Flynn, but Pierce was not the kind of guy who would let open leads sit unanswered.

"Let's call these folks from the Treasury first. You said their names were embedded in the inquiry you discovered the other day. Ginny, please dial the number for one of those Boston contacts," said Bill Pierce.

Ginny looked up the first contact, Alison Abrams, and called the contact number. When the phone rang, a call diverter answered immediately and asked you to dial a code or extension or dial 0 for assistance. Captain Pierce dialed 0, and Agnes answered the phone,

"Good afternoon, this is the Federal Reserve Bank of Boston. You've reached Alison Abrams' office. I'm her assistant. How can I assist you?" said Agnes.

"Good afternoon, this is Captain William Pierce, Chief of Detectives at the Barnstable Police Department. I'm looking to speak with Alison Abrams regarding an active investigation we have."

"Yes, of course, Captain. She's currently in a conference; can I have her call you back?"

"I need to speak to her immediately. Please get her and put her on the phone."

"All right then," said Agnes, "please hold," Agnes called over to the conference room and explained that she had the BPD on the other line and that he wanted to speak with her right now. Alison looked over at Winston.

"Let me take the lead on this," said Winston. Alison shook her head, but Winston had already pressed the conference button to grab the call.

"Good afternoon, this is Winston Glover, Director of Security and Systems Support for the United States Treasury Department. I'm with Alison Abrams, Special Investigator for the United States Treasury Department, and Michael Ross, Chief Information Officer for the Federal Reserve Bank of Boston. How can we help you, Captain?"

"This is Captain William Pierce, Chief of Detectives for the Barnstable Police Department. Thank you for taking my call. I'm sitting with Detective Matt Davis and Ginny Jensen, Senior Administrative Specialist, and we're investigating the death of Mr. Douglas Wood here in Barnstable. While researching his finances, we've come across some red flags posted by the Treasury. We've also noticed a significant amount of travel by Mr. Wood to the Cayman Islands just before his death. We are concerned that his death may not have been an accident, as it was first reported. Can you help us better understand Mr. Wood's finances and connection to the Grand Caymans?"

"Wait, what do you mean you've come across some of our account inquiries, red flags?" asked Michael.

"Well, yes, because Mr. Wood passed away, we searched data about him through NCIC and the FBI databases, and both searches have turned up Treasury red flags on some of his accounts, which limit our access to any of his account information," Ginny explained.

"Wait, I didn't know that the Barnstable Police Department was investigating Mr. Wood's death? What happened to him? Why are you involved in an investigation?" asked Winston.

"Mr. Wood died about a week ago, and as I said, we are investigating his death. Initially, we thought that he had an accident, but now we're reasonably sure it was intentional," said Captain Pierce.

Why haven't you contacted the FBI? They should be involved, don't you think?" Winston asked.

"Well, you know, we just found out that there was a financial connection between the Fed and the Treasury. It's not like you told us before we called you today!" Matt replied.

Bill Pierce took over again. "But let's get back to the accounts in the Grand Caymans. I'd like to know what you've found in the Grand Caymans. Was Mr. Wood hiding money or something? This information may be material to our investigation into his death." Bill was trying not to be too pushy, but he needed to get answers.

"Certainly, Captain, but I don't think we should be discussing this over the phone. Let's meet in person to discuss this in a proper setting, don't you think? We'd be happy to have you come up to Boston, or if you'd like, we can get in a car and come down to the Cape. Your choice, sir," Winston said.

"Well, why don't you come on down here – we can meet at our headquarters. The address is 1200 Phinney's Lane in Hyannis, right off Route 132, which is right off Route 6, a few miles after you cross the canal. Can you be here first thing tomorrow morning?"

"That's fine with me." Winston glanced over at Michael and Alison, who nodded in agreement. "We will all be there tomorrow morning."

"Thanks, Mr. Glover. I know it's short notice, but I appreciate this. We will all be here. I'll have coffee ready for you," said Bill.

Bill Pierce hung up the speakerphone and said to no one in particular, "Well, now we're getting someplace!" His face was red, and he made a clipped whistle through his front teeth.

Matt Davis turned to Bill and Ginny and said, "I think we should give Charlie Henderson a call to see if he knows anything about this big pile of money Doug Wood moved to the Grand Caymans. He should be aware of it, since they traveled there together and have some commingled investment accounts. Plus, the info from the NCIC indicates they were both involved."

Ginny found Mr. Henderson's home phone and dialed the number on the speakerphone in the middle of the conference table.

"Hello, who's calling?" Charlie said.

"This is Captain Pierce of the Barnstable Police Department – is this Charles Henderson on Sea View Avenue in Osterville?"

"Yes, this is Charles Henderson, and yes, I live on Sea View Avenue in Osterville. What's this all about, Captain?"

"We have some questions surrounding the death of Douglas Wood and your relationship with him. Would you mind coming down to the station on Phinney's Lane in Hyannis? This afternoon?"

"Well, yes. But again, what's this all about, Captain? What questions could you have?"

"Mr. Henderson, we have an active investigation surrounding the death of Douglas Wood, and we'd like to ask you some questions that may shed some light on the investigation."

"I've already spoken with Detective Davis. Do I need to bring an attorney or anything this time?" Charlie asked.

"Oh, nothing like that, Mr. Henderson. Just a few questions about your relationship with Mr. Wood, that's all. How about 2:00 p.m. today?"

"I'll be there. See you then."

Charlie told Barb he had to run out for a while and then called Billy Flynn from his car.

"Billy, I just got another call from the Barnstable Police Department; they want to see me this afternoon. I don't know what's going on."

"Nothing, Charlie – they probably just have some questions about your relationship with Doug – just tell them the same story you told that detective the other day, and for God's sake, don't worry. Give me a call when you're done."

"Are you sure that's all they want, Billy? I'm not too comfortable with the police, you know." Charlie was shaking his head from side to side as they spoke.

"Don't worry, Charlie, just answer their questions honestly and let me know how it goes."

"Well, do you think they know about the money – what do you think they have on us?"

"Nothing, Charlie, they've got nothing on us, so don't worry!"

Charlie smiled and said to Billy, "I'll have Jim O'Reilly meet me at the police station. It will make me feel more comfortable." And why shouldn't it? Jim O'Reilly was perhaps the single best attorney money could buy, and Charlie had him on retainer for any number of reasons. Jim was a Harvard Law School adjunct professor and a senior partner with Ropes and White on Cape Cod. Charlie had complete faith in Jim and his staff. He called Jim and explained the situation. They agreed to meet at the police station.

Charlie hung up, pulled his car onto Sea View Avenue, and headed toward the police station in Hyannis. He was only ten minutes away when his phone rang. It was Jim O'Reilly calling to tell Charlie that he was already parked at the police station and that he'd meet Charlie in the lobby on the first floor. Feeling slightly more confident, he called Billy Flynn back and told him that Jim was already at the police station waiting for him. He had another question for Billy.

"Did they call you, Billy? Are you going to have to meet with them too?" Charlie was nervous about this whole police thing, and he wanted Billy to know it. "Listen, Billy, if they ask anything out of line, call Jim and ask him to sit with you. Seriously, call my attorney. And then call me, and I'll tell the police to leave us alone. Get it? I don't want to have to deal with the police regarding anything, but especially regarding Doug."

"Calm down, Charlie. Call me the minute you are out of earshot, even if you're still in the parking lot. Call me right away and let me know what Jim thinks."

At the station, Ginny set out a coffee urn in the conference room and some chilled water bottles. Matt gave her a nod, and she left the conference room just as Captain Pierce walked in. She went to the lobby to ask the receptionist to bring Mr. Henderson into the conference room when he arrived. Then she thought better of it and decided to wait for Mr. Henderson to come, thinking she'd bring him to the conference room herself. So, she sat and waited.

Mr. Henderson was tall, well over 6 feet, and very well dressed, just as you would have imagined of a wealthy retired banker, with the look of affluence that went from his haircut to his expensive shoes. He was with another man, well-dressed and looking very much like an attorney she knew.

"Is that James O'Reilly with Mr. Henderson?" she thought. "I think it is. I should let Matt know about this." But before she could grab her cell phone, both men strode across the floor and went directly to the receptionist's desk. Ginny walked up to them, extended her hand, and introduced herself. They both shook her hand with a grip of confidence and a smile on their faces, but Ginny noticed there were a couple of frown lines on Charlie Henderson's forehead. And she thought, "That's funny, he looks a little worried."

"Gentlemen, please come with me," she said with a smile. She guided them to the conference room and led them to the table where Matt Davis and Bill Pierce sat. They both stood up and moved around the table to shake hands with each of the visitors.

"Oh, thanks, but we've already met," Jim O'Reilly said when Ginny introduced him to Matt Davis.

"We appreciate your time and assistance today," Bill Pierce said.

"Well, it's not like I had a choice, is it?" Charlie responded.

"Please have a seat." Captain Pierce gestured at the two chairs across the table from where he and Matt were sitting. Charlie sat down first, then Matt, and then Bill. Jim O'Reilly sat down next to Charlie after Ginny was seated at the head of the table, where she had placed a yellow pad of paper so she could take notes. She also had the conference phone and recording system controller and switches just within reach.

"Mr. Henderson, do you mind if we have Ginny take notes for us? It's standard procedure anytime our detectives have a meeting like this," Captain Pierce said.

"No, I don't mind her taking notes," Charlie nodded his head toward Ginny. "I'm sure you don't mind if Attorney O'Reilly also takes notes or speaks on my behalf. So, I'm wondering how we can help," said Charlie.

Attorney O'Reilly held his hand up and said, "First of all, it's my understanding that Doug died from an accidental fall – that Doug fell, hit his head, lost a lot of blood, and then had multiple organ failures due to that loss of blood. Is there something else that happened that we don't know about?"

"Well, I don't know about anything else right now except I do know that Mr. Henderson and Mr. Wood were friends and worked together at several different banks in Boston. I'm more interested in Mr. Henderson's relationship with Mr. Wood, and less about the details of his accident at this point." Bill Pierce leaned forward and tapped his pen on the table.

"Do me a favor, Mr. Henderson, and tell me a little bit about those red folders Detective Davis saw you take from Mr. Wood's house the other day and about the investments you shared."

"Well, as I already explained to Detective Davis, Doug and I had several joint accounts, actually joint investments, that were under both our names. We found that by doing joint accounts, we reduced our liabilities and greatly improved the financial performance of our investments. The red folders mapped the account data, which Doug kept in an online, cloud-based storage system. I needed the folders to help me identify my accounts and to ensure that Mrs. Wood has control of Doug's accounts now that Doug has passed away." Charlie glanced from Bill to Matt as he spoke. Attorney O'Reilly was nodding his head in agreement.

Captain Pierce set his pen on the conference room table and looked intently at Charlie. "We were surprised by your passport records to learn that you and Mr. Wood have been to the Grand Caymans several times, maybe ten or twelve times over the last few years. Were you aware that Doug Wood had recently visited the Caymans just before his death? He had visited the Caymans with Bill Flynn nearly ten times over the last five years. We also reviewed Mr. Wood's bank accounts and were wondering if you could shed some light on those specific accounts. Can you explain where Mr. Wood got all the money in his separate accounts and why Mr. Flynn was in the Grand Caymans at least the same number of times over the last five years? Are we going to find you complicit in any of the movement of monies from the United States to the Caymans or anyplace else, for that matter? You do have around $900M in shared investments, after all."

Charlie's face changed perceptibly – the smile was gone, and his expression was a blank stare, looking past Bill Pierce's face toward the windows on the other side of the conference room. The deluge of questions annoyed Charlie. He looked at Jim O'Reilly, nodded, then stood up and pushed his chair under the conference table. Jim O'Reilly did the same thing.

"I have no idea what you're talking about, but if you'd like a follow-up meeting with me, I will ask my attorney to check in with your town attorney to ensure that you have just cause. Good day."

Bill Pierce stood up, shook his head, and said, "Wait, I don't know why you're reacting this way. We only want to know what Doug Wood was doing in the Grand Caymans and if you had any suspicion that he might be hiding money there?" But Bill's words were lost in the moment.

Charlie and Attorney O'Reilly walked to the door, exited the conference room, crossed the lobby, and left the police station through the front door. They spoke for a couple of minutes in the parking lot and shook hands.

Charlie got into his car and pulled onto Phinney's Lane, headed toward Route 28. Charlie picked up his phone and called Billy Flynn on his 'fast-dial' keypad.

"How the hell did the police know that you, Doug, and I made so many visits to the Grand Caymans, and how did they know how much money we have in those accounts? How did they know that we've all been down there several times a year over the last five years? How did they know that, Billy? Both Jim and I were shocked that they knew about the trips and the money. Please get Felix on this call right now!"

Billy conferenced Felix onto the call, and Charlie asked him the same questions he had just demanded from Billy Flynn.

"How in the hell did the Barnstable Police Department know that we have $800 million sitting in a bank at the Grand Caymans, and how do they know that we've been down there a bunch of time over the last five years? It looks to me like they know as much as I do about what's going on. How's that possible, Felix?"

"Did they say $800 million?" Felix asked.

"Well, not that exact amount, but they knew a lot about our comings and goings," Charlie explained.

Felix started to say something, but Billy interrupted him.

"Charlie, they're just bluffing. Sure, they know we've traveled to the Caymans, they even may know how much money we've banked down there, but I can assure you they don't know any of the details and won't unless someone tells them."

Billy was trying to calm Charlie down and think on his feet simultaneously.

He continued, "Felix and I aren't talking, and Doug is not talking. So unless you say something to them, they won't have anything on us. Let's stay in touch and make sure we each know what the other is doing. I'll call O'Reilly and close the loop with him, and I'll call you back in the morning. There's nothing to worry about, Charlie, they're just bluffing!"

Charlie grunted into the phone and then hung up. He'd deal with Billy and Felix later.

Chapter Forty-Four

Winston decided to have Alison stop by for a surprise visit with William Flynn rather than try to get information from him over the phone. Winston suspected that a one-on-one with a pretty girl might get Mr. Flynn to tip his hand about the trips to the Cayman Islands with Doug and Charlie. Anything that Billy Flynn could tell them could shed some light on this money mystery. Alison decided to include Michael for backup in case there were any questions about using the bank's computers or networks.

Alison and Michael walked the three blocks from the Federal Reserve Bank building on Atlantic Avenue to the Bank of America building on State Street. After checking their credentials, the receptionist called Mr. Flynn and had a brief conversation. Then she turned to Alison and Michael, nodding at them.

"Please take that elevator up to William Flynn's office on the eighth floor." The office was private and located on a different floor from the Bank of America offices.

In the elevator, Michael said, "Now remember, Alison, we are here to get information, not to accuse him of any crime."

Alison flashed her blue eyes at Michael, then crossed her arms. She hated it when people had to remind her to keep her temper in check or keep her mouth shut.

When they arrived, Billy was getting off the conference call with Charlie and Felix. They introduced themselves, and he ushered them into one of his conference rooms, which had a sweeping view of Post Office Square and a partial view of Boston Harbor. He asked if they'd like some coffee, tea, or chilled water, but Michael and Alison shook their heads as they took their seats.

"How can I help you?" Billy smiled at Alison, leaned forward, and held out his open hands.

"I'm from Treasury," Alison said. "I was on that call this morning, the one you had with my boss, Winston Glover. I'm here with some follow-up questions regarding Douglas Wood and his bank accounts in Switzerland. I understand that you and Mr. Henderson have signature authority on all these accounts and that you recently moved the accounts from Seline Bank and Trust LTD in the Grand Caymans to a private bank at the Swiss Post Office. Do you care to comment?"

"Well, Ms. Abrams, first of all, those are private accounts with very limited access – I only have signature authority to move funds in case Mr. Wood or Mr. Henderson cannot direct the funds for any reason. I'm not aware of any account transfers you've described. I don't get involved with their banking unless my signature is needed instead of Mr. Wood's or Mr. Henderson's.

"Mr. Flynn, you've been to the Grand Caymans several times. I believe it was six times this year and at least ten times over the last five years. We know you flew there on a private jet as recently as last month. So, what were you doing in the Grand Caymans that often?" Alison paused and looked directly at Billy. He started to take a deep breath.

"Oh, and before you answer," Alison interjected, "I should let you know that we have copies of the bank sign-in sheets for every time you went to Seline Bank and Trust in the Grand Caymans, so we know you were at the bank for six separate visits this year and an additional fifteen visits over the last five years. What on earth were you doing at that bank so often? Opening new accounts or something?"

Then Alison stopped. She had never taken her piercing blue eyes off Billy Flynn, but now she looked away and shook her head.

"What kind of banking were you doing?" she asked again.

Billy Flynn was silent for a long time. Finally, he said, "Oh, just some deposits and stuff, nothing important. Nothing big or anything. Why?" Billy looked back at Alison, never flinching or taking his eyes off her.

"Nothing big? We reviewed the accounts in question – approximately fifty separate accounts, each with an almost $20 million balance. That is, until they were systematically closed; the funds were then transferred to the European Banking Clearing Center and subsequently to a private banking facility within the Swiss Post Office. In total, approximately $850 million was deposited in the Grand Caymans. But 'nothing big,' you say?"

Billy quietly watched Alison.

"Most recently, all the funds moved to Switzerland. Any idea who did this? Do you have any idea how Mr. Wood came into possession of $850 million? As a signature, you must be aware that you'll be complicit if there is any illegal business. Any comments?"

There was a very long pause as Billy Flynn gathered his thoughts. Then he grabbed a bottle of chilled water and gulped it until he started to choke.

"I don't know what you're talking about," he whispered as he recovered from coughing. "I don't know a thing about that money, and I certainly don't know anything about Doug Wood's fortune. However, I do know that from time to time, he asked me to go down to his home on the island and check it out. Sure, I might have brought some cash with me to deposit for him down there, but not $850 million – absolutely not. Nothing like that, nothing even close." Of course, Billy was lying to Alison about what he knew; the amount of money, and the fact that Doug and Charlie had homes on the island.

Alison smiled and said, "Who in the hell do you think you're talking to – do you think I'm an idiot?"

Michael was getting visibly uncomfortable. He observed Alison and then cleared his throat. Alison ignored Michael's warning and continued her questioning.

"I know what you and Henderson and that guy Felix did. You carried a large amount of money down to the Grand Caymans, put it into fifty separate accounts, and hid it from the United States government, including the IRS, Treasury, and anyone else you could think of. Now, where the hell did that money come from, Mr. Flynn? Where did you get that money?"

Billy cleared his throat again and turned away from Alison. With his back turned, he shouted, "None of your business, bitch!" Then he stood up and gestured with his arm toward the door.

"If you want to talk with me again, you better have a warrant, and if you do, you can call my attorney. I'm done with you – get out of my office!"

Alison started to say something, but Michael put his hand on her arm and turned her toward the door.

"Let's go, Alison," said Michael. They started to leave the conference room but not before Alison turned and gave Billy the finger. Billy just shook his head and then mouthed the words, "Fuck you" then turned and slammed the conference room door.

The elevator ride was full of tension. Alison was visibly upset, and Michael was shaking his head. He couldn't imagine a worse meeting with William Flynn. As they left the lobby, Alison started to say something, but Michael advised her just to keep quiet until they returned to the office.

When they returned to the Fed, Alison and Michael burst into the conference room where Winston had set up his temporary office. There was no holding her back now.

"How did your meeting go? Did you get the information we are looking for?" Winston asked.

"No," Alison said. "He's an asshole, and he's not going to say a word until we start to squeeze him. Then I think he'll roll over and tell us everything. We'll need to get Detective Davis to add some fuel to the fire and start squeezing him till he starts talking. I'll call the detective so he can put some heat on this guy. Then I think he'll tell us what we need to know."

"Hold on, Alison," said Winston. "Let's gather our thoughts and prioritize our actions. Let me call Detective Davis, and why don't you and Michael take a breather? I'll call you as soon as I get off the phone."

Alison and Michael took the elevator down to the ground floor. Once inside her office, Michael took her hands and squeezed them.

"Alison, I know you have a lot of passion, and you want answers from William Flynn immediately. I think that between Winston and Detective Davis, we will find some of those answers. You did a great job; now let's let them do theirs." He looked deeply and fondly into her eyes. He leaned over and kissed her on the forehead. She sighed and looked down.

"I hate having other people finish things for me. I hate it. I want to keep going."

"I know, Alison, I know. Let Winston and Detective Davis carry the ball for a little while, and then we can jump back into the fray."

Alison sighed and nodded. "Thanks, Michael, thanks a lot for your support." Alison smiled at Michael and kissed him on the cheek.

Michael hugged Alison and said, "You're the best. I know this is your case to solve, and I know you will."

Chapter Forty-Five

At this point, Matt Davis's office looked like one of those scenes on a television crime show when all the detectives paste suspects' faces and clues onto the big pinboard on their office wall. Matt had his whole whiteboard covered with names – C. Henderson, D. Wood, W. Flynn, J. Wood, the names of the two Treasury folks, A. Abrams and W. Glover, and the name of the IT guy from Federal Reserve Bank, M. Ross.

There was also a world map with lines and arrows from Boston to the Grand Caymans. But in Matt Davis's case, there was much more than meets the eye. He was pretty sure that the "accident" that befell Doug Wood might not have been an accident at all, but instead had more to do with money and the accounts that Alison Abrams had identified. He was reasonably sure that the individuals coming down from the Treasury and the Federal Reserve Bank of Boston would be able to provide a clear motive for what happened.

Matt wanted to pick the doctor's brain a bit more regarding the autopsy, so he called Dr. Miller.

"Hello, Dr. Miller, Matt Davis from the Barnstable Police Department. I'm calling to see if you've found any additional data or information regarding Doug Wood's accident."

"Well, Matt, I was just going to give you a call," responded Dr.

Miller. "We finished the second autopsy and found some omissions and errors, which necessitated a second look. Dr. Fernald and I have found bruising on Mr. Wood's shoulders and chest. These are consistent with being held and shaken, then pushed backward. There was also some bruising that may have been caused by a finger that poked Mr. Wood in the chest several times, you know what I mean, right? Anyway, they just finalized the updated autopsy report. I'll send it right over to you."

"Dr. Miller, are you telling me you think someone pushed Mr. Wood after all? Do you think we are looking at his being pushed as contributing to the cause of death? Well then, given this new information, I think this could be a possible homicide, Dr. Miller?"

"Yes, Detective Davis," Dr. Miller said as he sighed. "As you know, we determined the cause of death to be multi-system organ failure due to extreme blood loss from head trauma. But the bruising on his chest and shoulders indicates he had been forcibly pushed, causing him to fall backward and hit his head on the fireplace hearth. That gives us reason to believe that his death was not caused by an accidental fall but by someone shoving him backward."

Matt's brain was now in overdrive as the pieces to this puzzle became more transparent and confusing simultaneously. He asked again about the autopsy report.

"Yes," said Dr. Miller, "it's on the way."

Matt grabbed the fax off the machine when it came in and burst into Bill Pierce's office.

"Bill, take a look at this! They can confirm that someone held Mr. Wood by the shoulders and may even have poked him in the chest with a finger. They're saying it is very likely that he was shoved backward and hit his head."

Bill scanned the report and went right to the cause of death section. There it was in black and white: "Cause of death in part by multisystem organ failure due to extreme blood loss caused by head trauma, which may have been caused by a forceful shove backward, causing the victim to hit his head. We believe the fall may not have been an accident because there were marks and shadows representing pressure exerted on the front and back of the shoulders.

In addition, several marks on the left breast indicate that someone poked Mr. Wood with their finger or fingers before he fell backward. The shoulder marks could indicate that someone had their hands clasped on the front and back of both of Mr. Wood's shoulders. Mr. Wood was pushed backward and hit his head on the hearth."

"So, they don't think this was an accident, Matt? Are they sure this time? If they are, then I'd like to call the pathologist from the Medical Examiner's Office and chat with him about this as well." Bill ran his hand through his hair and took a breath. "And if we all agree that it wasn't an accident, I'm going to get Henderson and Flynn in here for some questioning. And I'm going to call the District Attorney."

Bill called Ginny and asked her to come down to his office, then called his assistant and asked him to run over to Dunkin Donuts and pick up three coffees and a medium box of Munchkins. The coffee was still hot when they were handed out. They all sat at his conference table and shared the donuts.

"So Matt, they're telling us that the accident may not have been accidental and that someone could have shoved Mr. Wood and that he fell backward and hit his head on the fireplace hearth?" asked Ginny.

"Yes," Matt said. "And here are the digital pictures of the marks and shadows of the bruises they found. They updated the report with this additional data. Now they are saying they can see bruises on the shoulders caused by someone holding or shaking Mr. Wood. It seems someone jabbed him with a finger on his chest and then pushed him back so he hit his head. We don't know whether it was intentional or still an accident, but we know that it is improbable that Mr. Wood fell on his own. Instead, someone seemed to push him, ultimately contributing to his death," Matt explained a little more from the autopsy report.

"Matt, make sure you update the case file to include this new information and insert the updated autopsy report into the case as well. Did you get in touch with Henderson and Flynn?" Pierce asked.

"On it, boss," said Matt.

"Now, I'm quite curious to see what the banking folks have to say tomorrow. I think they'll be able to shed some additional light on our case. Additionally, I want to intensify my focus on Henderson and Flynn now. Matt, I'd like to get Flynn here fifteen minutes before Henderson comes in. Then we'll walk Henderson past the conference room window into the Chief's office so they'll see each other – just to let them know we're questioning them both."

Matt nodded at Captain Pierce and left with Ginny. Matt returned to his office to call Charles Henderson and William Flynn to ask them to come into the precinct the next day. Captain Pierce just stared at his phone for a minute, then called his boss, the Chief of Police in Barnstable.

Bill Pierce was somewhat disturbed that no one from the hospital or the Coroner's Office had informed Matt about the new findings until now. It likely had a material effect on this case and would undoubtedly get Matt to ask some additional questions of Charles Henderson and William Flynn. "Yes," Bill thought, "these new findings will most likely change everything."

Chapter Forty-Six

Michael picked up Alison and Winston at their hotel at 7:00 a.m.; they were both ready to go, it was bright and early. Alison handed Michael a cup of Dunkin' Donuts mocha coffee and a jelly donut. "Thanks, Alison, it's my favorite," Michael said. She pointed to a Starbucks coffee in the cup holder, and Winston thanked her as well.

An hour later, they were driving over the Sagamore Bridge that the Army Corps of Engineers constructed during the rebuilding of the Cape Cod Canal. The Sagamore and Bourne Bridges were the only two ways to get over the canal and onto the Cape. By 8:30, they turned into the police headquarters parking lot and walked into the lobby just in time to be greeted by Ginny.

"Hello, I'm Ginny Jensen, Senior Administrative Specialist here at the Barnstable Police Department. Welcome. Please follow me to our conference room, and we'll meet Captain Bill Pierce and Detective Matt Davis."

Ginny led them into the conference room where Captain Pierce and Matt Davis greeted them.

Matt Davis outlined the case from the accident to the death of Doug Wood. He also included the update of the autopsy report, indicating that Mr. Wood may have been shoved backward and then hit his head, which could alter the type of case he was investigating.

Matt explained that this case would likely morph into a homicide.

Everyone looked around the table at each other. This had become a massive case.

Bill Pierce finally broke the thoughtful silence. "Mr. Glover, you mentioned to my detective here that you had something that might enlighten our investigation."

"Yes, as I mentioned on the phone, we've uncovered what might be evidence in support of your murder case. We've found that Mr. Wood, Mr. Henderson, and Mr. Flynn may have been depositing vast amounts of money into banks in the Grand Caymans and then transferring those funds to banks in Switzerland. We estimate the amount to be upwards of $850 million." Winston Glover tapped the folder in front of him as he spoke to the group.

Mouths dropped in surprise around the table. Matt whistled under his breath.

"Mr. Glover, did you say $850 million?" asked Bill Pierce.

"How on earth did they get their hands on that kind of money, sir?" Matt asked.

"We haven't been able to confirm all of our suspicions, but we do know at this point that they have been siphoning money away from the Federal Reserve System and certain banks here in the northeast, including their former employer, Bank of America." Winston paused to let that sink in and then continued. "We're following the trail of their activities starting as early as 2004. Somehow, they have managed to disrupt the electronic handshakes between the Federal Reserve System and some of its member banks. This allowed them to modify the data to reflect a new receipt location that points to the Grand Caymans. The transaction appeared to be completed accurately, but some data was diverted to their ghost accounts with no detection.

"We were fortunate that our Treasury Inspector Alison Abrams," Winston turned his head and nodded toward Alison, "was in Boston at the Fed on a special assignment to find out why select transactions occasionally failed. She pinpointed some of those failed transactions to the accounts controlled by Henderson, Wood, and Flynn. When we discovered the holding company, we noticed that all the funds in the 50 accounts had been transferred out of the Caymans. Coincidence?

I think not. It seems they knew we were watching, so they moved the money. We've spoken with Mr. Henderson and Mr. Flynn, but neither of them admitted any knowledge of the overall details of the account transactions. We're hoping you can shake them into telling us what happened."

"Well, Mr. Glover, we'll be talking with Mr. Henderson and Mr. Flynn today. We'll put them in adjoining rooms to ensure they can see each other upon arrival. I think we can apply some pressure and get them to talk. We don't have any other persons who were closely involved with Mr. Wood and could have known about the accident, so we think they may have some information that could help us. Nothing in his house was missing or stolen, and there was no evidence of a break-in. It seems that if someone shoved Mr. Wood in anger, ultimately by someone they knew and trusted." Bill Pierce glanced at the autopsy report as he spoke.

Alison leaned forward, looked at Detective Davis, and asked him a question she'd been wondering about for days.

"Who would want to kill Mr. Wood and why?"

"We don't know yet, Alison, but we'll find out for sure. Money is a big motivator. I'm confident that Henderson or Flynn can provide additional information to help us determine the answer to your question."

"Thanks, Detective. I have to agree, if someone with access to $850 million dies under suspicious circumstances, then it likely has something to do with the money. Maybe Mr. Wood was trying to take all the money, and someone didn't like that. Perhaps either Mr. Henderson or Mr. Flynn confronted Mr. Wood, and they got into a shoving match, after which Mr. Wood fell. Who knows, but it doesn't sound like someone entered Mr. Wood's home with the intent to rob or harm him. It wouldn't make sense."

"I think that someone got into an argument with Mr. Wood and accidentally or intentionally shoved him to the floor, and Mr. Wood hit his head on the fireplace hearth, eventually succumbing from that fall. Manslaughter would be the charge unless we find someone who intended to kill Mr. Wood. Right now, we only have two suspects, and both deny any knowledge of the accounts or the accident." Matt replied.

Alison started to tell them about her visit to Billy Flynn's office, but stopped short of sharing any details until Winston said, "Alison, we need to be very transparent here with the police."

"Well then, what did you find out, Alison? What have you got for us?" Matt asked.

Alison turned toward Matt and said, "Michael and I pushed Billy Flynn pretty hard, but all he said was he only went to the Caymans to deliver some paperwork to Doug and Charlie but didn't know details about the money. Then, he burst out that the money was none of our business. I think he's lying. He was quick to point out that if I wanted to chat with him again, he'd have his attorney step in."

"Did he mention anything about the money in Switzerland or how much money was in the Grand Caymans?" Matt asked.

"No, he denied knowing about other bank accounts, but I think he's lying about everything. I think he's right in the middle of this crime and may be complicit in Doug's death."

It was apparent that Alison was very passionate about solving this case.

"Mr. Glover," Bill turned to Winston, "I think you and your team should stick around while we talk with Henderson and Flynn. Then we can get together again after we're finished with them. We'll have you in a third conference room near Henderson and Flynn so they can see you. That way, they can worry about what else we may have on them. We'll bring you some lunch. Do you mind staying here for another hour or two?"

"That's fine, Captain. Anything we can do to help get them talking would be good for both of us." Winston had a wry smile on his face and nodded to Alison and Michael as if to say, "If the police can help us get our money back, then we're happy to cooperate with them."

They all shook hands, and Ginny led them to a different room where they scanned menus from local eateries and picked out what they wanted for lunch. They could see directly into the other two conference rooms where Charlie Henderson and Billy Flynn would be interviewed.

Chapter Forty-Seven

Charlie Henderson told his wife he was going to Hyannis for a haircut and would return home by noon. He drove to the Barnstable Police Headquarters, parked his car, and entered the lobby's front door. His attorney, Jim O'Reilly, was waiting for him. Charlie glanced at the three large conference rooms on the first floor and four smaller rooms used for suspect questioning. Each of the smaller rooms had a glass wall, allowing someone in the first room to see who was in the second, third, or fourth rooms. Both larger rooms provided a view into each other and across the lobby into each of the smaller rooms.

When Charlie and Jim O'Reilly checked in at the front desk, Ginny Jensen was waiting. She shook hands with each of them and asked them to follow her into one of the large conference rooms, where she presented them with chairs that provided a view into all the smaller rooms. Next, she offered each of them some coffee or bottled water and then left them alone while she walked over to the receptionist's desk. Ginny asked the receptionist to call Bill Pierce and Matt Davis to inform them that Charlie Henderson and his attorney had arrived and were waiting for them in Conference Room 2. Then she returned to Conference Room 2 and informed Charlie Henderson and his attorney that Matt Davis and Bill Pierce would arrive in a few minutes.

She met up with Captain Pierce in his office.

"He seems a little bit nervous, but not too much. I'll call you when Billy Flynn arrives, and I'll walk him right across the lobby in front of Mr. Henderson, so he gets a good look. We'll put him in the small room next to the police union office so that he's quite visible from your conference room. I have Sergeant Brady scheduled to sit with him until you're ready."

She returned to the conference room where Charlie Henderson and his attorney were waiting. She told them it wouldn't be long and then promptly left. After almost a ten-minute wait, Captain Pierce and Detective Davis entered the conference room.

"Good morning, Mr. Henderson, Attorney O'Reilly. Thanks for coming by this morning. We appreciate your assistance with all of this, and hopefully, we can clear up some additional questions we have regarding Doug Wood."

"Well, just a minute, Detective, I thought you asked us down here to talk further about Charlie's relationship with Doug Wood. What are you talking about now? I'm a little confused by what you just said. What additional questions, and what are you trying to clear up?" Attorney O'Reilly asked.

"We want to know where Mr. Henderson was on Thursday morning, the 28th, when Mr. Wood had his accident," Matt responded with a business-like tone.

"I already told you; I was playing golf over at Hyannisport. But that has nothing to do with my friendship with Doug." Charlie was trying not to lose his temper. He was trying to act impartial.

"What time did you start?" asked Matt.

"I think it was just before nine, maybe right at nine," Charlie said.

"Did anyone play with you, Mr. Henderson, or were you out there by yourself? And if you were alone, did anyone see you start your round?" asked Captain Pierce.

Charlie thought for a moment and then said, "I played alone, and I don't know if anyone saw me on the course. But, you know, you can jump on the course whenever you want if the tee is open. You don't have to check in at the pro shop–no real tee times at the Hyannisport Club."

"Well then, you don't mind if we confirm this with the clubhouse or the pro shop, do you?"

"No, please go ahead. I'm sure someone saw me Tuesday morning," said Charlie. "I just don't know who that might be. But I'm sure someone saw me there. Oh, I remember, one of the caddies, I think his name is Ted. He saw me tee off on the first hole. He complimented me on my tee shot – it was right down the middle about 245 yards. So, call the pro shop, and they'll confirm it."

"So how long were you gone from your house, you know, how long were you on the golf course?" Matt asked.

"Well, I only played nine holes, so probably three to four hours, tops," said Charlie. "But I did grab a beer before I headed home."

"If you had a beer after golf, didn't somebody see you?" asked Matt.

"I don't know if anyone saw me. There's a refrigerator on the patio; you get your own. I think there were some guys on the patio, but I'm not sure they know who I am. I didn't recognize them," said Charlie.

"So, Mr. Henderson, how do you know it wasn't four hours? How are you so sure?"

"Because I checked the time when I left the club so that I'd have an idea of when I'd be getting home," said Charlie. "So, by my calculation, I was gone for about three to three and a half hours – not quite four, though."

"Thanks, Mr. Henderson. I think that's all we need at this point. If we have any other questions for you, I'll reach out by phone or email."

Matt started to hold out his hand as Charlie got up from the conference table. Just then, Charlie looked across the hall and saw Billy Flynn in the other conference room.

"What the hell's going on? What's he doing here?" Charlie asked as he pointed to the other conference room where Billy Flynn sat with Sergeant Brady.

Matt Davis turned toward the other conference room.

"Mr. Flynn was asked to come by here to give us a bit more information about his involvement with the accounts that you, he, and Mr. Wood had control over down in the Grand Caymans. I'll let you know if we need to chat further; thanks again."

"Not so fast, Detective. I know Billy Flynn wants our attorney to sit with him, and since we're done here, please let Attorney O'Reilly join your meeting with Billy Flynn."

Detective Davis looked at Captain Pierce, who nodded and said, "Fine."

Charlie shook hands with Attorney O'Reilly and headed towards the front parking lot.

After Charlie left the police station, he stopped in Centerville to get his haircut on the way home. However, before entering the barber shop, he called Billy Flynn and left a voicemail, asking him to call back right after he left the police station.

"I hope he keeps his freaking mouth shut about this whole thing," thought Charlie. "What did that asshole even mean when he said 'more information?' What do they even know?"

Charlie could hardly contain himself while sitting in the barber's chair, thinking how stupid it would be if Billy Flynn said anything that could be used against them.

"Damnit, Billy, you better call me back the minute you're out of that police station, or I swear, I'll throw you under the bus myself," he thought. "don't forget to tell Felix to keep his mouth shut too!"

But Felix had already found something unexpected and told Billy about it. Billy had been quick to respond to Felix.

"We'll find out who's been snooping around the accounts, and when we do, I'll take care of them myself. Promise!"

It turned out that Felix had discovered that someone had been investigating their accounts in the Grand Caymans, and he was sure that it wasn't just a hacker looking for free money. The accounts were blocked off, so nobody could access the money, but it still made Felix nervous to know that someone might be able to circumvent the firewall and obtain ownership information. Billy was not going to mention this to Charlie if he didn't need to.

Upon exiting the barber shop, Charlie called Jim O'Reilly and left him a voicemail, asking him to call as soon as he left the police station. "That should cover it," said Charlie, "that should cover it." On the drive back to Osterville, he decided to stop for a drink at the

Wianno Club. He had a lot on his mind, and things were starting to get a little intense. Charlie needed to rein in Billy and Felix to ensure that each of them was on the same page as Charlie was. He was the leader, and they were the followers. The Vodka Tonic hit the spot, so he ordered a second one even before he'd finished his first one. When he got home, Barbara asked him how golf was. Charlie just smiled and got himself another drink.

Chapter Forty-Eight

When Matt Davis and Captain Pierce finally arrived at the conference room, where Billy Flynn was sitting and waiting with Sergeant Brady, Billy was already in a bad mood and distraught. But he smiled when he saw Jim O'Reilly walk in behind them.

He shook hands with Jim O'Reilly and said, "Hey, good to see you, Jim, but tell me, why the hell was Charlie Henderson here with you guys? What's going on? Why was I stuck here and not in with you and Charlie Henderson?"

Attorney O'Reilly put his hands up and said, "No worries, Billy, let's just see what Detective Davis and Captain Pierce want, okay?" He turned to Detective Davis and said, "Go ahead, will you, please."

"Thanks for coming down this morning, Mr. Flynn. We just have a couple of questions about where you were on Thursday morning, the 28th of this month. Let's say from about ten to noon. Do you remember where you were then?" Captain Pierce asked. He turned toward Billy Flynn and glared at him while he waited for an answer.

"Hm, let's see, I think I was up in my office in Boston all morning that Thursday." Billy was quiet for a minute and looked around the table, then he said, "Oh no, come to think of it, I was at my girlfriend's apartment all day. Yeah, that's it. That's where I was." He turned toward Detective Davis and Captain Pierce, nodding his head several times. "See, I was up in Boston all day. Now, what's this all about, and why are you questioning me?"

"Listen, Mr. Flynn, do you have any reason to believe anyone would want to hurt Doug Wood?" asked Captain Pierce.

"No one I can think of. Doug was a great guy. And that's why I think his death was just an accident."

At that point, Attorney O'Reilly put his hand up and said, "Unless you have some other questions about my clients' relationship with Mr. Wood, then I think we're done here."

Captain Pierce ignored O'Reilly and continued his questioning. He asked Billy if he knew anyone else who was aware of the bank accounts in the Cayman Islands. Billy said he thought only he, Charlie Henderson, and Doug Wood knew anything about the bank accounts down in the Cayman Islands.

"Do you know a Felix Brown?" Captain Pierce shook his head ever so slightly before he asked the question.

"No, I don't know a Felix Brown. Who is he?" Billy questioned.

Captain Pierce held his hand up in front of Billy's face, just like when he used to direct traffic and wanted a car to stop.

"We've got you talking with Felix Brown seven times just last week. Are you sure you want to deny knowing him?"

"Oh, you mean Felix Brown up in Boston. I thought you were asking me if I knew a Felix Brown down here on the Cape. Sorry! Yes, I know Felix Brown." Billy started to sound nervous at this point. Attorney O'Reilly cleared his throat and glared at Captain Pierce.

"Well, tell me, Mr. Flynn, how do you know this guy Felix Brown then?"

"He does some computer work for me. He did some work for Mr. Henderson and Mr. Wood in the past. That's all. Not much work at all."

"What type of computer work? What was Felix doing for you? And what was he doing for Mr. Henderson and Mr. Wood?" Captain Pierce asked.

Matt followed up with, "Did he have anything to do with the money and the accounts down in the Grand Caymans? What about the money in the Swiss Postal System? Give me an idea as to what exactly Felix Brown was doing for all of you."

"I don't know anything about Switzerland and their Post Office; I don't know what you're talking about. I don't know what he did for Charlie or Doug. Why don't you ask Charlie? He was here when I arrived in the other room with you guys. Why didn't you ask him – he might know more than I do?"

"We did, and he said you could fill us in on everything, that you were the one who reached out to Felix, and he said he didn't know anything," Pierce explained.

"He's lying. He's the one who reached out to Felix and had him call all the banks to ensure that everything was handled correctly. I had nothing to do with that. I run a security company and provide security to people like Charlie and Doug – nothing else."

"So, tell me then, how do you supply security to Doug Wood and Charles Henderson when you're up in Boston, and they're down here on the Cape? Do you drive down here every day to make sure they're safe? How were you protecting Mr. Wood when he fell and cracked his head open? Were you there watching out for him?"

"I wasn't there as I told you. I was up at my girlfriend's apartment in Boston. Did you check if Charlie Henderson was there?"

"Oh, that's interesting," said Captain Pierce. "Were you aware Mr. Henderson was at his golf club over in Hyannisport playing golf when Mr. Wood had his accident? He said he thought you might have stopped over to see Mr. Wood the day he fell and hurt his head."

Billy Flynn was quiet, but Attorney O'Reilly interjected, "If you guys don't have any other questions, I think we're gonna head out now." Both Matt Davis and Bill Flynn ignored the comment and continued.

"Mr. Flynn, we're going to check your phone to see if it traveled down here on the 28th. Cell phones always connect to the local cell tower, and your carrier saves that data in a file. Any chance your phone will tell us that it was over in Osterville on the 28th?"

"Captain, I was not down here on the 28th, and neither was my phone. But go ahead, call Verizon. They'll tell you that I was at my office in Boston all day. So go ahead, call them."

"Oh, we already called them, and yes, your phone was in Boston all day on the 28th. However, your car wasn't. I'm sure you're aware that you pay for that OnStar safety system for your car. Did you know that the OnStar system installs a computer chip in the vehicle that tells the OnStar folks and the dealer where your car was on a particular day? Did you know that your car has an OnStar chip? Of course, we did, so we called your dealer and asked them to request that OnStar send us the telemetry information for your car. Guess what, Mr. Flynn? We have the report right here. Want to tell us what it says?" asked Matt Davis.

Just then, Captain Pierce waved a computer printout of the report in front of Billy's face.

"My client has nothing more to say, gentlemen, other than he was not at Mr. Woods's house on the 28th. So, unless you're going to arrest him, we're leaving. Next time you see my client, I'll ask you for a warrant. If you don't have one, then we'll not be talking with either of you," said Attorney O'Reilly.

Billy started to stand, but Matt Davis was up in an instant and blocked his exit.

"Listen, Mr. Flynn, we are pretty sure that you or Mr. Henderson were over at Doug Wood's house on the 28th and may have had something to do with his not-so-accidental fall. If you were there and we could prove it, this would not go well for you. You'll become a suspect in the murder case of Doug Wood, and we will arrest you. But, if you cooperate with us now, we'll see what we can do for you – it's your choice."

Billy Flynn turned toward Attorney O'Reilly.

"What are you talking about? Doug Wood fell and hit his head. My client had nothing to do with that, absolutely nothing. He said he wasn't here on the 28th, and that he didn't do anything to Doug. He was a friend, and he would never hurt him. You've got this all wrong. He didn't do anything, but if you continue this kind of harassment with my client, I'll have a meeting with Jon Cantor, your town's attorney, and it won't be a friendly meeting at all! I'll let him know that the Town of Barnstable and you, in particular, are harassing my client."

Matt Davis stood back and let Billy Flynn and Attorney O'Reilly walk toward the conference room door, but spoke to Billy in a firm voice.

"Remember, Mr. Flynn, it's your choice to cooperate and save yourself… or not."

Billy Flynn hesitated, then walked quickly through the conference room door into the lobby. As he and Attorney O'Reilly turned toward the front door, Billy Flynn saw Alison, Michael, and an older gentleman sitting in another conference room. They all stared at him. He stopped and gave Alison a menacing look that sent shivers down her spine. Then he and Attorney O'Reilly turned and walked out the front door, heading for their vehicles. Billy Flynn's last gesture was to raise his left arm and give the police station the middle finger.

When he got to his car, he turned to Attorney O'Reilly.

"Keep them the fuck off my back, would you please? This is getting very bothersome, and you know, Charlie and I don't like to be bothered now, do we?"

Jim O'Reilly nodded as he turned and walked toward his car.

When Billy got into his car, he checked his phone and saw that Charlie had called him and left a voicemail. Billy skipped the voicemail and called Charlie directly instead.

"Charlie, it's Billy. What's up?" But he didn't let Charlie answer. Instead, he continued, "You know those bastards are accusing you and me of being complicit or something with Doug's death, and they're threatening us. They said if we didn't admit we were at Doug's house the morning of the 28th when Doug got hurt, there would be big trouble for us. You know Charlie, Jim told them that he was planning to reach out to the town attorney if they weren't careful. What the hell, Charlie?"

"Listen, Billy, keep your mouth shut, and don't tell them another goddamn thing. I mean it – nothing. And get on your phone and call Felix, and tell him to keep his mouth shut in case they want information from him too. Tell him not to say a damn thing – got it, Billy?"

Billy said he understood and then asked Charlie, "What are we gonna do, Charlie? What are we gonna do about Doug? Should we have a meeting with Jim?"

Charlie thought for a second and said, "No, nothing, Billy, we're not going to do anything right now, nothing at all."

Chapter Forty-Nine

Matt Davis was the first to speak after Billy and his attorney left. "They're both lying. Billy Flynn and Charlie Henderson were both probably at Doug's house, and chances are pretty good that they know what happened. We just can't prove it right now, and I don't think either one of them will help us. They're not stupid enough to admit to anything."

"And now they've got their attorney involved, and he's bound and determined to keep us away from both of them," said Bill Pierce.

"And be that as it may be, I'm still gonna treat them both like suspects because they are," said Matt.

Bill Pierce nodded his head. He also didn't think either one of them would talk. They needed more proof, and they needed it before the funeral. Mrs. Wood was already not cooperating with the police because she was treated like a suspect, and she would certainly be less likely to cooperate once her husband was in the ground. The evidence was somewhere in that house, but nobody, including Matt, Ginny, or Bill Pierce, could find anything that conclusively proved that Billy Flynn or Charles Henderson was there the morning of the accident.

Matt got up from the conference table, shook his head, and walked out of the room. Ginny and Bill Pierce followed. They returned to the other conference room to thank Winston, Alison, and Michael.

"Well, guys, what happened? Did they crack, you know, confess?" Alison asked.

Bill Pierce turned toward Alison and said, "No, not yet, but when Billy Flynn saw you here, he seemed to get more agitated."

"I have that effect on him." Alison smiled.

Bill Pierce nodded but said, "Their attorney probably won't let us have any more time with either of them." Then he turned to Winston and Michael and said, "Thanks for coming down. Let's stay in touch just in case anything new comes up."

"How about we get the FBI involved? Think they'd be more cooperative if we got the FBI on their case?" said Alison.

Winston shook his head and said, "Let's forget about that for now and let the Barnstable Police go after them. We can always call the FBI later if we need to.'"

Winston, Michael, and Alison stood up, shook hands with Bill Pierce, Matt, and Ginny, then walked out of the building and got into their car for the trip back to Boston.

Matt turned to Ginny and Bill Pierce and said, "I'm heading to the bank before it closes. I'll be back in fifteen minutes. Let's talk again. Do either of you need anything while I'm out?"

"No thanks," said Bill, and he turned toward the elevators and headed back to his office.

Ginny was already walking to her office, but turned to Matt and said, "You'll figure this out. You'll get them, Matt; I know you will." She smiled and got into the other elevator.

Matt waited in the drive-thru line at the Cape Cod 5 Bank, dwelling on the case. He tried to figure out why he was having so much trouble getting more evidence on Billy Flynn and Charlie Henderson. Fingerprints in the library were irrelevant because both of them had been into the house a hundred times before the accident. No proof there. He just couldn't think of what else he could do to get some evidence that would stand up in court. Matt leaned back in his seat and stared in front of him while he continued to try to find an answer that made sense from a legal perspective.

"What the hell happened there? What happened to Doug Wood, and how can I link Flynn and Henderson or Mrs. Wood to the scene?" Matt asked himself. "Someone obviously must have shoved him, causing the fall. But was it intentional, or was it an accident? How do we prove that it was intentional?"

Just then, he shifted his focus from the car in front of him to the bank's video camera mounted on the ceiling of the drive-thru near the corner of the roof. "I should have heard from the crime scene guys by now about the missing files on the surveillance computer. Damn it, I should call them right now and see what they have for me. Maybe the files were backed up somewhere else."

Matt pulled out of line, parked in one of the parking spots next to the bank, and called into the main switchboard at the station.

"Hi, it's Matt Davis. Please send me over to the crime scene office, thanks."

Someone answered quickly.

"Yes, this is Detective Davis. I need to know what you found out about the deleted files on that surveillance computer you took from the Woods' house."

The individual explained the complexity of the situation, which led to a lengthy processing time, but stated that they had made progress with the security company. Matt thanked them and said he wanted to hear from them the minute they got the file backups.

Next, he called Captain Pierce.

"Hi Bill, listen, the crime scene folks have figured out that the surveillance video computer is backed up over at the surveillance company using one of their servers. If the backup files from the 28th are intact, they might contain a video that could prove that Billy Flynn, Charles Henderson, or even Jenn Wood was at the home that day. Even better, the camera file might show what happened to Mr. Wood. I'll be right over, meet you there," Matt said.

He backed out of the parking spot, turned around, and drove toward the police station. He went over to the crime scene team's office and asked if they had the backup files yet. They said no, but one of the officers just left to go to the surveillance company's office to hopefully pick up the backup files for the 28th.

Bill Pierce was just coming into the office when Matt was leaving, so they stood in the hallway, and Matt brought him up to date.

"Listen, Bill, the crime scene folks are on the way over to the surveillance company to get the backup files for Mr. Wood's surveillance system. They should have it back here in no time. Then we'll be able to see who was at the house that morning and maybe who shoved Doug and ultimately killed him. They'll call me when they have the backup files back here."

"It's the key we've been looking for," Bill said. Matt smiled and then explained what the laptop was and what it contained. He said he had permission from Mrs. Wood to keep it for a few more days. An hour later, the crime scene folks called Matt to come down to see the video.

With the backup file loaded onto the computer, they scanned the dates until they found the 28th and activated the video scan to replay the day's video. The screen was blank. They typed in a command-level call, and the computer replied, "NONE."

"What the hell's wrong? Where's the video scenes from the 28th?" Matt asked with a hint of frustration.

The tech nodded at Matt, retyped some command-line strings, and then shook his head. "Matt, the video's backup file has been deleted. There's nothing from the 28th. Someone erased the whole day on both computers, so we're screwed now."

"There has to be a way to find it – come on!" He turned to face Ginny and said again, "There has to be a way to find it, right?" Matt nodded his head as he spoke.

Ginny said she'd call her friend at the FBI to see if she knew how to retrieve the deleted video data from the hard drive or the cloud backup, even though it'd been erased. Matt just shook his head and closed his eyes.

Her FBI contact, Gail O'Riley, was not in her office, but her secretary told Ginny she'd have Gail call her back as soon as she found her.

The phone rang about an hour later. It was Gail calling back.

"Hey, Ginny, how are you? How's that dreamy detective? What's his name – Matt? Are you guys getting serious?" Ginny smiled at the mention of Matt's name. But she was somber in her response.

"Gail, we've got a problem here. I have a Dell laptop video processor from a possible murder scene, but the files from the date in question were wiped off the hard drive. The backup server at the security company was hacked, so their copies of the files were also deleted. Any chance you can help me get the images lifted off the computer even though someone deleted the files?"

"Yes, it is possible. I have a few external specialists who can do that; one at the Federal Reserve, one at Homeland, and a couple of independent contractors. Whom would you like me to reach out to?"

"Well, that is convenient. We're already working with the Fed on this case. Who is that person?"

"He's up in Boston. His name is James Clark, and he's one of the world's experts on data trapping and removal. Contact Mr. Michael Ross, his boss. I've got his number right here."

"I don't even need the number; I've already got it, Gail! Mr. Ross was just down here yesterday. I'll give him a call right now, thanks. Give my best to Bobby and Bobby Jr."

She ran into Matt's office and filled him in on the good news. Matt swung around in his chair and offered Ginny a seat at his conference table. They dialed Michael's number right away.

"Hello, this is Michael Ross with the Federal Reserve Bank of Boston. Can I help you?"

"Hi, Michael, this is Ginny Jensen and Matt Davis from the Barnstable Police Department. Have you got a minute for us?"

"Sure, Ginny. Hi Matt, what can I do for you?"

"Listen, Michael, we have a Dell laptop that Doug Wood used as a video server at his home. We reviewed the video files from the 28th, and they've been wiped clean. Then we got the backup files from the surveillance company, but those files were also erased. Is there any chance you can help us reconstruct them? It's crucial to our case down here; it might even be helpful to you guys."

"Hang on for just a second," Michael said.

He called Jimmy Clark into his office and explained what had happened before putting the phone on speaker.

"Hi guys, I've got Jimmy Clark here with me – he'll help us out," said Michael.

"Hi," Jimmy said. "I'm going to skip looking at the hard drive and go right into the cloud server that the surveillance company uses to back up their computer files. Give me just a minute."

Jimmy went straight for Amazon Web Services (AWS), Amazon's secure cloud computing storage. Next, he asked Ginny for the username and password for the Dell laptop. He typed them both into AWS and said, "I'm into their AWS account; just give me a minute."

Matt turned toward Ginny and gave her a questioning glance. Ginny mouthed the words, "I don't know," in response.

"What is AWS?" Matt asked.

"Oh, sorry, it's a new off-premises storage service offered by Amazon. You use their servers located in their data center, accessible via the internet. Pretty great stuff," Michael explained.

"You said the 28th, right?" Jimmy verified. "Well, okay, I'm in there, and I've got the whole day's video up and running. Let me send you a copy right away."

"You're not going to believe what this shows. Shit, I think this should be all the evidence you'll need." Michael took a deep breath as he spoke.

Ginny opened the video file and started playing. Matt leaned closer to the laptop's screen and stared at it with his mouth agape. He turned to Ginny and Bill Pierce, smiling.

"I think we've got them. This proves they're both culpable. Both of them!"

"Look, Matt, make sure this video is stored on our system, not just in the cloud. You never know who might be able to delete it. Then it's gone as evidence," said Bill Pierce.

"Do you mind if we put a copy of this video on our server here in Barnstable?" Matt asked Michael and Jimmy.

"Go right ahead, Matt," said Michael.

Matt turned to the Crime Scene Tech and said, "Save it in-house, please."

Chapter Fifty

Jenn scheduled Doug's funeral for 10:00 a.m. on Tuesday, two weeks after the accident and only two days after the ME released Doug's body. It gave her enough time to contact everyone to let them know that there would be a Mass at the church and a gathering after the funeral at Jenn's house. Jenn decided to skip formal visiting hours since the hospital had kept Doug's body for so long.

Barb spent every day with Jenn helping with all the arrangements. She helped organize the Mass at Our Lady of the Assumption Church in Osterville and called the caterers from the Wianno Beach Club, who would take care of the post-funeral reception at the Wood home. Jenn was also planning to have Doug's friend, Commodore Brinkley from the Yacht Club, bring the family, Charlie, and Barb out into East Bay on Doug's big boat. There, they would spread some of Doug's ashes into the waters he loved so much.

Both of Jenn's daughters and his granddaughter were already in Osterville and did their best to stay out of the way. Charlie offered to run any errands if Jenn needed anything.

By Monday night, everything was ready. Charlie suggested to Jenn that everyone leave the house and come over to the Wianno Club for dinner. Jenn thought it was a good idea, so Charlie called over and reserved the Sea View room for dinner, which had a separate entrance that would offer total privacy. He knew Jenn would appreciate that.

Barb confirmed that Father Ryan would join them for dinner. Not too big a gathering; Jenn, her two daughters, her son-in-law Rick, her granddaughter, Charlie, Doug's younger brother Bob, and his wife Megan were all confirmed for dinner.

Jenn took Barb aside and gave her a big hug and a kiss on the cheek. "Barb, thank you for this – I couldn't have done it without you. Thank you, my dear."

Barb just smiled and gave Jenn a big hug. The two started to cry together as they sat down on the couch in Jenn's family room. They looked out at the Eel River, where Doug's boats were tied to the sides of the dock, and just held hands.

"I never thought I'd lose Doug so soon. I thought we'd be together for another phase of our lives. I thought we'd all be traveling, that Doug would see both of his daughters married with children, just as he'd dreamed about since before they were born. This hurts so bad, Barb, just so badly." Jenn quietly sobbed.

Barb put her arm around Jenn's shoulder and tried to offer comfort.

"Jenn, be strong for the girls and be strong for yourself," was all Barb could think to say.

Dinner at the Wianno was a wonderful celebration of life for Doug Wood and his family, including Charlie and Barb.

Chapter Fifty-One

The service on Tuesday at Our Lady of the Assumption was very pleasant, and even Father Ryan was brought to tears during the eulogy that Charlie shared with everyone.

"Doug is my best friend. He has helped me through life with guidance, love, and affection, demonstrating a great understanding of my faults and what needed to be done to help me through some difficult times. Doug is with me today, helping me through this most difficult time. I'll miss you, Dougie, and I'll see you again in heaven when my time comes. In the meantime, I'll think of you forever. I love you." Charlie ended the eulogy and wiped a tear from his eyes. He thanked everyone for coming and celebrating Doug's life. For Charlie, it was the single saddest day he could remember, and that included the day he learned that both his parents had been killed in a car accident in Florida.

As the organist played "Adagio for Strings," Jenn and her girls went to the back of the church to greet everyone and thank them for coming. Barb whispered to Jenn that she and Charlie would run right over to the house so someone would be there if anyone arrived early before Jenn did.

Doug's house was just a short ride from the church, and Barb and Charlie drove in silence. Each of them was lost in their memories of

Doug. When they got to Doug's driveway, they saw that the caterers from the Wianno Club were all set up and ready to receive the guests. Charlie grabbed a cup of coffee and went into the library to look out the rounded backside of the room onto the river.

"Damn it, I'm going to miss you, Dougie. I miss you already, my friend." He said out loud.

Barb entered the library, put her hand around Charlie's waist, and said, "He loved you, Charlie, and I know you loved him."

Charlie spent part of the day holed up in the library and only came out to check on Jenn and ensure she didn't need anything. He just didn't want to share his grief and worries with anyone. Barb came in periodically to check on Charlie and eventually suggested that he should join everyone out in the kitchen. So, Charlie followed Barb out to the kitchen, and they all sat at the large kitchen table the rest of the afternoon, telling and retelling "Doug stories" from the old days. Charlie was happy to share many anecdotes about Doug at work and some of their private times.

Charlie thought about Doug's cancer and the fall he took. Poor Doug just couldn't catch a break, and now he was gone. He could hear Doug's voice at the hospital saying to Jenn, "Help me, please." Charlie began to sob, a deep and vibrating sob like the one that took over his body when he found out his parents had died. Charlie was suddenly alone. He could still hear Elton John's "Goodbye Yellow Brick Road," which was on the radio the summer his parents died. It was a great song, but it was a terrible summer.

At some point, Charlie took Jenn from the kitchen to the living room, where they could be alone and look out onto the Eel River and Nantucket Sound. He tried to stay calm during all of this. However, between the death of his friend and his concerns about finances, he was feeling the pressure.

"Jenn, I was happy to do the eulogy. Doug was my best friend, and I'm proud to have known him. And I'm sorry, Jenn, but I'm not ready to accept Doug's death yet. I can't help it." Jenn thanked Charlie and then walked over to the big couch that faced the back of the living room and a wall of glass.

She gestured to Charlie to come and sit with her and said, "I did love him too, you know." Jenn nodded, and they both started to cry.

Then Barb came in and said to Charlie, "I think it's time to go now, Charlie. Jenn is exhausted. Jenn, if there's anything you need, just let me know. I'll see you tomorrow."

The two of them hugged Jenn, and Charlie said, "I don't know what to say, Jenn, so I'm just going to say I'm sorry, and I'll miss Doug. See you tomorrow." As he took Barb's hand to leave, Charlie fought back tears.

Jenn walked them to the front door.

"See you tomorrow at 11:30 a.m. on the boat." Barb added.

Jenn nodded, threw them a kiss, and thanked them again for all of the support and love.

When they got to their car, Barb said, "Charlie, I'm so sorry about Doug. I'm sorry for Jenn, and I'm sorry for Emily and Hannah, and I'm sorry for me. But right now, I'm the sorriest for you. He was such a big part of your life, and now you've lost him. I'm so sorry, dear."

Barb started to sob and shake. Charlie kissed Barb and put his arm around her. Once she stopped crying, he started the car, and they were home in five minutes. Charlie left her at the front door and pulled the car into the garage.

"I'll see you inside, Barb."

Charlie came up the side steps into the kitchen and asked Barbara if they could go on the back patio and sit for a while. He was pretty beat by all the day's activities and the stress. Mostly, he was tired because he had lost his best friend, Doug.

Barb led him out of the breakfast area doors to their outdoor seating area. She offered Charlie a chair and took the one beside him.

"Charlie, I'm so sorry this all happened. It was completely unexpected; no one could have ever anticipated it. Let's relax and try to get a nap before dinner."

Charlie nodded and then closed his eyes. He started to move his hands back and forth on the arms of the chair in tandem with the ocean waves breaking below on the beach. He was already asleep when Barb looked over at him. She smiled and closed her eyes as the tears began to flow down her cheeks.

Chapter Fifty-Two

The next day was Wednesday, and the Commodore had Doug's big boat backed into the slip, standing at the cockpit entrance to offer a hand to everyone coming aboard.

"Good morning, Commodore. Thanks for helping out with this today. Jenn appreciates your help." Charlie was always a gentleman.

"Good morning, Charlie. I'm happy to assist, and so sorry about what happened to Doug. It just isn't right."

"No, it certainly wasn't right. Death never is, is it?" Charlie stayed at the stern of the boat to assist the Commodore. Once everyone was aboard, they pulled in the lines, and the Commodore headed the boat out to the center of East Bay. Jenn was to say a few words and spread some of Doug's ashes onto the water. Jenn started to cry, but was able to say goodbye to Doug. Then she took some of the ashes from the urn and gently spread them off the stern into the waves of the bay.

"I'll miss you forever, Doug, and I'll love you forever, my friend and loving partner. One day, we'll be together again," she said in a voice just above a whisper.

Both daughters took some of Doug's ashes and spread them onto the water, then handed the urn to Charlie and Barb, who did the same thing. Charlie said a few words, and then the Commodore headed east toward the Eel River and pulled up to the dock at Doug's house.

For just a moment, Charlie had a flashback to the day Doug told him with total excitement that he'd just bought his first boat. He begged Charlie to go with him to Burr Brothers boatyard in Marion, where they had just taken delivery of Doug's brand-new Tiara 39, which Doug named Bonanza.

It was Doug's first big boat, and he kept it for five years before moving up to a Viking 45, named Bonanza II, and then on to his current boat, a Post 56 Convertible, named Bonanza III. Charlie smiled, knowing that Doug loved him almost as much as his boats.

Charlie helped Barb and Jenn off the boat and walked them down to the end of the dock. As he helped them down the steps from the dock to the brick path that led to the house, he noticed someone sitting alone on the patio on the other side of the pool. As he and the family got closer to the house, the man stood up. Immediately, Charlie recognized him as Detective Matt Davis. He approached them and extended his hand to Jenn.

"I'm so sorry about your loss, Mrs. Wood. You and your family have my deepest sympathies."

Then he turned toward Charlie and Barb, grabbed Charlie by the wrist.

"Charles Henderson, you are under arrest for the murder of Douglas Wood!" Matt said in a low voice.

As Matt Davis walked Charlie to his car, he could hear Jenn and Barb shouting.

"What are you talking about? Not Charlie!"

"Charlie, please say it's not true. Please!"

But Charlie couldn't hear them. He was already amid a flashback when he and Billy Flynn were over at Doug's house the morning of the 28th, and Doug had told them he was dying of cancer. Doug explained he wanted to confess everything, how he had helped Charlie steal all the money from the Federal Reserve Bank of Boston and several member banks. He wanted to come clean about the fact that they had stolen nearly $900 million over the past decade.

"No, Doug, you can't tell anyone, no one!" Charlie had shouted at Doug.

But Doug kept shaking his head, saying that he had to tell them to clear his conscience and tell the whole story before he died.

Charlie leaned into Doug's face and poked Doug violently in the chest.

"If you do this, it will ruin everything for you, me, Jenn, and Barb. Do you really want to do this?"

Doug continued to shake his head.

"Doug, you can't tell anyone about the money, no one!"

But Doug shook his head again and said he had to confess it all. So, Charlie grabbed him by the shoulders and shook him like a rag doll.

"Yes, I will, and you can't stop me!" Doug shouted back.

Then Charlie shoved him backward with all his might. Doug struggled to stay standing but eventually tripped, falling backward and hitting his head.

Billy Flynn saw the blood first and said, "What the fuck Charlie, what the fuck did you do?"

But it was already done. The fall had cut Doug's skull open, which started a massive bleed out that would eventually cost Doug his life.

Charlie now remembered turning to Billy Flynn and saying, "Let's get out of here before Jenn gets home."

Billy looked at Charlie and said, "What the hell, Charlie? We should call 911!"

However, Charlie was already at the front door and wasn't planning to turn around. So, Billy followed Charlie and ran to his car. Charlie had been silent on the drive back to Hyannisport, reflecting on what had happened. The last thing Charlie remembered was his anger toward Doug for threatening to reveal the truth about the money to everyone.

Billy had picked Charlie up at the golf course earlier in the morning so Charlie could leave undetected. Much like Billy's alibi when he left his car at his girlfriend's apartment garage and then rented a car to drive to the Cape. When he dropped Charlie off back at the course, it looked as if he'd been there all morning. When Billy returned the rental car to Boston, he walked to the parking garage, jumped in his car, and drove home. It looked as if he'd been at his girlfriend's all day.

Charlie had come out of his dream state as Matt Davis was putting him in the back seat of his patrol car. All Charlie could see now was the awful look of disbelief on Barb and Jenn's faces as he stared back at them.

Charlie took a deep breath and thought about what had happened to Doug when he shoved him backward.

"Oh my God," he said. "I've killed him. I've killed Doug. I killed him over money. I killed my best friend over money, and he'll never come back. Never. Oh my God, what have I done?"

Matt backed his car out of the driveway and headed back to the Barnstable Police Department, all the while thinking, "Charlie, was it worth it? You've killed your best friend and put yourself in prison for the rest of your life. Was it worth it?" He looked in the rear-view mirror and saw Charlie staring at him.

Charlie asked, "Detective, how did you know?"

"Greed always leaves some kind of evidence, always!" Matt replied.

THE END

Acknowledgements

Writing this book has been a long-held dream of mine. Over the years, I have had advice and support from my family and friends, to whom I am very grateful. In addition, there are some specific individuals I would like to acknowledge:

I want to thank Sharon Anderson for her ongoing support.

Additionally, I would like to thank Caitlyn Siderwicz for her assistance in editing this book.

Many thanks to Kate and Bill Plettner, Peter Moody, as well as Fran Doyle and Alvina Baxter Moran, for their valuable insight and critiques of this book, and their support.

I would also like to thank Jim Coogan for his guidance.

Of course, a big thank you to Kristen vonHentschel for her help with the book and cover design.